LIAM FOR HIRE

A. ZUKOWSKI

Beaten Track
www.beatentrackpublishing.com

Liam For Hire

Published 2018 by Beaten Track Publishing
Copyright © 2018 A. Zukowski

ISBN: 978 1 78645 244 3

Cover image: Sean McGrath, 2009
Cover design: A. Zukowski, 2017

Beaten Track Publishing,
Burscough, Lancashire.
www.beatentrackpublishing.com

ACKNOWLEDGEMENTS

To my mother. I miss you.

To the guys in Cork. You are my Village People.

To J. or P.B. Why the hell did you get so fucked up?

Thanks to the following for their insightful comments or beta reading: Laura, Steven Milian, Eric Westfall, Johnny Williams and Kerry Genova. But I am solely responsible for the errors and the bad language.

Massive thanks to Debbie McGowan at Beaten Track, and Alexis and Jor for their careful proofreading.

The views towards Catholicism are fictional and do not represent my opinion.

ACKNOWLEDGEMENTS

CONTENTS

GLOSSARY

Aggro: UK slang for aggravation

Bedsit: usually a room in a shared flat

Craic: Irish slang for fun

Fag: UK slang for cigarette

Fag hag: a woman who hangs around gay men

Flat: an apartment in American English

GAA: Gaelic football league. It is played and watched all over the Republic of Ireland

Greasy spoon: a low-cost café

Hackneyed: clichéd

Irish Leaving Certificate: the school graduation exams in the Republic of Ireland

Overground: local trains in London, as opposed to the Underground

Queer: the term has been used to refer generally to LGBTQ

RTE: Irish public broadcaster

Shattered: very tired

Snog: kiss and cuddle, equivalent to make-out in American English

Tannoy: loudspeaker

Toke: pull on a cigarette, a joint etc.

Whore: the characters call themselves and each other whores. They are not meant to be insulting.

*The author acknowledges the following trademarks: Shrek, Pokémon, Grindr, Bushmills, Jameson.

LIAM FOR HIRE

PROLOGUE

HAVE YOU ANY idea where Sasha may be? Who's taken him?" the male detective demanded.

The glare of the light bulb made me squint. I was too withdrawn and exhausted. Tears blurred my vision as my body screamed for drugs. I became aware of how I stank. The room in the police station was closing in on me. "Max. He runs things around Elephant and Castle."

He frowned at me. "What do you mean 'he runs things'?"

I started to shake. "Have you got a smoke?" Any drug would be better than none.

The policewoman found a packet, drew one for me, and lit it. My hands trembled. The whole fucking world did, as if a tsunami had hit London, but I knew it was only due to my sorry state. I inhaled deeply so the smoke filled my lungs.

"Well?" The male detective impatiently tapped the desk with his pen.

"Max's men sell drugs. They have young men and women working for them in brothels and on the street. I don't know the details, and if they find out I'm here telling you about it, they'll fucking waste me."

But I told his henchmen to come, and they took Sasha. I was a stupid idiot. I was too young to realise how dangerous it was when love turned to envy and desperation. I'd be forever guilty of betraying and hurting Sasha, someone I'd claimed to love. Maybe I was not born to find it. I'd be punished.

I rummaged in my pocket and dug out the name card the East End gangsters had given me. The number was almost illegible now. I handed it over to the detectives. "Here. Go and find him," I pleaded. Tears finally fell and I couldn't stop them.

~~~

I'd woken up and remembered that Sasha had gone.

The owner of the greasy spoon on the way to the South Bank showed me the local paper. I read about how Max and his gang got busted, and the police found trafficked victims who were forced to sell themselves. The police had found Sasha and rescued him from the gang. Sasha was not one of the trafficked boys, but he'd been living and selling himself on the streets after running away from foster care. He'd survived.

Sasha had always been a fighter. The fucker. I loved him to bits.

A few months later, I'd found out that Sasha was going to college. I wanted to make sure he was really alive. I didn't try to go into the college building, though. I didn't think the staff would let a homeless junkie like me in anyway. Instead, I hid in the shadows across the street and waited to see him. I was afraid to approach him after I'd nearly got him killed. I wasn't sure how long I'd waited but when he came through the glass doors, my heart leapt at the sight of him. He was well wrapped up with a hoodie and woollen beanie. If I could just hold him one more time.

"I'm sorry," I whispered. I couldn't stop myself from watching him as I stood there transfixed, feeling guilty but happy to see him even though it was from a distance.

Jay was there to meet him. Of course, Sasha's boyfriend. He kissed Sasha's cheek, and wound his long strong arm around Sasha's shoulder as if protecting him from the cruel world. Jay seemed nice. Hot too. A mixed-race boy who'd taken much better care of him than I ever could. Not the stupid state I was in, anyway. I watched the two of them walk away until I couldn't see them anymore. Yet, I stared and stared. My heart ached and my body froze in the unwelcoming wintry wind.

~~~

See what you've become, Liam? A beggar playing fucking 'Danny Boy' on the dirty street? You should be ashamed. I'd told myself that the drugs had fucked up my life, but that would have been too simple. It was the life I deserved; that's what I'd always been told.

I took more and more drugs. Being alone wasn't doing me any good. I knew I needed to do something with my addiction.

It could have been any night. I'd earned enough money begging on Oxford Street to get myself a bundle. In my confused mind, I'd even thought I was buying some for Sasha, too. How fucked was I?

Just a little bit more. Yeah, tomorrow's another day and I'll find more money. I wasn't worried about running out of skag. *Shit! What the fuck!* I couldn't see anything. It felt peaceful, though. So fucking calm.

My vision. No, I couldn't feel my arms. My heart was thumping faster and faster against my ribcage, as if it was trying to escape. I must have passed out at some point. I don't know how long I was out of it. When I came to, I tried to sit up. *What's that sticking to my hair and face? Christ!* It smelt disgusting. I wiped the sick off myself.

There was more. Something on the floor, and the dirty mattress caught my eye. Red, metallic smell filled my nostrils. *Holy fucking shit.* I screwed up my eyes and looked again. It was blood, fucking blood. *Whose?* I was stunned silent. *Focus, Liam. Please, don't let me be the one bleeding to death here.* Panic set in, and I crawled until my fingers bled too.

More blood on the wall. My arm. I tore the needle away from it, and a small rivulet of blood squirted out from the puncture.

I'm OD'ing. Well done. I grabbed the first thing I found—a dirty rag or a T-shirt—and dabbed on my arm to stop the blood.

I'd never coped with an OD before. The closest experience I'd had was when I saw a guy I'd known in someone's flat a few months back. Horror descended upon us. An ambulance was called, and his mates hauled him out onto the street to wait for help. I saw his lips turn blue while life drained out of him. I'd run after that, because I didn't want to be questioned over the dose. I ran and ran with no destination.

I'd heard he didn't make it. The dread chilled my bones, and yet I was drawn to the darkness as if I was born for the same destiny. I carried on, injecting junk to achieve the sweet feeling that'd last a little while.

My thoughts were hazy but I realised I might die alone, just another unwanted addict in a filthy room. Who'd raise an alarm? I'd smell in a few weeks, I supposed. I forced myself to open my eyes wide. Had I managed to stop the blood? I stood but my legs were like jelly and the white spots returned. My heart pounded. I thought I could feel the blood travelling to my head. I steadied myself on the wall, and tottered over to the door and pushed it open. *Where's the nearest fucking hospital?* The mental hospital nearby also offered drug services. I didn't even know what time of the day it was and whether it'd be open. I couldn't remember where exactly the hospital was.

It wasn't fucking funny to walk around London looking like a zombie, but that must have been how I appeared to the other pedestrians. Half dead and blood on my clothes and arm. I fell into the reception of the hospital when the automatic doors opened, and collapsed onto the cold tiled floor. A woman gasped. My vision was blurred as I gazed up at her. She was wearing a blue uniform. A nurse. *Help me!* I wanted to shout but no sound came out. Yet, my body screamed. I shut my eyes because the bright light was making me see stars again. Two, three faces were hovering over me, though, when I half-attempted to open my eyes once more.

"OT eight," someone shouted. "Which doc's on duty?" Crackling noise and a reply.

"Get a move on. He's not going to make it."

Strong arms lifted me and I was on a stretcher, being wheeled through the corridors. Green and blue uniforms bustled around me. Someone put an oxygen mask on my face. "Stupid drug addict. Waste of our resources." Yeah, they were probably right about me. My dad would agree. I imagined Mum's lined face hovering above and staring at my misfortune.

Sasha wasn't going to cry if I died.

I'm sorry. You're better off without me. It was my last thought for a while.

~~~

I awoke in the hospital feeling as though I had died. And it wasn't Heaven I'd ended up.

"What's your name?"

I struggled to stay awake. The nurse's eyes were bright. Her face was round and full of kindness.

"Liam." I sounded distant. My consciousness had departed a while ago.

"Liam, I'm Dr. Foster." An older man stared down at me. "We've stabilised your heart rate and breathing. The antidote has worked. We don't have the facility here for you, so we can discharge you or find you a placement with a rehab."

My body was already screaming for drugs and my brain felt like mush. "Discharge?"

"Yes, you can go home," the nurse ventured, hesitant because she could probably guess where I'd been living.

Home. I might have started to laugh because they frowned at my hysteria.

The nurse was calm. "Rehab normally takes months to arrange, but we can help." Yes, very helpful. Because I was a despicable homeless addict and I'd nearly fucking died, I'd earned a fast track to medical services.

I stopped laughing and gazed at them both. "Please. I want to get clean."

My resolve didn't last long. The actual journey to the treatment centre was a blur. I could still hear my own screams. Good job they'd strapped me down.

"Just let me the fuck out, you fucking bastards! I want to die. Now!" And I repeated the same, again and again.

Those words would haunt me for the rest of my life. *I want to die.* The two-week public health detox programme was so brutal that if I'd known how to escape, I'd have done so.

The room closed in and I knew I was sitting in my own filth. Vomit or shit I couldn't tell. They'd hosed me down earlier. *Was it yesterday?* In that room, I'd lost all self-respect and all sense of dignity.

I'd hear music. Prokofiev. It was ridiculous. Rehab was no place for beauty. *And you're a sick fuck. How can you care about classical music?* I'd cried and cried when I remembered I sold my flute for drugs. I'd gone and done the one damn thing that I'd promised myself never to do. That flute had been my lifeline since I was six. I used to play it in the squat, and Sasha would tell me off for wasting my talent. When I remembered what I'd done with my flute, I ran to the pawn shop to try to steal it back. I had no money. It had gone. It had been sold to someone who deserved it.

I'd taken enough drugs to forget about that, but I dreamt about the flute often. And the rabbit. I'd kept Skip in a cage in the yard. I looked after her for a long time.

Dad hit me so hard one day, I'd run away and hidden in the fields. When I went home eventually, I fell asleep. I'd found Skip motionless in her cage the next morning. Whether she was starved to death or died of a sickness, I'd never found out. I was distraught but Mum thought I'd cried so much because of what Dad had done. Perhaps. I'd learned that physical and emotional pain was never far apart. If I numbed myself enough with drugs, I'd feel no pain.

They put me in a scalding bath, but my skin felt cold as if it'd melt in the heat. I tried to push them away but they kept me down. "Let me go, you fuckers! I need skag," I'd shouted until my voice was hoarse. Then I'd bawled and whispered the same. *Anywhere but here. Death is better than living a life of indignity.*

I found myself sitting on the narrow bed with tears streaming down my cheeks. There was a small window in my room, and I stared at it every morning, wondering. *Will the bed sheet work? I have a strong neck.* Then I laughed and cried until I was gasping. Without the drugs numbing my senses, debilitating emotions flooded my whole body. I clearly deserved this life.

The worst part was sitting in the group therapy sessions, which nearly killed me. I didn't want to talk about my feelings. It was the whole point of taking drugs. Yes, I was abused physically and verbally. Not the worst upbringing, I'd say. The tears kept coming at night after the aches subsided. I stifled them with my fist, then I hit the wall with it until my knuckles reddened and swelled.

After two weeks, I was tossed out onto the street. *Sorry, the public health service doesn't have the resources. You're on your own, mate. Go to the outpatient clinic and get a prescription for buprenorphine.* Right, as if it'd help. The physical symptoms had gone but I wasn't ready. I knew that. I stayed in a homeless shelter because there was no way I wouldn't go straight back on drugs if I returned to squatting and panhandling.

The guy from the next bed paced backwards and forwards half of the night. Then he sat on the bed and faced the wall. I couldn't tell if he was asleep or not. And so, I watched him as he was illuminated by the moonlight. I imagined myself being the broken man, living out my wretched life in a shelter like that. I was afraid to leave the accommodation, but my sanity was deserting me. Every night, I contemplated what'd driven my neighbour insane. I thought of my own darkness, my imaginary high beam from where a quick departure might be arranged. Every night, I cried myself to sleep after contemplating the different methods of permanently relieving my agony.

I lasted less than a week in the shelter. I went and found Chris's apartment and knocked on his door. He was the only acquaintance I had who didn't take drugs, apart from hash. I'd also never fallen out with him. I might have borrowed or stolen from Chris, but he'd been cool with me when I'd last seen him a few months back.

"Can I kip on your couch or your bed? I'll be your sex slave. Just until I'm back on my feet." I fidgeted. I held a small carrier bag that contained next to nothing, a reflection of how little I'd achieved in my twenty years on Earth.

Chris raised his eyebrow sceptically, a cigarette dangling from his mouth. "I have no use for a sex slave. You can stay with me, though."

He opened the door and showed me in.

PART ONE
HIS MAN THURSDAY

CHAPTER 1

Eighteen months after Sasha left.

I N MY DINGY bedsit room, I get ready to go to my appointment
with someone new. I consider my skinny jeans and tight shirt
in the mirror. I often wonder what the johns see when they meet
me for the first time. I'm not what you call a stunner, but I'm
good-looking enough. I have dark hair, pale skin and thin lips. A
few freckles make me appear a little younger than my age. It costs
to keep my hair under some control, but I have to do it for the
sake of my job. I run my fingers through it again. My Old Spice
deo. *Shit, where is it?* Found. Apply. I give myself another once-
over before heading out to face the world.

To save money, I ride the bus to my meet. I sit upstairs where
I can disappear into my own thoughts for a while. Through the
smeared window, I see the dirty streets of Haringey turn into
the greener Islington, inhabited by people who have money and
class. The streets here are arranged into these clean lines like the
kind of life the well-off lead.

Seeing how the other half lives reminds me of my time
surviving in squats and the reasons why I love and hate London
at the same time. I like it for its openness; it's a place that absorbs
people from all over the world and all walks of life. But it's
unforgiving to those who have nothing, like Sasha and me when
we were younger. We used to laugh at ourselves; I was the stray
dog and he the alley cat. I'd watched Sasha sell himself on the
street but I was too hopeless to help him. We were not creatures
who could be good for each other. We'd been co-dependent and

we'd eventually destroyed one another. The city swallowed us—two homeless kids with no prospects—and then unceremoniously dumped us in a deep dark hole without resources to crawl back out.

While I pass the time pondering about my past, the bus soon reaches my destination. I get off and take the short walk to this neat town house off Essex Road with a small but organised front garden. I feel my usual nerves about meeting a new john. Every time I go to a client's house, it's as though I've stepped into a film set. I play a street punk pretending to be a confident escort. No matter how long I've been doing this, the first time is still strange. I take a moment and gaze at the dark-green door. Deep breath. I check myself again and ring the bell.

I don't expect the man who opens the door to be this good-looking in an unassuming kind of way. Most of the time, my clients scowl and furtively glance around, as if I wear a big sign announcing to the neighbourhood that they've ordered an escort. But the guy in front of me smiles, revealing straight white teeth. He holds the door wide open. Once inside, he shakes my hand, his palm firm and warm. Then we hug awkwardly, and he introduces himself. "I'm Ali. It's short for Alastair."

"Liam." I grin back.

I guess he's in his thirties, and fit, wearing a simple blue shirt and dark jeans. He is a couple of inches taller than me, making him about six feet. His hair's light brown and his eyes are clear green like two pools of tropical sea. They are striking and unmissable. It is a cliché to say eyes are the window to the soul, but they do tell me a lot about the men who hire me. And this man here has beautiful eyes. My eyes, on the other hand, are dark; I like to think they may make my soul impenetrable.

"Want a drink?" Ali asks, while I am still contemplating him. I've kicked my worst drug habits but I still indulge in cigarettes, dope and the occasional beer. I say no to a drink, though. Maybe later. Alcohol makes my nerves worse. No matter how long I've been selling sex, revealing myself to a stranger is not easy.

He pours himself a small shot in the wood and chrome kitchen and takes a sip. The house smells clean. I can glimpse the TV and the books in the sitting room, and a sofa covered in cream canvas. I like the décor, which seems as understated as the man, even though it'll have nothing to do with me. I only expect to use the bedroom, not the rest of the house.

He gazes at me. "Shall we?"

I nod, and he leads me to his bedroom upstairs, which is clean and tidy. It feels cosy. I see the plump bed and wonder for a moment what it's like to sleep there at night. I bet Ali sleeps well. *Does he have worries and regrets? Does he suffer from insomnia, like I do?*

Get a fucking grip, Liam.

"Okay. You want a fuck, right?" It's all too common when I turn up for an appointment, the john wants something completely different from what he's originally requested. I'm not a miracle worker. I can't prepare myself if I'm not forewarned.

He nods. I ask for the money up front.

A small frown appears on his face for a second, but he opens the bedside cabinet and retrieves a wad of cash to give to me. I count it quickly and put it in my pocket.

"You want to fuck me? Yes?" I check again. Uncertainty and apprehension fill me.

"Yes." He hides his hands behind his back.

I sit on the bed and take all my clothes off. I don't feel self-conscious about my body anymore. It's my job. Ali stares at me with wide eyes, but his feet remain glued to the same spot. I put on my charm face and give him my best smile. "Get ready for me, then. Don't be shy."

Ali strips too, slowly, and my eyes are drawn to the taut abs and the cool tats on his arms. His body is not sculpted from gym work, but it's solid and bold. He must play a sport regularly. One of the tattoos is a Celtic knot; I'd like to ask him about that, but I don't. I don't want to be intrusive. On his other arm is a wood or a forest that wraps around lean biceps. Not bad at all. I've seen his narrow wedding band too and the picture on his bedside table. I've trained myself to quickly get a sense of the men I sleep with. Call it survival instinct.

In the photograph, Ali and a pretty young woman with long blonde hair stand somewhere sunny and hot. They are happy and smiley as if they're a perfect couple in the middle of a lifestyle advertisement. That's what I imagine, anyway, because I've never experienced that kind of life. The good life. What the fuck is he doing hiring a prostitute when he seems to have everything and a pretty partner? I close my eyes for a moment, but I can't sense the woman's presence in the house. Damn, he's probably another closet case. I've met enough men like him in my line of work.

Their wives and girlfriends are out of town or staying with relatives and friends, so they call me up for sex. Or, they're getting a divorce or separated from their partners. I'm their once-a-month indulgence.

I open my eyes again and get on with business since his circumstances have nothing to do with me. His hard dick is pretty large, the way I like them. That, together with the strong body. Shit, I'll probably want to jerk off when I go home later.

I stroke his erection, making it even harder. I smile. "I can see your cock likes me already." That earns me a shy grin from Ali.

I take a condom out to tool him up. "I'll be down on all fours. Is that okay?"

Ali manages to nod. I position myself on the bed then and raise my lubed and readied arse to let him see it. I half-turn to see him approach me with uncertainty. He's reticent for whatever reason, so I add, "Tell me if there's anything you want to try, okay? It'll feel good as long as you tell me what you want. I promise." I consider myself professional and I do want to satisfy my clients.

"Okay."

I look back to see him finally moving to position himself just above me; his eyes consume my nakedness.

I shift slightly forward, opening myself wider for him. I feel him aligning himself; his hands on my arse cheeks tingle me in a good way. They are warm and steady and they cup my hips firmly.

"Let me know if you want me to stop, okay? Any time," he says, voice low and gentle. *Fuck, really?* That's a new one. I feel the pressure as he breaches me but it doesn't hurt with the lube, honestly. He inches in tentatively, as though afraid he'll hurt me. I arch back even further to give him more access. I like the sensation of the movement of his hands on my back as he explores my skin. He leans down. His hot breath wafts lightly across the back of my neck. He gradually fills me and his thrusts quicken, but I can tell he remains cautious. I half turn again to see his face, which is blushed. Sweat has beaded on his forehead. Okay, he's aroused, but he can do better.

Ali comes forward and asks, "Can I kiss you, Liam?"

I chuckle. "'Course you can. Don't believe the myth."

"A myth?"

Really? The man hasn't heard but he's respectful enough to ask if he can kiss me?

"You know, the one that says whores don't kiss." I turn my head around more, so my face is pressed against his warm cheek. Honestly, I'll have whiplash if he continues to be so hesitant. I like my john bold and straightforward. Paid. In. Out. Gone. I can't deal with other shit.

Ali frowns, then he kisses me lightly with hesitation. "It's my first time."

I guess he means he has never used an escort before. An inexperienced john treats the prostitute too kindly. He'll soon learn. I arch back and give him another deeper kiss, just to show him it's okay.

I was addicted to heroin and crack, and sometimes meth. I'd tried everything—a habit financed by begging. I despised myself for both my drug addiction and the fact that I was basically a charity case. The downward spiral of self-loathing and disgust. But I was too fucked up to deal with it until I knew I'd be dead if I didn't do something about my sorry life.

I gave up drugs, and I've been an escort for a year since I became clean. I couldn't go back to panhandling, but passing my Irish School Leaving Certificate didn't exactly qualify me for many jobs that paid the rent in London. The bedsit costs £900 a month because I had no deposit or reference. I need fifteen fucks a month minimum, so I keep obsessing about how many more times I have to bend over to make ends meet.

I haven't had many sex partners recently who are not paid hookups. It's a bonus that Ali is attractive. Still, I am undecided whether this is merely tolerable or if I am a little excited by his erection deep inside me. It'd be good to feel aroused while on the job. *Okay, don't think about feel. Mind back on the job, Liam.*

Ali is holding me tight, so I can feel his pulsating heartbeats on my back.

"And you can go as fast and hard as you want, man. Don't worry about hurting me. I'm used to it."

He listens to me and now picks up speed. I can tell he's close. He plants more kisses around my neck and back as he thrusts into me, still not as harsh as most clients. The pressure builds. He mumbles something incomprehensible and comes. He continues to embrace me while he slowly calms down and withdraws. As he releases me from his hold, my hard-on has gone, but that's okay. I turn back around and watch his face, while he takes his condom off.

He surveys my body once more, no doubt noticing my limp penis, and scratches his head. "Uh. Should I take care of you?"

I scrutinise him. The man is pretty, with glowing cheeks from the exertion and shimmering sweat all over his skin. I would have liked to stay and play but it wasn't exactly the deal.

I smile at his suggestion. "No, Ali. I'm all right. Thanks for the thought."

I do get clients who like to be fucked or to blow me, but it still feels like work rather than 'being taken care of'. I don't typically dally after an appointment. After all, I'm not paid for the overtime.

We both get up and dressed.

He sees me out. While we're in the entrance hall, he kisses my cheek and says, "Thank you, Liam." His almost innocent gesture is so tender it makes me shudder. I have to blink a few times to remind myself this is a job. Thinking about emotions is pointless.

"You're welcome." I give him my most charming beam and a wink. "Book me again if you had a good time, yeah?"

His grin makes the crow's feet that are just appearing at the corners of his eyes more obvious. I like them on the man, though. I don't think I have a type, but a 'daddy' is definitely not one I'd normally go for. But then, he's probably only ten, fifteen years older than me. *Hell, shut up, Liam. Quit over-analysing. It's not like this hot guy is going to be interested in you beyond paid-for sex.*

I'm probably horny, missing a lover or a regular fuck buddy who would be better than nobody. I miss one person most but he's gone, found his true love and he's doing well. I am happy for him despite the ache inside me when I think back to the hard times I shared with Sasha and the love I felt for him. Some days I wish I could turn back the clock. By the time I told Sasha I loved him, it was too late, but regrets are a luxury for someone like me. I betrayed him because I was young, jealous and foolish. I nearly got him killed by the East End gangsters. I need to redeem myself but I don't know how.

With all those messed-up thoughts crowding my head, I bid farewell and leave Ali, an unlit cigarette in my hand ready for when I go out into the cold. I smile to myself, comforted by the feeling that he'll ask for me again.

But I soon forget about Ali and get on with my week. I love the craic and I used to party a lot. I've calmed down a little lately. Sometimes, I have a few beers and smoke hash with my flatmates. Our resident dealer Dmitri usually has some good stuff for sale. Besides, I don't want to spend my hard-earned cash in overpriced bars in London. Having been homeless means that I'm hyper-aware of poverty, of how I could lose everything with one mistake. I see that time and again with fellow homeless souls. Right now, I care only about surviving and keeping clean.

Back in my flat, Dmitri sells me a quarter. It will last me a few days if I go easy. I notice the 'foreign cunt' print on his T-shirt. Ironic, given he's Russian.

I smile and point to his shirt. "*Pizda*."

His brown eyes widen. "Hey, you know Russian?" Dmitri is dark, intense and seems to be perpetually jittering, probably because he's a part-time drug dealer. I've come across so many men like him I recognise the traits. When I say part-time, though, I have no clue what else he does. More wheeling and dealing, I guess.

I laugh. "No. My ex is Polish. He only taught me that word and *suka*. They are the same in Polish and Russian, right?" Sasha used to call me a *pizda* when I was particularly insensitive. I deserved it most of the time, too.

Dmitri agrees. "Yeah, the most overused words in my country because we are all cunts and bitches."

I shake my head, not believing it for a minute. Apart from Chris—my other flatmate—we're all foreign cunts and we're all in some precarious situation in this country.

He regards me. "You're gay." Ah, the telling pronoun.

I've just melted a bit of the cannabis and now crumble it on the tobacco. "Yup."

My sexuality has not come up in my conversations with Dmitri. I tend to keep a comfortable distance from the guys in the flat, and we respect each other's privacy. Chris knows me but the others don't. Chris is also an escort, and I met him through some common acquaintance when I first arrived in London. He was the one who helped me when I came out of rehab, and gave me the idea of hustling when I couldn't find a legitimate job. We both make no secret of our profession to the other sharers.

"Why do you ask? Do you have a problem?" I hope he's not homophobic. I don't want to share a flat with a gay-bashing asshole. I'd hate to have to deal with the aggro in my own accommodation.

"No, of course not." He shrugs, showing indifference which, luckily, has been the most common reaction I've encountered in London. No matter what else is wrong with this city, I feel safe most of the time as a gay man and that's cool enough for me.

"You and Chris are, hmm, boyfriends?" I rather like Dmitri's Russian accent, kinda thick and harshened by the tobacco, making him sound older than his age.

I chuckle. "No, Chris is not really anybody's boyfriend, y'know?" Or girlfriend, for that matter.

Chris is twenty-six and the oldest of the residents of this dump. He's gorgeous. I mean he's proper top-notch model material. I never ask him why he does what he does. He must make a shitload more money than I do. Chris will shag anyone, too, and he has a new lover every few weeks. I don't know how he does it because I wouldn't be able to explain myself and my job to someone new all the time. Some days, I watch him and try to figure out his story. I've come to the conclusion that everyone has a tale, though some people have more colourful ones than others. Chris and I have occasionally slept together, but we're both realistic enough not to think we have genuine affection for each other just because we fuck. Dmitri doesn't need to know all that.

"It's none of my business," he concludes.

I am about to retreat to my room with my joint when he whispers, "I can get other stuff, you know."

Fuck. My heartbeat races. That's all I need. At least once a day, I feel the urge to go back out there for the hard drugs. It'll be damn difficult to stay clean when the temptation is so near. "What kind of stuff, exactly?" I ask even though I'm afraid of the answer.

"Coke, Special K. Tell me what you want." Dmitri lights up a joint and watches me, his dark eyes sharp. He most likely recognises a recovering drug addict a mile off.

It's so fucking tempting. So. Fucking. Tempting.

"I'm good. Thanks," I reply eventually. "I'll bear it in mind, though."

Without waiting for his response, I retreat back to my room, feeling dizzy all of a sudden.

I have to remind myself of the horrendous rehab. The pain and nightmares. The sweating and itching. Feeling sorry for myself, completely losing control. Suicidal and emotional. I can't go through that again.

When I'm not working these days, I play the flute to occupy myself. I bought one recently with the money I managed to save. Now my drug use is under control, I make decent money escorting. I was totally out of my mind to give up my flute for heroin. Playing it now reminds me of what a despicable and desperate homeless junkie I was. The tin whistle was good for panhandling, but the flute is my true instrument. I practise as much as I can and vow never to be apart from it again, ever. When I play, I can lose myself in the music and forget about everything else in my life.

~~~

I have built up some regulars. Together with a couple of new clients this week, I'm on the right track for the month's rent money. Even so, Ali's next request makes me smile.

I approach his house with an image of his strong body. The warmth inside surges. I try to steady myself before ringing his bell. *Come on, now. What's up with you?*

He gives me a heartfelt beam when he opens the door, as if he has genuinely looked forward to my coming. I've worn my tight shirt and skinny jeans to come to the appointment. They've become a sort of work uniform; I'm more a hoodie and tracksuit bottoms kind of guy when I'm not working. Tonight, Ali's attire is quite similar to mine but with an extra layer of maturity and wealth. He doesn't exactly seem to lack cash, given he lives in a house in Islington, one of the wealthiest boroughs close to London.

Thursday night again. I wonder if his wife is at an evening class. Some of the men I service are in the closet. I don't have the moral compass to judge people who cheat, and frankly, I don't care. In the back of my mind, though, I worry about being beaten up by their wives or whoever. I don't have hang-ups about my work but I know what most people think about sex for cash. It's not a profession to be proud of. At least I've not consciously hurt anybody in order to earn money, even when I was addicted to drugs.

When we are still standing in his hallway, he passes a wad of cash to me. After I've counted the amount, I raise an eyebrow as a question mark because he's given me more than what I charge for a fuck. Ali mumbles, while wringing his hands, "It's a tip. Don't worry."

Staring at the notes in my hand, I frown. "You don't tip before I've delivered the service, mate." I may be a prostitute but I don't accept payment when I haven't worked for it. I'll be vulnerable to peculiar demands later on.

"I want you to have it." Ali shifts his feet uncomfortably. He gazes at me for a long moment, seemingly debating what to say. "I...I want us to have sex as though we're making love."

Making love? Jaysus. I scratch my head. I am at a loss why the words scare me. It's not like I don't understand what it's about, theoretically. "Okay. You mean more kisses and shit?"

Ali laughs. "And shit." His face lights up and he looks about ten years younger. "Like cuddles."

Cuddles. Hugs. Kisses. Luxuries for other people.

Sex has been only sex to me in the last few years. I guess grown-ups sometimes need some tender loving care. Fuck knows why Ali wants that from me, but if it's what he fancies, it's not the weirdest request I've ever heard. "'Course. The customer is always right." A frown appears briefly on his handsome face.

I take his hand and lead him into the bedroom. We are still standing when I start kissing him, slowly at first as if I need to taste his lips and savour them. All the while, I try to think of him as someone I want. Strangely, it turns me on more than I care to admit. As I undress him, each small button of his shirt I undo brings expectation that thrills me. His strong hands seem too big for the same task, but they are delicate at the same time with the act of revealing my body.

Soon, we are both topless and breathing heavily with anticipation. Even with my boyfriends, I have always been a fuck first, think later kind of guy, so this is brand new. Ali is in no rush, as his smooth hands touch the skin of my chest, circling to my waist and pressing on my abs. His caresses send hot currents through me. I follow his example and explore his earlobes, neck and nipples with my lips. His skin tastes sweet and salty. Ali reciprocates with his perfectly shaped mouth. I moan softly, even though I normally try to suppress any sounds I make when I'm on the job. I'm not supposed to be the one enjoying himself here.

He pushes me onto the bed and continues with the kisses while I return the favour, absorbed by his lips and tongue. We are both hard, but before I can do anything, Ali unbuttons my jeans and pulls them down. He scoots back and licks his lips when he sees how hard my cock is. His warm hand wraps around my hard-on and strokes it until pre-cum oozes from the slit. He uses his fingertips to massage the swollen head, making me harder. Oh, crap. That is supposed to be *my* job.

"Fuck." I groan. All I can do is to bury my fingers in his soft hair. I become conscious of the fact that I haven't even taken the trousers off my john while he's giving me a hand job.

I am also hyper-aware of my performance, wondering whether it is living up to his request, when Ali shifts and goes down on me, catching me by surprise. I can tell he doesn't know what he is doing, but the heat and the suction soon take care of me. He gazes up to meet my eyes, making me want to shout out his name, someone's name, anybody's name, but I realise I don't have anyone.

Since Sasha, I've been all alone in the world. Friends and acquaintances, yes, but no one who cares about me. Drugs are a form of immunisation against feelings, so with abstinence comes a flood of emotions that needs to be suppressed. I'm good at going through the motions and not getting involved. Mindless sex helps to drown out the loneliness that eats at my heart.

I whimper something incomprehensible, even to my own ears. The arousal Ali causes is the best thing that has happened to me in a long while. Notwithstanding his lack of technique, I am loving his tussled hair and admiring eyes. Hot damn. Just like that I am on the verge, so I pull out because I don't want my client to swallow my seed. We haven't talked about this but I don't want him to complain. I jerk myself off quickly, my fist desperately completing what he has been trying to do. I squeeze my head and stroke my shaft with some force. I gaze at him as I do so. The pressure feels right; my desire for release soon takes over. I spill on the edge of the bed sheet, coming in waves. I turn to see Ali watching me come with bewilderment, his eyes wide and lustful, as if he wants to devour me.

Seeing him like that makes me impatient. I yank his trousers off, freeing his erection that stands tall and proud, as though it's waiting for my lead. I push him back on the bed, and I straddle his thighs and lean down to take all of him in. I relax my throat to let him fuck my mouth deeply. His hands are in my hair and his bright-green eyes focus on my face with admiration. Is that what he means by making love? The passion he shows on his face? I don't dwell on it because I can tell he's about to combust. I find my discarded trousers and take a condom and lube out of the pocket and shield him. I move to inch my arse onto his erection. Bliss, despite my still-sensitive hole from another trick this afternoon.

Ali sighs, "Oh, Liam."

His voice is hoarse and sensual, reaching out to me in an unexpected way. I ride him like a motherfucker on heat because he's turning me on. Job or not, I want to see him come. I need him to enjoy this. If he thinks it has anything to do with the L-word, so be it.

This way, with me riding Ali fast and hard, he can't fight it, can't slow down to try to protect me. His eyes betray nothing but fire. I desperately need to light that fire, to set his eyes ablaze. I continue to push myself up and then sink back down to the hilt, so his cock impales me again and again, my hands resting on his washboard abs and supporting my weight.

"Fuck," Ali yells.

"I'm on it."

Ali smiles. He draws his knees up and opens them wide to give me better leverage.

I am kneeling now, his hard dick sliding in and out of my arse. I speed up even more. He soon plateaus. Ali shouts my name. He bucks his hips up to meet me repeatedly until he stops pushing into me. I relax my arse that had clenched around him during sex. He flops back, his chest rising and falling fast. Beads of sweat spread across his body like tiny pearls. Beautiful.

I wait until he has completely calmed down before moving off, disposing of the condom and cleaning him up with a flannel from the bathroom.

Ali watches me as I do so. He whispers, "Thank you, Liam."

I smile. "You're welcome." I consider the man and how good sex felt just now, but then I shake my head. It's a job. Nothing more. I put my clothes on quickly as I always do.

"I'll let myself out." I think he can do with a rest after the intensity.

He sits up and starts dressing, too, with a grin on his face. "No. I'll see you out."

CHAPTER 2

A s I say goodbye to him in the hall, Ali hugs me and plants a kiss on my cheek. It is such an innocent gesture but it lights up my insides. It's been forever since someone treated me so sweetly. I stare at him, wondering why I should react this way.

Ali distracts me from my train of thought when he touches his chin and asks, "Hey, do you want that drink now?"

I consider it. Why the hell not? I don't have another appointment after him. Most of the time, I try to get away from my meets as soon as I can. Tonight, I really fancy that drink with the gorgeous man in front of me. One drink. And I give in to the temptation.

He leads me into his modern kitchen. The spice rack and the hanging pots and pans show that Ali and his wife cook. That's for sure. I sit by the island, feeling embarrassed. It's ironic that I can take my clothes off and have sex with a stranger, but insecurity fills me just because I'm about to have a drink with him.

"Well, what can I get you?" Ali stretches to open the drinks cabinet, where an assortment of neatly shelved bottles can be seen.

"I'm having this. It's a good Scottish single malt." He holds up the whisky bottle.

I don't know much about its Scottish variety, but I enjoyed the odd glass of Irish whiskey when I was an older teenager. I reply, "Whisky sounds good."

Ali gives me a generous one before pouring himself another.

"Is it all right if I have a smoke?" I take a cigarette out of the packet.

"Yeah, come outside." He opens the patio door, then grabs both the glasses.

I follow him. We step out into his backyard and sit on two metal chairs. Ali turns on the patio light. I can see that the garden is small but it has some semi-wild flowers and plants, like a little oasis in the middle of the urban jungle. Ali passes me the whisky. I hold the glass with my left hand, while I put the cigarette in my mouth and light it with the other.

I watch his face spread into an open smile, as though he is really pleased I've stayed. It feels good to be treated like an equal by Ali. With some clients, I sense an underlying disdain for me even though they need my services.

"Cheers!" He touches his glass to mine and takes a sip. I have a mouthful of whisky too. The alcohol burns my throat in a good way. The fragrance of the drink, the herby scent of the garden and the tobacco are making me light-headed.

"You've got a nice garden." I inhale the smell of herbs. I'm a farmer's son, so I don't know much about town houses and domestic gardens. I only feel calm sharing Ali's space in the dusky evening.

"Thanks. I quite like gardening. I don't plant too many flowers, though. They're mostly herbs, and some veggies and fruits." Ali wrings his hands. "It's an old man's hobby, I'm afraid."

I shake my head and offer no comment. I thought about his age during our first appointment. Judging from the way he is in bed and his lean toned body, Ali's fitter than all the other johns I have. But I typically stay away from their personal lives unless they want to tell me.

After finishing the cigarette, I feel on edge again, sitting here in the unfamiliar backyard. "Do you mind if I roll a joint?"

"No, feel free."

I take my small bag of hash out and break up a cigarette in preparation. He watches me with interest. When I am done, I offer, "You want some?" I light it and take a toke.

Ali accepts the lit cigarette I hand over and inhales. Watching the thin line of smoke, he is deep in thought. "It's been years since I smoked dope."

He passes the joint back to me and I suck in another bellyful of smoke, wondering if he's as straight-laced as he seems. Emboldened by the hash, I probe, "How old are you, then?"

He laughs lightly. "Too fucking old for you. I'm forty-five." Ali looks at least five years younger. I thought he was in his thirties. Most of my johns are older guys, so I'm not surprised, and I don't think he's 'too old', whatever that means.

He shakes his head as if bemused by the revelation of his own age. He watches me smoke with a patient smile. "Are you really twenty-one?"

I lick my lips. "Yup. Nearly twenty-two. Why?" It's going to be my birthday in a few months.

"I thought people lied about their ages online." He rests his head on the back of the chair and continues to gaze at me, the turquoise of his eyes set against the enveloping dusk.

I managed to upload some pretty decent photos onto the escort agency's website, and I was mostly honest about my personal stats. When I say decent, they are the complete opposite, and erotic, revealing the top of trimmed pubes and my bare arse, that kind of thing. Chris helped me with them because he loved shaving and dressing up. That's Chris's story.

Anyway, the images will be scandalous for respectable folks like my ma and pa, so it's just as well they will never know.

"You don't need to lie about your age to be untruthful. I don't have anything to hide." The only thing no client will get from me is emotional attachment, as hackneyed as it sounds. It's not good for me or for them. I need to protect myself. No one else will.

He nods, as if he understands my reasoning. After finishing the joint, I light up another cigarette and take a large sip of the whisky that clouds my head. I realise I'm enjoying the conversation. Here in this little garden, I am able to relax. Living in my box room in the crowded flat isn't good for contemplation. But then, who am I to complain? I can hardly afford anything else.

As we listen to the hum of the London suburb and the distant sirens that cut through the city's streets all night, Ali's curious gaze fixes on my face as though he really wants to know the real me. "And you're Irish, right?"

My accent is unmistakable. "Yup. Born and bred in West Cork."

Ali plays with his wedding band and he takes a gulp of his whisky, almost finishing it. "So, how long have you been in London?"

"I came to London nearly four years ago." But most of the first three years were shrouded in a drug-induced fog. I'm not proud of it.

"Do you miss home? Do you ever feel nostalgic?" Ali stares dreamily at the shadows of the garden. I wonder why he's the one who seems to be pining for something.

I look intently at the dark sky as I consider his questions and finally I realise what 'home' means to me. Even with a roof over my head I'm still homeless in my heart. Bricks and mortar don't mean anything. I'm not sure if I want a real home right now, somewhere I belong. Not that one is on offer or available to someone like me. Some days, I long for the freedom of the streets, strange as it may sound to anyone who has never been homeless. My bedsit and the job are like a hamster's cage, giving me temporary shelter but making me go round and round in circles.

I reply, "I don't miss the actual places. I miss the stars and the inky nights. Sometimes I think I can smell the seaweed on damp sand and hear the sound of the waves on Inch Beach if I close my eyes. I yearn for the thunderstorms and the crystal dewdrops clinging to long grass. I want to hear the tunes played on a bodhrán and the low notes from the clarsach." I inhale deeply, then slowly breathe out, thinking about those beautiful things I once shared with someone I thought I loved and would spend the rest of my life with.

It stings to remember that mossy evening in deep winter. We sat on a bench in St Stephen's Green, Dublin. The chill in the Irish air always seeped into your bones. The grass wore a beautiful white dusting of frost. I'd hoped that something so pure remained between Cillian and me. I was wrong, as always, because I'd had it drummed into me that what we did was wrong. *It won't last because it's not natural.* We had known each other since we were ten and we'd been boyfriends for four years. For all that time, I cared about no one but him. I can picture it now: a scene of two young men saying goodbye played like a modern tragedy.

I asked Cillian to come with me to London. It seemed like the logical next step. We'd left behind a small village in West Cork, arrived at the capital, which changed everything that I thought Cillian and I had. I thought we could save our relationship somehow by leaving the country together, so we could start somewhere afresh. He avoided looking at me. I wanted to scream, to make him acknowledge how he'd been hurting me.

"I don't want to leave. I've got friends here," he replied, gazing at the span of grass and the duck pond beyond.

I lit a cigarette. "I'm your friend. Your best friend. Soul mate. They're your words, Cillian." *I love you. I want us to be together forever.*

"We were kids. How'd you hold on to promises like that? I've just got a job here and I've made new friends." His voice was small but every word still landed on me like arrows. *Fuck you, fuck your stupid new friends. Stupid fucking queens who are always drinking in The George.*

He'd more than made friends in Dublin. He'd started fucking around and didn't even bother to hide it.

I bawled like an impetuous child and called him every name under the sun, my voice breaking, shattering any trust I had about love. *You fucking prick. Get ye hole filled every night by gobshites.* I cried until I couldn't breathe.

He'd promise me the world and then forget about it. I don't know how long we sat there and whether I was still crying, trembling with grief.

Cillian eventually stood and backed away, muttering, "I'm sorry, Liam."

That was how we parted ways. Cillian was my first and only lover then. Afterwards, I'd convinced myself falling in love at fourteen, or perhaps at any age, was a big fucking mistake. I used the last of my money from back home to get a one-way plane ticket, and arrived in London penniless and homeless.

I shake my head to clear my mind of these painful memories. Ali raises one of his eyebrows but he doesn't comment on the things I miss about Ireland. Or the fact that I'm shaking from thinking about Dublin and Cillian. I can pretend it's the night chill.

After quite a while when he appears to be thinking about what I said, he tells me quietly, "My mum's from Kerry."

I remember his Celtic knot. "Aye. The dara."

Ali beams again. "Yeah, well. I can't say I know a whole lot about her, but the knot was tattooed in her honour." He goes back into the house and gets himself another glass of liquor before re-joining me. I've almost finished mine and should be getting going, although Ali doesn't hurry me at all. He is so laid-back. I have only been in his company twice but I feel comfortable in this space. His house and his presence.

"I chose the knot because of her name." He offers this piece of information like a riddle for me to solve, so I consider his face. It looks strangely familiar. Brown hair. A perfectly balanced face. A mouth that can pout but won't. I wonder for a second if he's related to one of my numerous relatives. When you come from a small place, you're infinitely connected, and those social webs eat you up until you become someone others want you to be. Or, you escape the snare like I did.

As if sensing my thought, Ali offers more clues, "You may know her. I understand she's rather famous on Irish television."

I consider his face some more. Oh. The strong nose, the twinkly green eyes.

"Dara O'Shea?" I guess. He nods to indicate I am right. She's a big star if you like RTE, the Irish public broadcaster, but I don't. She's probably in her sixties now. Anyone Irish would recognise the actress with the flaming red hair and vivid green eyes like a pre-Raphaelite beauty.

I whistle. "Holy smoke, but you grew up here, right?" Ali has a clear London accent. There's nothing Irish about him. I wouldn't have guessed if he didn't tell me, but that was not unusual given how many Irish immigrants there were.

He opens his palms. "Yeah, well. She didn't want too much to do with me. I was left with my father." His eyes twinkle in the dark as he watches the night.

"Why did she leave?" I try to think if I recall anything about the actress's personal life, but unfortunately no, I haven't paid much attention. Provincial television and the gossip press are not my thing. I had always imagined the world out there waiting for me to explore. Growing up, the only thing I escaped to was music and later fantasies about men. And I'd imagined going somewhere with my one-and-only when I grew up, away from home. How does it feel growing up without a mother, knowing she's abandoned you for an audience of millions out there?

Ali bites his lip, "She was pretty and young, and wanted to be a big star. I guess having a kid might get in the way." I find it hard to imagine how a mother is more interested in being famous than caring for her son. Despite being poor, my parents wouldn't have abandoned us. I have to respect them for it. Even when they couldn't accept my gayness, they didn't exactly kick me out. My father's fist and the scorns. The pressure and the oppressiveness. They'd felt like waves that drove me away. That's all.

"I'm sorry," I offer. He shrugs, his eyes still distant, as though he's thinking about his absent mother.

"What's your dad like?"

Ali takes another gulp of the whisky. "He was a scriptwriter. He wrote screenplays for the BBC. He used to shut himself in his office, writing for most of the day. I became very good at entertaining myself. I'd retreat into my own little world." He forces a smile but it couldn't have been easy. I try to imagine what his childhood was like: a lonely boy who reads a lot. He seems like the studious type to me. It's an upbringing completely different from mine. I wouldn't know too much about growing up alone or staying indoors and studying.

"I don't know what's worse. I'm the middle of five kids, so I never had any peace. No one took any notice of me, either, and I had to look after my younger brother and sister all day long." We were pretty much left to our own devices, so I single-handedly brought them up. I could be responsible if I really tried.

Ali gazes at me again. "It must have been hard." Well, it was not the worst. I liked taking care of them in a way, and my younger brother Finn used to look up to me. Then he got picked on at school for having a poof for a brother, and that was that.

"Do you get on with your dad, though?"

Ali smiles. "I do, actually. It wasn't easy for him. He was a reclusive writer and forced to become a single parent. He's such a closed-off person but I didn't feel not connected. We are quite similar in many ways, so I guess I empathised with him instinctively. I'm definitely not a very social kind of person." He shrugs again in an apologetic kind of way. He's luckier than me, though, if he gets on with his father.

I don't know about Ali not being a social person, either. He has been good company, given the circumstances. I don't ordinarily try to befriend my johns anyway. But conversation with Ali comes naturally. As we talk, I finish my cigarette and the drink. I want to stay and chat like this, but it's not exactly in my job description.

"Well, thanks a million for the whisky. Thousands of Irish people would be proud to have fucked Dara O'Shea's son. Sadly, I'm not one of them. Sorry, I don't do TV."

He laughs. "Still. You should tell me more about Ireland sometime. I've never been."

Boy. I love those mesmerising eyes and his broad grin. He is thinking about booking me regularly if he wants me to tell him about Ireland, right? That's cute.

"You don't pay me for that shit." I chuckle inside in anticipation of more appointments with Ali, so I take out my phone. "Talking of which, can I give you my mobile? Contact me directly. You and I don't pay commission that way." Business is business. It's better to go through the agency with new clients. You can't be too careful these days, especially in London. I've come across my fair share of wackos out there. But, I have good feelings about Ali. No way is this guy a serial killer. So, there's no point paying a middle man. He beams, too, and gets his phone out for us to exchange our numbers.

~~~

I am glad when he calls me the following week. Thursday again. His voice reminds me of these prim and proper British actors. My Irish accent is fading and softening after four years away, but it's still smoky and, I've been told, sexy. The West Cork lilt is pretty distinctive.

"What's up? You want me to come round later? I can avail myself." I hope my smile comes through even if he can't see me.

"Well…" He sounds uncertain even though this is going to be his third appointment with me. Is he still uncomfortable about hiring me?

"It's okay. I'm sure I've heard the request before. Just tell me what you want." I try to sound as jovial as possible.

"I...I remember your ad mentions all-night appointments." I wait for him to finish but he seems to be debating. I can imagine his frown when he struggles to express himself. "Uh, hmm."

To spare Ali further embarrassment, I finish the request for him. "Do you wanna book an all-nighter with me?"

"Yeah, that's it." The relief in his voice makes me smug.

"No problems. When?" I'm quite grateful for the night rate, especially with someone I'd probably fuck without getting paid. It does happen occasionally.

"I'd like to see you tonight. Sorry it's very last-minute. We can make it another night if it's more convenient." His voice is soft and gentle. "I just want to spend more time with you."

It sounds so intimate to my ears, as though he's asking me out. We're meeting at *my* convenience because he wants to spend more time with *me*. Can one do an invisible happy dance? I know I shouldn't mix business with pleasure, but keeping his business is a bonus.

I have a john before him, though. "I can be there about eleven. Is it too late?" It's better late than nothing. I quote him a price. This way, I am already some way towards the month's rent and expenses after only a day's work. Another eight or nine fucks to go.

After the earlier appointment with another client, I go home first to shower and change, then take a taxi to Ali's. The same sense of welcome greets me whenever I am near his place. We hug briefly after he lets me in. He explains why he's in sweatpants and a T-shirt—"I came back from swimming a while ago." I like him in shirts but the casual look suits him well.

Once inside, I shrug off my leather jacket. I bought it in a second-hand market a couple of months ago. I can't refuse my regulars even when I don't need the money because I have to keep them happy. So, sometimes I have extra to spend on luxuries, like better clothes. I refuse to feel bad about being an escort. It's a job like any other. It enables me to eat, to dress well and have a roof over my head.

Ali takes my jacket, gives me a peck and asks, "Are you hungry?"

I have been too busy to remember to eat. That happens a lot when I'm working; my stomach must have shrunk from my begging days. Sasha and I would go for days not eating very much, spending all our hard-earned cash on drugs. We'd made the trip to the soup kitchen when we were desperate.

"I am, actually. I haven't eaten dinner." I follow Ali to enter the kitchen and sit down at his dining table.

He turns to look at me. "Liam, you'll waste away!"

I love the concerned tone in his voice. I consider my arms. Okay, I'm on the skinny side.

His eyes travel the length of my body and he shakes his head as if he disapproves of my lack of self-care. *If only you knew how little I cared for my body in the past.* He takes some food boxes out of a takeaway bag. "Let me feed you tonight, anyway. I didn't know what you liked, so I ordered a Chinese takeout. Hope it's okay." He puts a container in the microwave and turns it on.

Ali places a bottle of beer in front of me and smiles.

"I eat everything," I reply. I sometimes get chips or kebabs, but takeouts are treats. I'd rather save the money so I didn't have to work so much. Mostly, my meals at home involve bread—beans on toast, sausage sandwich and more toasts with one thing or another. Okay, Ali has a point about my diet. It's not exactly healthy.

When one food box pings, Ali puts another one in. Soon, the dining room smells of rice and something delicious. He lays the food out and gives me a plate and chopsticks.

"Wow. Can't use these, mate. You've got a fork?"

He seems amused again, and gives me a knife and fork with a smile. I don't hold back and put rice and whatever's in the boxes on my plate and stuff myself. I didn't realise how ravenous I was until the food was in front of me.

Ali sits down too and spoons some food for himself, but he doesn't have a lot.

"Am I eating too much?" I ask as I put some noodles in my mouth.

He laughs. "No, please. Like I said, I didn't know what you liked, so I ordered a selection. I'm glad you're enjoying it." He continues to watch me eat.

"Beggars can't be choosers," I reply with a mouthful of stir-fry.

He observes me while I stuff my face some more, his curious eyes on me. "Do you see yourself a beggar?"

That's an unfortunate turn of phrase. I put my fork down and gaze at Ali. Do I want him to know my personal history? I decide that I can talk about my experiences with Ali, even though it's more difficult than being naked and having sex with him because it's exposing myself on a more intimate level.

"Ali, I used to panhandle on Oxford Street. This is a definite step up." I sometimes told people I was a busker, but I knew no one gave me money purely for my music. I lived on guilt money and I wasn't comfortable enough with that. But then, I was too messed up to stop myself from doing it, to survive, to pay for drugs.

I watch him to see if he's disgusted but his facial expression doesn't change. "I don't want you to ever feel sorry for me or anything," I add. I have a degree of pride left since I cleaned up my act.

There is a little concern on Ali's face, but otherwise he is still the same kind and open man. "I don't. I often wonder about the reasons behind people becoming homeless and begging, but you don't have to tell me anything."

It's not a story I want to share with him right now. "I won't bore you with the details."

"Okay."

He puts his chopsticks down, and I honestly can't fit any more in my stomach without being sick on him when we have sex later. So, I set my fork aside.

"Thanks, Ali. That was delicious." I ask, "Have you got anything planned for tonight?" I am aware we've already wasted a good portion of the night having a late dinner. I am there for sex. Despite the title, I don't escort anyone and I am not asked to go on dates. I have no illusion what I do for a living.

He turns shy again. "No. I mean nothing special. I didn't feel comfortable that we had sex and you left. I'm not like that."

I consider the man. Really? He already said he liked 'making love' and now he doesn't want me to fuck and go? I frown. "What's wrong with having sex? You want to kiss and cuddle. We can do that but you don't need me all night long. You have your wife for that, Ali." I notice how he plays with his ring a lot when he talks.

Ali's eyes narrow and he blinks. Then he utters quietly, "My wife." Abruptly, he stands up. Not letting me see his face, he takes the plates and dishes into the kitchen. With his back to me, he stacks the plates and dumps the cutlery in the dishwasher, his spine full of tension. I may have touched a raw nerve if he is separated or getting a divorce or in the closet.

I follow him into the kitchen and take his hand, distracting him away from whatever he pretends to be doing with the crockery. "Come on. It's cool. I want to fuck, okay?"

I lead him to the bedroom. I don't know why I treat him so differently from the other johns. I feel bad for upsetting him. It's as though I need to be particularly gentle with him. He's too fragile for my usual brand of insensitivity. I should be the one to show him the ropes. If he's been in the closet, it's perhaps what he needs.

Once we're in the bedroom, I take my clothes off and I help him out of his. The man is gorgeous. His shoulders are broad, and his body's solid without him coming across as a gym rat. His mother is a pretty woman and Ali has inherited her good looks, except that there's something deliciously masculine about his features. He will make good boyfriend material, though it has to be difficult if he is still married and isn't out.

"You're so hot, man." I lick my lips.

I push him down so he's lying on his back. I lean down to kiss him from his mouth to his neck and chest, tracing down the faint line of hair along his front, and wrapping my mouth around his hard cock.

He moans, "Liam."

I only utter a *hmm* while I tease him some more with my tongue, focusing on his erogenous spots. With all-nighters, there is less rush to get them there and get out. My appointments with Ali never felt like that in the first place, but I want to take it easy tonight.

As I am still thinking about how to pleasure him, he asks, "Can you top?"

My eyes snap open with surprise. I can bottom, obviously, since a lot of the men want a tight hole to fuck. But topping is my preferred position. I've forced myself to be versatile since I started turning tricks. My answer is to rim him, teasing him with my tongue, and playing with his balls and hard dick. Low moans reflect Ali's appreciation. "Is this what it feels like?" he asks softly.

I try to digest what he means by that, but my erection is twitching with excitement and distracting me from more introspection. "Hmm?"

I reach for the lube in my discarded jeans and squeeze a generous amount on my hand and fingers. I wipe my hand around Ali's balls and perineum, and push two fingers inside of him until he arches up and onto my digits, as if he's starting to fuck them. By the time I finish with his p-spot, he is gagging for it. Time to put the condom on and apply a great deal more lube to my cock. I consider him again, noting the angular lines of his face and features, his lips apart, eyes with fire burning bright in the dusk of the room. My heart is thumping happily, telling me that this is not only about being physically aroused.

I plunge in then because I can't wait a second longer. His tight arse felt so good, I would have liked to yell if I wasn't on a job. From the ecstatic expression on his face, he loves it, too; he enjoys me being rough and his obvious desire turns me on enormously. I hold on to his thighs and pull them apart more to allow myself access.

"Is this all right, Ali?" I check, just in case, even though his heavy breathing already tells me this is what he wants.

He manages to nod.

"It shouldn't be hurting anymore." I pull out and move in again, angling my cock to brush his glands.

Ali's grin spreads. "It feels good. I feel…full, but it doesn't hurt."

I want to make him feel even better, so I close my still-lubed hand on his erection. I milk him along the rhythm of my movements. He fucks into my fist. I shift to deepen my thrusts. Ali's face is a sight to behold. His cheeks are flushed, and he fixes his gaze at me with an intensity that makes me dizzy. I want to see him come first, so I heighten the pressure on his cock and massage him; he peers out of half-closed eyes and groans. Pre-cum gives way to ropes and ropes of jizz as he explodes, violently thrusting into my fist until he's spent.

I follow, and delve into him hard enough for him to draw up his legs and curl his toes. I hold onto his knees and fuck myself dry, abandoning all inhibition and wanting the man in front of me to lose himself as I take him. All the time, his big eyes are fixed on me. The flushed cheeks, parted lips and unrestricted lust all laid out for my desire. Post-orgasmic Ali is exquisite. Why he ever needs to buy sex is beyond me.

I soon come in waves, feeling the heat that courses through me. Then I collapse on him. He holds me. I mean he properly cuddles me and cups the back of my head so it rests on his firm broad chest. *No, no.* The yearning in me, for tenderness, for all the good things in life that I don't deserve. I only ever felt like this with a couple of men: Cillian and Sasha. When they'd seen the darkness inside me, they left. I don't want to think about them right now, and compare Ali to them. Ali is a client, for fuck's sake. And someone so decent would never be interested in a man like me.

So, I bolt up. "I'll clean us up and I need a cigarette."

CHAPTER 3

I ESCAPE TO THE en-suite bathroom. I wash my hands and splash some water on my face. Then, I grab a flannel, wet it, come back to Ali, and meticulously wipe him clean. I put on my trousers, and go out to his little balcony overlooking the back garden and roll a joint. The blast of cold does my head good. The rush of hash calms me down, too, so the confused emotions I felt while I was having sex no longer flood my brain.

A fragrant scent wafts through the night air. Lily or lavender, I cannot tell. I inhale deeply. Just like Ali, his place fills me with serenity.

Ali's put on a pair of boxers and a T-shirt, and comes out to join me. In the darkness, it's hard to read him. I offer him my joint but he shakes his head. We lean against the railing to admire the dark shades of the night.

After a long silence, he says quietly, "You talked about my wife."

I exhale, waiting for him to continue.

"She, eh, she died last year," he tells me quietly.

Shit. It's tactless for me to bring her up then. "I'm sorry." I meet his eyes which contain barely healed sadness. "She must have been young." From the photograph, she was younger than him. They made a beautiful couple.

He rubs his nose bridge. I notice it's another one of his signs of insecurity.

"Yes, Emily was only forty. She died from breast cancer. We were together for twelve years." His voice shakes slightly, or is it just my imagination because of the breeze?

I feel awful for reminding him of her, but I'm also interested to hear more about his life. It's strange because I normally try to stay away from my johns' stories. I prefer to get in and get out. Some of them are lonely gents who need someone they can talk to. Unfortunately, I often become that person, in addition to providing the sexual services.

"You can tell me more if you want to," I offer, despite my reluctance, because the man in front of me clearly needs a sympathetic listener. If only I had one of those.

Ali nods and continues, "She collapsed on her way to the bathroom one night, and I couldn't resuscitate her. She died in my arms here in the house. I was trying to give her CPR and wishing it was the end at the same time. I felt so guilty for wanting her not to suffer anymore, and seeing my wish come true..." Ali's eyes are watery, making them look like green sapphires against black velvet, illuminated by the moonlight.

I move closer and hug him. It is nothing sexual, but a friendly, supportive kind of contact, and I plant a light kiss on his head. He smells of expensive lemony shampoo and sweat from sex. "Hey, I understand."

He stares at the dusky city and tells me more. "She had been ill for two years. At first, we had hope. So much hope... She was far too young..."

He rubs the tears from the corners of his eyes.

"I took care of her here. Couldn't bear to send her to a hospice. I couldn't do anything other than bathe and feed her, give her drugs, and read to her. It was as if that was my whole purpose—watching her fade away. I thought I was being punished but why was she the one who suffered?"

Punished for what? But I don't dare to ask, as I hardly know him. I let him carry on.

When we part a little, his mild smile comes back. "Well, I've tried to come to terms with it. It's still hard some days." I squeeze his arm and he leans into my embrace. We are very different, but we also share a difficult past that haunts us. Every day, I try to resist returning to drugs, to survive and keep my head above water.

"I'm sorry to bore you with this."

I plant a platonic kiss on the side of his head again. "Hey, I'm not bored. You can tell me anything you want." Damn if I'm going to say this to every client, but it actually feels good to be the one he's talking to. My profession is probably more useful than most people imagine. Like a psychiatrist's couch on the cheap.

"Let's not talk about me anymore." He asks, "Do you have anyone special?"

I almost laugh. It is kind of strange to be intimate with a bunch of men, then go home to a bedsit room and feel the loneliest in my entire life. But I try my best to conceal my feelings by lightening the mood and avoiding the question because it's not Ali's problem. "Is that a roundabout way to ask whether I'm really gay or am I gay for pay?"

Ali cocks his head to gaze at me. "No. I don't suppose it's any of my business." He fidgets, too. "I told you, it's kind of hard for me to have sex with someone without knowing him."

I laugh out loud this time. "Then why have you called for a prostitute?" Most men buy an escort's services because they want anonymous sex. They don't want to get to know him. I light a cigarette and regard him, waiting for an answer.

Ali looks away. When he turns back to face me, his eyes are a little glistened. Fuck, my big gob. He's such a sensitive type. I shouldn't have mouthed off like that. Sometimes I do wonder how I manage to keep any regulars. I mean, I'm businesslike and I don't pretend I am into them, or anything like that. But I deliver. I'm discreet. I'm pretty good-looking with a decent enough body.

Ali...I'm not sure why he needs someone like me, and wants to understand me.

"I found out I was attracted to men about five years ago, but I loved Emily in my own way. I didn't want to hurt her, so I never told her. I thought I'd just suppress my feelings. Lots of men do that, right? Stay in the closet for the sake of their wives and children. Then she got ill. It was even more difficult, then, for me to come out."

I meet his gaze to encourage him to continue. Now I understand why he blames himself.

"Every day I was burdened with the guilt of not coming out to her. I'd be able to say the three small words. She might be angry and upset, and we might have to divorce, but I'd be free. But those words just wouldn't come," he tells me. "I have a confession to make."

I hold my hands up. "Whoa. I don't trust confessions. Don't ever use that word with me."

Ali nods with understanding. "Sorry. I forgot you were probably Catholic."

I shrug to show that I'd got over the effects of a religious upbringing, but I decide to tell him anyway. "My family was religious and I grew up attending all the observances—Sunday mass, confirmations and baptisms. We had something at church every week, and we were always under pressure with the question, 'Have you any sins to confess?' The priest used to ask me if I had any unusual thoughts to tell him. I thought about some boys in school, and I found out how to jerk off when I was maybe nine or ten. I knew better than to tell him *those* peculiar feelings. I remember answering, 'I am only a boy. Of course I have no weird thoughts!'" I laugh.

Ali nods.

I was never any good at lying. Neither the church nor my parents could accept me the way I was. *You're a disgrace. It's immoral.* My dad took out his disgust on me physically, as if he'd beat the gayness out of me, reasserting what he saw as masculinity or some shit like that. As far as I was concerned, my liking boys was no different from other teenage boys and girls who were at it. A couple of my siblings—my sisters Marie and Niamh—were supportive. Finn decided that I embarrassed him when he started secondary school, telling me to fuck off when I tried to take care of him. It hurt to be rejected by my dad, my older brother Patrick and then Finn. That's why I learned to shut down my emotions before they'd get to me.

The only person I trusted was Cillian. We became inseparable when we were fourteen.

I couldn't fucking stand the constant nagging about me being abnormal and disgusting anymore. By the time I finished the Leaving Cert—the first chance I had—I left with Cillian and we went to Dublin. The capital was more tolerant, and he decided it was more fun to be young and single. He was right. We were only eighteen and should've been having the best time of our lives. Still, I felt betrayed to come home and find some dude hammering into my boyfriend in our bed. *Fuck that.*

Tears threaten to fall from my eyes, so I blink hard and look away, hoping that Ali can't see me in the dusk. I should be past caring about what people back home may think of me, but talking about Ireland with Ali has brought the feelings back. It's been four hard years and no one there will understand what I've been through. And fucking Cillian. I wish I could stop crying for that bastard.

Ali looks at me and is deep in thought for a moment.

At last, he quietly says, "I want to tell you that you're my first male sex partner, Liam. Just now, when you were topping. It... it felt so right and natural. Thank you." Ali touches his ring and rubs his chin. "It's pathetic to be so clueless at forty-five, isn't it?"

I get it then. He thinks a professional may help him find out what sex with men's like. I'm glad to be the first man to sleep with him. It must have been a good enough experience for him to keep using me.

"Hey, I dig it. There's nought wrong with gay sex, speaking from experience." I grin. "You know you are into men now. That's good," I try to reassure him. I'm glad that I've achieved something by helping Ali figure out his sexuality.

"You think so?" His eyes brighten. "One of my colleagues, who's gay, suggested the escort agency. I thought it was a crazy idea, but then I became curious and browsed the website one day.

I wasn't actually going to use it. But I…I saw your profile and, well, y'know. You somehow caught my attention." He cards his fingers through his hair, smiling embarrassingly.

"Hey. It must be my Irish charm." I give him a broad beam to show that it's okay. I am genuinely grateful. It's good to know that I'm attractive enough for him to notice me. "Can I ask you something?" My curiosity is really running riot tonight.

"Hmm. It depends!" He smiles.

"Why didn't you just check it out back then? Why couldn't you have called an escort?" I add, "I'm not advocating cheating or anything."

Well, I don't think deeply about the rights and wrongs of anonymous sex. Otherwise, I wouldn't be in my profession. But I also understand how a lot of people believe in fidelity and what it involves. I guess when you find someone you truly love, you won't want to be with anyone else. I once thought that myself. Now, I don't dare to imagine myself in a committed relationship. What I thought I had with Cillian and Sasha only ended in someone getting badly hurt. I'd blamed myself for my failures. I wasn't good enough. That had to be the reason.

He sighs. "I'm way too honest. I'd have felt so bad that I had to tell Emily. The most I did was watching gay porn secretly and jerking off. But even then, I felt utterly awful, as if I *did* have an affair behind her back."

I gaze at his face.

I can only talk about the present, a safer territory. "I'm glad you tried me. Was I what you expected? You know, sexually?"

I can hardly remember my first time. It seems so long ago now. Cillian and I were both virgins and we didn't know what we were doing but we were horny enough to get each other off on his narrow bed. I thought we loved each other and it was the most important thing for me then. I was actually innocent once.

The first time I sold myself was quite memorable. He was a big man and his dick was fat, but he didn't know how to use it. Subtlety is not a trait of most of my clients. It'd hurt despite my preparation but I managed to shut my emotions down. I soon got used to it. I'd shared my life with Sasha, and I'd known other rent boys when I was on the streets.

Selling myself seemed a logical step more than anything else. I knew what I was getting myself into. Doing it through the agency means a slightly better class of clientele, and more money than standing at street corners. A few hundred sexual encounters later, here I am trying to talk to someone twice my age about losing his gay virginity to an escort. Is this irony or just life? I'm not sure.

"Yeah, you...you were great." Colour rises on his cheeks. "I was a very lousy lay with women. For years, I thought there was something wrong with me sexually, but I never figured out what. I couldn't understand why I found it so hard and it took me so long to have an orgasm, and why it didn't feel right thinking about women while I masturbated. It all made sense when I realised I was attracted to men, but then I became consumed with guilt and shame. I wish I had told my wife at the end." He shakes his head, eyes shimmering with unshed tears once more.

I try to imagine that. It is easy to be convinced when everyone around assumes you're straight. I recall how I realised at such a young age. I was in primary school and I had crushes on a couple of the older boys who were gorgeous in my eyes. I would think of them in the bath or in bed and love the tingling feelings in my groin. I fantasised about their naked bodies and their muscular arms. I soon learned to touch myself, though I wasn't sure if the two things were connected. When my classmates started to talk about girls, I looked at photos of famous female stars and celebrities and tried to stare at their boobs, but I felt nothing. My eyes were always drawn to the actors instead. It was simple really.

To show I understand, I reach out and caress his face, and wipe away the moisture around his eyes with my fingertips. "Hey, you're definitely not a bad lay." I smirk to show I am joking, soothing his pain with humour. "You're more than adequate."

He leans into my palm, and then chuckles. "And you should know. I mean, I envy you. From what you said, you are sure about your sexuality."

That makes me laugh again. Envy me? Hot damn. "You're jealous of a whore because he knows his sexuality? You're weird, man." Somehow, Ali sees the absurdity in it too and laughs, sounding like ringing bells. I add, "And yes, I'm definitely gay. I've never been with a woman."

He's still grinning. "See! You're twenty-one and you already know your own mind. I didn't find out till I was twice your age. I'm glad that I can explore my sexuality now."

I shake my head. "Come on, crazy. Let's have a shower and we can have round two. You're wasting your cash on talking to me." I walk back to the bedroom and head towards the bathroom.

He follows me. "By the way, I don't like you calling yourself a whore. And it's not a waste. I like talking to you."

I don't feel ashamed about what I do. For me, on that bench in St Stephen's Green, I left behind any idea of exclusivity, loving the one and only and happily-ever-after or even happy-for-now. I am definitely not remotely happy for now or the foreseeable future. I really think Ali deserves a happy ending, though.

"Well, I'm what I am. I joke about being a whore all the time. It's fine." I hit his arse. "I think there are other things you may like to do with me apart from chatting."

He smiles and we shed our clothes to get into the shower.

We blow each other under the jet of hot water. I wouldn't know what he was like with women, but sex between us has been getting better and better. Ali is no doubt a natural at gay sex.

As we sleep later, Ali holds on to me, spooning me from behind and I have to admit it feels damn good. I need the contact of the warm skin and the solidity of his body. Most all-nighters are hard work and the sex can be relentless. With Ali, it feels like I am staying with a boyfriend. I sense his hot breath on my shoulder and his faint snores are soothing. I'm a light sleeper. It makes it easier to turn tricks at night, but tonight I let myself be held and enjoy the closeness. I manage to sleep for a few hours with some pleasant dreams for once. It hasn't seemed like work. I've felt valued and cared for, which is a brand-new experience for me.

The next day, I should have left early but I give him a lazy early morning blow job instead, before getting dressed to leave. Because Ali has shown me respect, I want to provide the best service to him.

"See you soon." I sit on the edge of the bed and give Ali a peck on the cheek while straightening my shirt. I can't help but smile when I gaze at him.

He reaches out to touch my back and asks sleepily, "I guess Thursday again next week?"

I nod. "Yeah, text me to confirm, okay? You had a good time?" I caress his face with my fingertips. It's still warm from sleep.

He sits up, his fingers combing through his tussled hair. "Yes. Shame I can't afford all-night appointments all the time. You're good for my soul but bad for my purse."

I grin. I've never been told I'm good for anyone's soul before.

He's getting hooked on me, though, which is flattering. My price, however, is non-negotiable. "The only thing I'm good for is your dick," I tease him.

He narrows his eyes and shakes his head, disagreeing with my statement.

An idea comes to me. I've always been quite a party animal when I can afford it. I suppose that's why I became addicted to heroin and crack in the first place. These days, I rarely go out to save money and to reduce the number of tricks I have to do. Besides, I don't feel as horny as I used to. Am I getting old? At the age of twenty-one? Sometimes I'm too tired after work, and all I want to do is have a joint and go to sleep. Getting off seems too much hard work, even if it's for my own pleasure.

Ali in the morning is cute, sleepy and confused, but highly adorable. I feel impulsive and reckless. So, I break my own rule about escorting. "Listen. You wanna go for a drink before the next appointment? It's not part of the service but we can go to a gay bar, if you like?"

I knew he wouldn't have been into the scene. Otherwise, he'd have no use for me. Bet he can get a hookup in seconds if he signs up to Grindr or goes cruising.

Surprise flashes across his face, but then he agrees. "Ah, sure. I'll pay you, of course."

I take my first cigarette of the day out of the packet, ready to walk and smoke in the early morning. "Damn it. I fancy a drink. Just pay me for a fuck like you normally do, all right?" Before I can change my mind, I continue, "I'll come round at eight."

He nods and smiles.

I walk out, feeling lighter on my feet. The day has just broken, as though Ali's grin has penetrated the darkness inside of me.

PART TWO
HIS PIPE DREAM

CHAPTER 4

I TURN UP AT Ali's door on time. He's in his usual plain shirt and jeans. A faint scent of cologne seduces me as Ali and I sit in a taxi to go to Dalston in East London. I have an urge to hold his hand while we sit side by side, but instead, I stare out of the window to see the changing lights as the car glides through the darkness. While avoiding physical contact and conversation, so I can hide my interest, I observe him through the soft reflection, his face blurred by the surface of the glass. The butterflies in my stomach flutter, and I silently curse myself for being a stupid idiot. We're going for a drink. I've already had sex with the man numerous times. Why should I be apprehensive?

Because it's a kind of intimacy that may lead to more, and I'm afraid of what it entails. My past experiences will jinx my chance of finding and keeping a friend.

It feels a little awkward sitting in the bar together since Ali and I don't know each other well. His presence calms the nerves I felt on the way here. Being there with Ali has grounded me, as though we do this kind of thing all the time. I'm glad to have asked him to come out. It's not like I have a lot of mates to go bar-hopping with anyway. These days, I avoid going to bars too much. It's much cheaper to get some cans in and drink with the guys in the flat. And I don't run into drug addicts and dealers that way.

Ali buys the first round of drinks and we sit in comfortable silence as he surveys the bar, which is all stainless steel and modern, with pale wood flooring and large glass windows that would let plenty of light in during the day. He glances around, soaking in the atmosphere, while taking a generous gulp of the beer.

I clean up the foam on his upper lip with my fingers. Ali smiles. The connection between my hand and his face sends slight currents that course through me. I enjoy the little electricity I sense whenever I touch him like that. I can indulge myself in that kind of tenderness tonight. *Maybe.*

"It's the sort of cool joint some of my colleagues would love, gay or not," he comments, still casually appraising the bar.

I take a large sip of my ale and probe, "What do you do? I never asked."

"I'm in special effects. My office is right in the middle of Soho but I never frequent the gay establishments." He chuckles, his shoulders shaking slightly.

"You mean special effects in movies and all that?"

He nods. I don't know what I find more incredible: his job or the fact that he never goes to the gay bars in Soho while working there.

"Wow, you're kidding me, right? Which movies have you worked on?"

He reels out the titles like they're nothing. The man has done the effects on lots of the major Hollywood animations and blockbusters. I can't believe that not only is Ali the son of a famous Irish actress, his job is also totally glitzy.

"That's so fucking cool!" My eyes are wide, as if I've just met a Hollywood A-list.

He frowns. "You seem surprised."

That makes me laugh. "Sorry. I kinda expected you to do something sensible, like working in an office or accounting or some shit. Maybe a schoolteacher." I can't help the chuckling. Usually my johns' personal lives present little interest to me. I shouldn't try to guess what they do. Appearances can be deceptive. I don't think deeply about most of them. Ali is an exception, though he isn't someone I'd normally go for. It's not only his age but he's gorgeous, well-dressed and appears to be highly educated. Class. That's it. Compared to me, Ali is a class above. No doubt about it. There's no way someone like Ali will be interested in me. Yet, I'm sitting here and I want to know his personal history. That's intimacy at a level I'm not sure I'll be comfortable with.

"That's..." He looks pained, biting his lip. "I'm insulted that you think I'm a boring office worker or a stuffy teacher!" But then he regards me for a second. He can see the funny side and he joins me, giving me a face-splitting laugh.

I grimace. "Sorry. I'm not insinuating that you're dull. But you've got a proper well-paid job. I don't associate with people like you." The more I find out about him, the more I realise that he's a seriously cool guy under the clean-cut appearance.

"People like me, aye? There goes the theory that I'm rather unique." The smile on his face reaches everywhere, showing much amusement.

I kiss him lightly, tasting the hint of dark beer on his lips. "Of course you are. Of course."

He laughs, enjoying our silly conversation. "Is that what you tell everyone?"

"No, I don't tell anyone anything." Flattery is not my strong suit. Besides, Sash used to say I was the most tactless guy around and he was not wrong.

Ali shakes his head, still chuckling.

"If you're in showbiz, how come you're so fucking shy about being gay?" I am guessing that people in film are flamboyant by nature. I try to imagine him with these creative types, but he is not like how I picture those kinds of people. He is so not Tinseltown. Perhaps the London scene is different.

He sets his beer down. "I'm not shy about being gay, Liam. I'm shy. Period. The job is perfect for a computer nerd. I'm not an actor. I'm the guy thirty steps away from the finished product. I'm the man who draws Shrek's nose hair."

"You did that? That's way too cool." I snigger. I had a computer when I was at home in Ireland, but I wouldn't know anything about being a nerd.

"No, I didn't. I was giving you an example." He laughs so hard his face has turned red.

When he finally stops, he turns serious again. "Besides, I was married to a woman until a year ago, I wasn't out for that reason, too." He reminds me he has only recently 'come out'. "It still feels strange to think of myself as a gay man. Told you I'm quite pathetic."

Now, I feel like crap for laughing at him. "You're not pathetic, Ali."

He smiles again. Gorgeous. "I like you too." The truth is I like Ali a lot. But I am afraid to admit it.

The ale is pretty smooth, and I become more relaxed around Ali as we settle into our evening. I have not felt like this with anyone for a long time, enjoying easy companionship. When I was living on the street, I had acquaintances but they came and went, some tragically. I couldn't relax because there was always danger lurking around the corner when I was homeless.

"So, did you go to college? How do you get into special effects?"

He nods. "You remember I told you I was always by myself when I was a kid because my father ignored me? I taught myself to programme and it went from there, really. I completed my undergraduate degree and a Master's in computer science and got a break. I've been in this job for over twenty years."

"Nice!" It's so easy to speak to Ali that I find myself opening up about my past.

"I should have gone to university after school, but I forfeited that privilege when I left home. I had the grades for it too. I may sell my arse for a living now but I am no dummy."

Apart from Sasha, I'd not told anyone this much since coming to London. Sasha and I shared something deeper, but ultimately, he never felt the same about me as I did about him. I'd learned early on that the streets were dangerous, so the less other people knew about me the less they'd use it against me. I had to be on high alert all the time which was stressful. That's why so many of us ended up with mental health issues. I had trained myself to shut off emotionally.

"You're not stupid at all, Liam." Ali shakes his head.

"Thanks! So, when I was in my nappies, you were already creating Pokémon to sell to us kids." I smile, flashing my white teeth. It's much easier for me to joke about things than to talk about myself.

He pokes my chest in jest. "You cheeky sort! I had nothing to do with Pokémon." He laughs, though, and I really like the fact that he never seems to get upset when I'm being a brat.

To change the subject, I go outside for a smoke. Ali comes out with me and stands by my side, his eyes on me the whole time. As I savour my smoke and flick the built-up ash off, I try to direct the conversation to him again. Out of the two of us, Ali is the safer topic by far. "So, how did you find out you were into men?"

He scratches his head. "I…I had a crush on someone at work."

I raise an eyebrow. "You mean you fancied him?"

"Uh-huh. Sort of. He was a few years younger than me and worked in my department. Like I said, I couldn't hurt Emily, so…" He may be blushing but I can't see too well in the moonlight. "I'd only feel guilty about it."

"What happened to him, then?" I light another cigarette while he talks. "Did you tell him you're into him?"

Ali squints under the streetlamp. "He left the company. That's it. He knew about my feelings…" He shifts position. "We didn't act on it. We didn't do anything."

I watch him intently, still trying to understand his past.

"You mean he also fancied you?" He's reluctant to talk about things. I ask because he's got my interest. It sounds like fucking *Romeo and Juliet*. "But you wouldn't have an affair."

Ali nods, his eyes dull for a second. "He left the company because of me. I was…" He wipes down his face with his palm. "It was just painful."

Oh, shit. I recognise too well the ache in his voice. I let him carry on.

"I felt like I cheated on her and I let him down anyway. One kiss. That was all we allowed ourselves. And we said we wouldn't spend any more time together. He decided he couldn't do that and resigned." Loyalty clearly meant a lot to Ali. "Do you think I was being old-fashioned and stubborn?"

I think about the predicament. Theoretically, yes, I guess that's what most people in committed relationships would struggle with, but I haven't had that kind of personal experience. When I expected Cillian to be devoted to me, he'd only thrown my trust back in my face.

"I honestly don't know what I would have done in your situation. You're asking the wrong person about relationships and being faithful."

Ali's mouth forms an 'O' shape. Yeah, right. I would love to find a boyfriend at some point, but I'd have thought the chance of that happening to me was slim to none. My family had drummed into me that there was something wrong with me. And now, it's hard to see any decent man being involved with me.

"But, are you sure you're not bi?" Ali has said that he loved his wife in his own way.

He sighs, "I wish I were. At first, I thought I might be, too. And after ending my relationship with Matt, that's the guy's name, I wanted to get back to being married to Emily. Just forget about being gay." He tries to laugh, but tears pool in his eyes again. "Sorry, I don't mean to say it's not right to be gay," he says.

I shake my head. "I know that's not what you mean. So, you gave up the chance to be with this colleague. Then what?"

"I tried to forget the whole episode, dismissing it as a phase, like some stupid homophobe…" I can't help it, but I move closer to Ali and wrap my arm around him. Encouraged by my embrace, he continues, "My love for Emily was…more platonic. It was not the same anymore. I noticed other men. The things I thought about when I jerked off… I watched gay porn when Emily was not at home. It's a different kind of attraction. I knew and it was difficult to admit that I made a big mistake and I was hurting her whether she knew or not."

"Why did you come to me?" I ask. I find myself fascinated by Ali's story, even though my heart breaks for him.

Ali gazes intently at me, his eyes still glittery with unshed tears. "She's been gone nearly a year. I'd like to find someone but…I also wanted to know if I'd like to be with a man sexually. I'm sorry."

"There's no need to feel sorry. It's my job."

Ali swallows. I see his Adam's apple moving along. When he speaks, his voice is soft, as if he's pleading. "Only because it's your job? For me, I like being with you. It surprised me because I wasn't expecting that given our age gap."

I gape at him. What is my reason? Why am I taken by Ali? I'd invited him to come out to the bar. I scratch my head. I've allowed myself to follow my heart, and for him to break through my defences. "I like you." Is it enough reason to ignore my escort's professional code?

Ali smiles. "It's enough for now. Don't you think?"

I should ask him 'enough for what?' but I'm afraid of the answer. This something that I'm feeling urges me to stay on the pavement outside the bar, to listen to him talk about his life, and be the one who comforts him when he needs. *Why am I doing this? Am I expecting the same from him? Someone who cares about me, despite what a fuck-up I am?*

I shake my head to get rid of my confusing thoughts. I light another cigarette, just for something to do. "Are you out to your colleagues and friends now?"

Ali squeezes his hands together. "Yes. Mostly."

"Uh? What do you mean by that?" I ask.

Ali cocks his head as though considering how to explain things to me. "I have a lot of friends who were also Emily's, so it's awkward." I run my palm along his arm to try to help him talk. Ali gazes at me and shivers but I don't think it's from the chill of the night.

"I lost most of those so-called friends. They thought I'd betrayed her somehow. Emily's family and sister don't know. I'm not sure how I can explain it to them. Her parents live in Spain now, so I haven't had to deal with them yet." He swallows. "People at work are fine but they try to set me up."

I frown and attempt to understand these social situations. I think I can empathise. It's strange how coming out can be difficult whether you're forty-five or eleven.

I stub my cigarette butt underfoot. I feel a pang of pain thinking about Ali getting a boyfriend. I know he said he liked me but I'm only an escort he's hired. If he wants to find out about gay sex, he's had enough practice with me now. There's no reason why he shouldn't be out there getting laid, or finding a more suitable partner. "Is there something wrong with the blokes your workmates hook you up with?"

Ali definitely blushes this time and he rubs his chin. As he gazes at me, his eyes glitter under the hazy moon. Instead of answering me, he leans in and kisses me, his arms drawing me closer to him, trapping me between his broader body and the wall.

Our kiss deepens as we explore each other through our tongues and lips. The combination of the faint scent of cologne and the taste of Ali's mouth is intoxicating. It feels tender and intimate, and I don't know what to do with it. I only know I want to be kissed by him and I want to be held by him this way. We are out there for a long time tongue-fucking until there is a wolf whistle from someone walking past, and I realise my hands have been all over him as well, caressing his arms, back and his tight arse while he continues to hold me close. We break away and grin at each other.

When we go back in the bar for another drink, I ask him to tell me more about how he creates the characters and the scenes. Ali drinks from his pint of beer. "Unfortunately, I no longer get involved with the small parts now—the line drawing and filling in, the detail work. That's because I'm a project leader." When he talks about his work, his eyes light up and he uses his hands, as if he's trying to draw in the air. He must love his job.

"I oversee the creation of characters in our unit. It'd be a small animal or a side character. We—my team—will build it from how the whiskers are, to the way it looks, showing different emotions, various postures and poses. What the character looks like when it's angry, happy, excited. I still love the hand-drawn part, more than when it goes into digital realisation."

Ali clearly knows his stuff. He has to be pretty good and experienced if he's leading a team.

"It sounds intense." I try to imagine the work. Art wasn't something that I was wild about but I did grow up watching some of the films that Ali had worked on.

"It really depends on what the producers and directors want. After the detail work, we'll use green screen for the movements. Do you know what that is?"

I shake my head and he explains the procedure to me. As he speaks, he's so animated for someone who is usually reserved. I can really see his passion for his creations. I'm pretty ignorant when it comes to anything technical. I'm okay with my mobile and using the apps, but even having a phone has been a new development for me. I wasn't one of those beggars who could afford one. Now, I do need it constantly in order to get the jobs.

We are sipping our second beers when he asks, "Tell me to shut up if you want, but what do you do when you're not working?"

That's easy. "I listen to music and play my flute."

Ali's eyes sparkle as he looks attentively at me. "Why do I have a feeling you're a very good musician?"

I smile. "Yeah, I'm pretty good." It's been a very long time since I've been reminded that I'm not a complete loser and that I'm actually good at something. "I've been playing music since I was four or five. I was in the school orchestra, leading the flautists."

He listens with great concentration and replies, "I'd really love to hear you play some time."

"Maybe." It's nice having someone interested in my music, but we're not yet friends. I have to keep repeating that to myself as the conversation continues. "I played the tin whistle when I used to beg. You might have heard me." Or, Ali might have been like all the other people who ignored me, who thought of me as garbage that littered the streets in London. Even now, I'd feel the curious mixture of self-loathing and survival instinct.

"I think I would have noticed you too! Oxford Street, you said?"

I nod.

"I really can't recall a tin whistle player, I'm afraid." He frowns. "But I tend to leave some coins for anyone living on the streets when I walk past."

"Most people don't take much notice of us." Most people probably think I'm crazy to be nostalgic for my homeless days, but sometimes I think back on them and relish the sense of freedom. Freedom that also ended in hell and an addiction that shackled me to physical survival. Now, I'm clean and I work but I feel like a buoy not quite anchored anywhere.

"I try to, though," Ali answers, with clear concern on his face. "Why did you end up homeless in London in the first place?"

Thinking back to that time hurts but I don't have a reason to lie to Ali. He's perhaps the first person who's cared enough to want to know since I cleaned up my act. I find myself trusting him and opening up.

"I wasn't only homeless. I was addicted to heroin and crack." My fingers circle the rim of the glass and I avoid looking at Ali as I confess to him about my past drug use. He grabs my hand, though, and wraps it in his big warm palm. I could almost hear my dad's voice in my head about how worthless and disgusting I was. "I lived in a squat with someone. I loved him but I was so fucked up that I'd let him go and sell himself. We were destroying each other."

I tremble but his hand remains steady on mine.

"But you survived."

"Barely." I look up and I'm met by his beautiful green eyes. "I'm a fucking idiot."

He shakes his head. "You're too hard on yourself. You managed to come off drugs. It must have been traumatic. How old were you?"

"I was eighteen, nineteen. My boyfriend...Sasha...he was a year younger. I can't tell you how hooked we were. It was as if I wasn't myself anymore. I didn't have a thing to my name, and it's easier to cope with the cold and the abuse on the street if you're wasted, y'know?" I feel myself cracking, losing my voice, but Ali kisses my cheek.

"It's okay." His hand gently touches my head, my neck, grounding me.

"I let him down. I not only watched him deteriorate, I got jealous cuz he met another boy. Sasha'd never loved me. He wasn't in a state to know how to love anyone. I should have known." A tear falls on the table. Then another.

"I should have taken better care of him but I was too drugged up most of the time. We held on to each other for survival for a while. When I was high, I'd only think about where the next hit would come from. Junk was all that mattered." My voice breaks.

Ali kisses my hair. "You don't have to tell me any more if you don't want to."

But tonight, a little gate has opened. "My life was ugly." *I'm filthy inside too, just the way I was born. That's what they kept telling me.*

"But you can live a different life, Liam."

I gaze at him again through blurred vision. I want to believe him. He wipes my face and plants another kiss on my forehead. I stare, wondering how I'd change my life.

"I'm sorry. I don't mean there's anything wrong with your life. I don't know how…" Ali whispers.

I nod. "It's okay. I told you my life's shit."

"You're off drugs now, though?" Ali is scrutinising me thoughtfully.

I down my beer. "Yeah, except hash and cigarettes but you know about that." I've got emotional, talking to him, but his attentiveness tells me I can. I appreciate that. I haven't talked about myself so much since coming out of rehab. Opening up to Ali is a relief, even though I am a little afraid of how he may respond, how he will see me knowing my past. He hasn't reacted negatively or shown any judgement.

"But that's enough for tonight. I don't want to go on about my fucked-up life. I've got a better side that I think you'll like more." I force a smile, and try to think about business again.

Ali grins. "Yeah, the back side."

I join him in chuckling. "Likewise."

Ali is finishing his drink. "Am I allowed to flirt with you?" He turns serious for a second.

I continue to laugh quietly. Have we been flirting with each other? That kiss outside of the bar. Wow. It was the most sensuous, teasing kiss ever. "Of course you are. I'm an action-louder-than-words kind of guy, though, when it comes to sex."

Ali smiles. "I, uh, like your actions."

"We'd better head back, then, so I can put on my Action Man suit and fuck the hell out of you."

Ali breaks into a peal of laughter. "That's not flirting. It's a threat. A damn good one. I can't wait."

Geez, what the fuck am I doing? Breaking my rule, seeing him for a drink, and fucking enjoying it. It's dangerous. Very uncool. But I consider his striking face and feel calm. Feel good without additional chemical substance. I shake my head, as if I can ditch all the deeper thoughts. I am quite aware that this 'relationship' isn't healthy, not in my escort's rule book. If going out with Ali is reckless, it's also totally exciting.

With all these musings crowding my head, I'm mostly quiet travelling back to his house in a cab. I become vaguely aware that Ali has been looking intently at me. We sit close together. Ali reaches out and takes my hand, our fingers lacing together. Ali seems so radiant next to me; I feel like I'm glowing inside.

As soon as we arrive at his house, and after he closes the door, he shoves me back against the wall in his hall. We kiss. There's nothing slow and tender in this one. Our tongues dance. Ali only breaks away to lead me upstairs. As we climb the short flight, he toes off his shoes and starts to take his shirt off. I see eager and all I can do is follow.

It's as if we're in a rom com when we leave traces of our garments from the hall to his bedroom. We stumble into the room. I can't help but laugh and Ali beams. His shirt's off, top buttons of his trousers already open. I peel my T-shirt over my head. He takes his trousers and boxers off, exposing how hard he already is. Likewise, I pull my jeans and briefs off.

"How do you want me?" I smile, feeling giddy and tipsy. Ali seems to be, too, and his drunken energy is not only from the alcohol. We're continuing the sexual force from our earlier kiss outside the bar.

He climbs onto the bed and drags me towards him. "Fuck me. I'm so ready." It's not an Ali I see much, but I like it.

"Okay. Okay." I take out lube and condom as he plants himself face down. This is one of the occasions that calls for speed. I quickly drizzle and spread lube, put the condom on and without hesitation plunge in.

Ali mumbles some incoherently delicious words that totally go over my head. I am concentrating too much on how to please him and my urgent need to get off. Ali's rubbing himself against the mattress and I push in deeper and deeper. Then pull back and bury myself in him again.

We fuck in a primal and desperate way. As I near orgasm, I can no longer tell what our relationship is.

Ali thrusts his hips while I fuck him.

"Jerk yourself off."

He grabs hold of his cock and uses the friction against the mattress to help him. When he comes, I feel his hole contracting around me and I soon follow him, emptying myself into the condom.

I'm so fucked, in a good way, and in a totally unprofessional way. I shouldn't have gone for a drink with him. Shouldn't have let him kiss me like that outside the bar. And we shouldn't have fucked like lovers.

CHAPTER 5

I LOOK FORWARD TO Ali's night every week. He makes me feel so cared for when he requests an all-nighter. Ali usually orders food or he cooks for me. When he finds out I enjoy the Chinese takeaway near him, he buys from it the most. It's the first time since I left home that I am treated like someone who matters. I wouldn't have thought that a client would make me pine for Thursday nights as if they're dates. I have no fucking clue what I'm going to do about his obvious interest in me.

I do know this: I can't hide the excitement in my stomach anymore as I approach his house every week.

Occasionally we do something that seems almost ordinary, like this one night we go to his local pub in Islington before our appointment. I really like these old bars in London. The stale smell of beer mingles with the sticky red carpet, patterned wallpaper, the wood panels and faded décor, all things that trendy Londoners shun now. They remind me of the pubs at home, except in London we don't find the old men staring at *the queer boy* whenever I enter this kind of establishment because no one here knows me, and most proprietors don't give a shit about my sexual orientation. And the music. I sometimes imagine the Irish music I grew up with whenever I sit in a pub like this. Ali seems to prefer the traditional drinking holes, too, rather than the glitzy modern ones.

The local ale is smooth and dark, and it soothes my throat nicely. Ali is pretty quiet and I am still insecure about how I should behave around him when I'm not working, so we mostly sit and grin at each other. Ali and I behave as though we're a couple getting to know each other on our first date. The warm feelings are winning me over bit by bit, despite all my trepidation about getting attached to someone.

For the umpteenth time, I notice how deep and green his eyes are. How they light up when he laughs, which is often. My heart rate increases. I should call it quits while I'm on top. *But I want to see him.* It must be my need for a friend. Someone who seems to like me for being *me.*

Ali stops my meanderings when he suggests, "How about we have a game of snooker?" I look over at the table where a few guys have just finished a game.

I don't even remember the rules. I played a few times when I was in Dublin, but Ali has to show me how to position the cue properly and the order of balls to aim for.

"Okay, let me demonstrate how it's done." He leans over, his long legs stretching, accentuating his lovely backside. I practically salivate over how his fine arse fills his jeans. He concentrates, his left hand beautifully placed on the edge of the green, strong veins supporting his action. The cue makes a clean strike, and one of the red balls glides along to the far pocket. There really is an art to playing snooker and Ali has the showmanship for it.

He repositions himself and hits the black. He beams at me, then moves to take the black ball out again and puts it back on the table. Ali glides along like a large cat, I've decided, and I'm surprised at how good it is just to watch him and the killer glint in his eyes.

I tease, "Show me how I'd hold the cue again." I lean over the cue and gesture him to come and hold my hands. He does, his solid body covering mine, and his sturdy arms holding me in position. It's like a prelude to sex. *Hmm, being bent over the snooker table...*

"I'm still not getting it, Ali. Hold my hands again and show me?" The amusement in my voice is quite obvious.

He does. His face is so close to me that I can feel his breath. He whispers, "I love it when you play dumb. It's endearing."

I chuckle and he moves back, releasing my arms and hands. I miss his body heat already.

I take my turn and manage to pocket three balls in a row.

Ali's grin widens. "Are you sure you're not lying to me and pretending to be a novice?"

I shake my head. "I think it's purely beginner's luck."

As if on cue, excuse the pun, my next hit completely misses the mark, and the ball rolls over to the opposite side of where I intend it to. After that, I lose easily because Ali is a damn fine player.

When we sit back down and take up our drinks, I sip my beer and make fun of him. "Okay. This is not fair. I bet you've been playing this longer than I've lived."

He shakes his head and smirks. "There's got to be a few things that I'm good at because I have age on my side. I started playing snooker when I was at college."

I consider him. I honestly don't feel Ali's age most of the time. Okay. When we have sex, I'm the more skilled. When we talk, I never feel I don't have enough to say because of the age gap. I guess my past experiences have made me mature beyond my years or I have simply skipped a part of growing up all together.

"Do you play anything else?" I ask.

"Not really. No team sports anyway. I go swimming every week." I know about that. A couple of times during our appointments, he told me he'd come back from the pool. "What about you?"

"I run. It's the cheapest way to keep fit."

I try to stay healthy, to look good. It's better for business. I am quite lucky because I don't really tend to put on weight even when I remember to eat. I'm aware that my body shape makes me a twink, even though I'm a bit too tall for one.

Ali nods. "Swimming and snooker. I seem to like sports that are a bit technical. I'm geeky like that."

I can't help but make fun of him. "So, how do you think you've performed so far, sexually? It's quite technical, you know."

He smiles and shakes his head, realising I'm joking. "I still feel a bit weird being able to enjoy sex but…thank you for 'coaching me'." He makes the quotation marks with his hands, and gazes at me with warm eyes. "You're the more experienced one here. How much do you rate me out of ten, Liam?"

"Hmm. I can't do that." In my heart, I want to give him full marks for his effort. In fact, in an alternative universe when I don't think about sex as work, I'd definitely sleep with him for free.

He finishes his beer and cocks his head. "Why not?"

"If I'm going to start grading my clients, I won't have any left." I laugh to hide my nerves about discussing the other men I sleep with in front of Ali.

Ali narrows his eyes for a split second, but then lets it go. "Well, if there's a rating system for you, I guess I may have to give you a pretty high score."

I can't help but laugh at that. Imagine being ranked on the escort agency's page. It'd be embarrassing. I can only deflect with the lifting of my glass. "Cheers! I guess you can't compare anyone to me since I'm your first and only…unless…" It's presumptuous of me to think Ali hasn't explored other options since he had sex with me the first time.

He scratches his head. "No. Uh. Just you, since you're perfect for my needs."

"Perfect for your needs, huh?" I feel proud. Most people would probably think it's pathetic for an escort to be happy because a john praises him for his services, but I don't care. I know Ali's sincere about that, just like he's honest about so many things. He makes me feel good about myself. "For that, you've earned a drink." I pick up our empty glasses and head to the bar.

On the way home, Ali stops outside a group of greasy takeaways. "You hungry?"

"Ah, yeah." I skipped my dinner again. Now with a few pints in my stomach, I could do with some food.

We're just outside a kebab shop that sells chips, pizza, and probably every other kind of fast foods if the price is right. I raise my eyebrows as a question mark. Ali only shrugs. We must have been a little drunk to think the cholesterol feast is a good idea.

Ali and I enter the shop and purchase a couple of kebabs. We eat like two college kids as we walk back to his house, picking up bits of reconstituted meat and onions, with sauces covering our fingers.

He glances over at me and laughs. "This is so undignified!"

"That'll teach you. You're the one who wants to go out with me. You're lowering your standards, Alastair." I chuckle.

He stops, chewing on his food and scrutinising me, as I also come to a halt.

We are surrounded by the dusk and damp, sogginess seeping through my thin jacket. I hadn't noticed it had started to drizzle. I stand still and regard him, while sucking on my greasy fingers. Something between us has changed, and it's as thick and sticky as the rainy air tonight.

Ali shakes his head. "What do you know about my standards?"

I am lost for words. It is true. Perhaps I don't know him enough. We fuck like rabbits once a week and I enjoy having sex with him. But that's not it. I like how we share and how he treats me like an equal. In bed, we are versatile with each other. Ali is as much a giver as a taker, which makes him a great lover. I'd say he sets a high standard for himself, and he treats everyone with the utmost care and respect. After all, he's been tremendously generous and friendly towards a sex worker. I can't say the same for many of my other clients. The man in front of me is a gem and I'm lucky to know him. I want to know him better.

Shit. Hot sauce is sliding down my hand. I have to rescue it with my mouth. I run my tongue up and down the affected fingers and suck on a blob of the sauce.

The seriousness of a moment ago has evaporated. Ali laughs once more. "Damn, Liam. Don't expect me to have a sensible conversation with you when you're licking your fingers like that!"

I do look like I'm sucking a small dick off. I recognise, then, what I've been doing and join him in chuckling. Yeah, that's right. I'm often accidentally sexy. It makes my job easier. I grab hold of his hand, grease be damned, and pull him towards his place. I can't wait to use my fingers on him and get them sticky again.

~~~

I've found out what makes Ali tick, so I made a purchase specially for him. Extra service. Star escort and all that.

His eyes widen when I present him with the small box. "Oh, is that what I think it is?"

"It is." I grin.

Considering he has only recently discovered gay sex, Ali is happy to experiment and will trust me to do anything. Trust. The fucking idiot.

"It'll feel good if you let me." I can totally understand it if he doesn't want to go so far, though.

His lips turn up and he soon smiles shyly. "Yeah, all right. I trust you."

I consider him, my heart surging with delight. Trust. What a small but powerful word. No one—my family, Cillian, Sasha— thought highly enough of me to trust me, while at those points in my life, I let myself love them and expected the same in return. Now, this gorgeous man believes in *me*.

I shake my head and try to focus on my task. I eat his arse, thoroughly prepping him. With plenty of lube, I carefully insert the little electric plug inside of him, checking all the time that he's happy with it.

He frowns at one point. "Hmm."

My hands stall. "We don't have to…"

Ali cocks his head. "It's okay."

He gradually gets used to it and I patiently arouse him the best I can. Then, I ride him like there's no tomorrow. To say whatever goes on between us is like fireworks would be too clichéd, but the sex is definitely spectacular. I don't have the words to describe my thumping heart as I watch his come-face.

When he calms down, he burrows down to blow me. He has grown to love it; though not at pro standard, he makes up for it with care and passion. I chuckle after I come. He looks up, his big eyes wide.

Releasing me with a plop, he asks, "What? Did I do something wrong?"

I try to stop myself from laughing. "You were a gay virgin a few months ago, Ali. It's really funny to see you with a butt plug and blowing like a champ."

His response is to hug me and rub his head against my neck like a cat. I enjoy Ali's clinginess, making it really difficult to leave after my appointments with him. I smell his musky hair now and inhale the lingering scent of sex, which has become so familiar and safe. He plants kisses all around my shoulders and neck, tingling me so tenderly.

When he looks up again, his gaze is intense. "Liam. I'd never experienced orgasms like this. As though...sex is finally right."

I don't know what to say but I rub his head and kiss him deeply. "Sex is never wrong." I do empathise. I'd been told my sexuality was unnatural so many times when I was growing up. At least I know now consensual sex should be a good thing. I add, "You're great."

He purses his lips as he thinks about it. "Emily and I tried for a baby. She wanted to be a mum, like a lot of women of her age. That's also another reason I thought there was something weird about me. And after I discovered I was attracted to men, I was glad we didn't have children. I felt really shitty about that."

I'm sure if Ali did have a child, he'd have loved him or her to bits, though. "I'm sorry."

He sighs. "I was just so upset for Emily because not having a kid was one of her regrets when she found out she was dying. I couldn't help but wonder if it was my karma."

"I don't understand." I frown.

"I know it's irrational, but I almost made myself believe that because I was gay, I couldn't make her pregnant and it was all my fault. I should be the one who was punished. And yet, she had cancer and it's unfair. I couldn't help it but that's how I felt the whole time she was ill."

I feel sad for him, imagining all the difficult emotions he'd gone through in the last few years.

"Thank you, Liam. You made me realise it's okay for me to try to enjoy my life. I'm not hundred percent there yet but I'm fine for now."

"I helped you realise it?" Uncertainty floods my brain.

"Yes, you. That's why I came to you again, after the first time. You helped me see that it's okay to explore my sexuality. I'd see that you didn't have much of a hang-up about it. I hope I don't sound dumb." He scratches his head.

"No…" All of a sudden, I'm burdened with a sense of responsibility. In a good way. I swallow. "Okay. Thanks, I guess. I'll put that on my CV. Specialised in helping men feel positive about gay sex."

Ali laughs. The sound warms me up so nicely, I want to stay and cuddle.

Eventually I get up and leave, much later than is necessary for a fuck. I bend down and kiss Ali, who still reminds me of a large feline—a lazy tamed tiger who is watching me put my clothes back on.

I press a brief kiss on his lips. "Don't get up. I'll let myself out."

I circulate his house and the surrounding streets a couple of times. I like the tranquillity around here at this time of the night. It's nothing like where I grew up, though, where the countryside would be pitch-dark at night, and the only sounds were from small animals. I'm used to the city now but I will never be completely at ease. A few people shuffle along, hurrying to go home to their loved ones. This feels reckless but I'm going to brave the consequences.

Before I can change my mind, I find myself back in front of Ali's little house and I ring the bell. It takes him several minutes to come down. Perhaps he's still getting dressed. I can hear some faint noises in the house and smile to myself, trying to imagine him hurrying to open the door.

"Liam?" His face is priceless when he sees me—happy but at the same time worried why I have come back.

I barge in before I can persuade myself to run away. I take my leather jacket off again. "No, you didn't ask for an all-nighter and you won't be paying for it. But can I stay here tonight?" I think I'm blushing with the request, as though I'm asking for something illicit.

I am sick of my small room and waking up on my own. I dig why he wants me there all night. Besides, I have no more bookings after Ali, so, I am officially off. My time is my own. That's my justification for breaking my rules about escorting. I must be getting to trust Ali too.

He gives me a face-splitting beam and takes my jacket. "Of course. Come in and get comfy." I go into his sitting room, somewhere I'm pretty well acquainted with now.

He cracks open a couple of beers and hands me one as we sit on his wide sofa. "Do you want to watch a film?"

I nod while taking the bottle of beer from him. "I'd like that."

Ali lets me choose, so I go for his DVD collection. I pick out an animation film I know he worked on. We converse intermittently when he tells me something about what was done behind some of the scenes. I feel so comfortable in his presence.

Midway through the film, I shift closer to him and kiss him, deeper than I would have done on a job because I am off the clock. He reacts, his hands automatically searching my body. He cups my arse and our erections rub against each other through our trousers. All I know is I want him even if it's against my principle of not giving away freebies.

"You're so hard, Ali."

I kiss him, my tongue searching and teasing. We get lost in each other's taste and sense until I can't quite breathe. I don't like this loss of control, and yet, I want to give in.

Ali's hands knead my arse cheeks, pressing me closer and closer to him. "Yeah, I'm always desperate. I think it's you."

I try not to think about that. At this moment, I'm just as turned on as he is. I want to see his ink so badly. I tear off his top and sit on his thighs, our hard-ons straining to the point of being painful. With ragged breaths, I lose my shirt and pants, and unzip Ali and pull down the waist of his jeans and boxers to free his dark shaft.

I suck my fingers and explore him. At the same time, I lean down and kiss him once more, suffocating his moans.

When I'm sure he's ready, I lean back again so I can admire his face. All the time, my fingers continue to play with him and I use my left hand to massage his balls. As I stroke him, his face turns into a picture of pleasure, flushed and vulnerable. My fingers are obviously better than the sex toy we used earlier. He stares at me with admiration like nothing I've seen before. I am becoming breathless and turned on by the sight of Ali.

I plant a wet and sensual kiss on him again, and as I am so close to his face I see myself reflected in the turquoise pools of his eyes.

"I want you so much," he whispers in my ear, his voice hoarse with arousal.

That's all the encouragement I need. I pull off his trousers completely and turn myself around, prop him up with a cushion and spread him wide so I can taste him. My arse would be in his full view. Holding on to and spreading his thighs, I greedily eat his arse, lick his balls, and drag my tongue around his perineum and then all along his erection to the darkened tip, and I drink his pre-cum and love his musky scent.

Ali cups my arse and rubs the cheeks with his big hands. He's rough and tender at the same time.

I can't see his face but the sounds he's making are exquisite. After I've devoured him and sucked his dick, I turn back and scoot up.

I grab the trousers I've discarded on the floor and take out a condom. I roll it on Ali and ease myself down. I am still sensitive from our earlier round of sex.

"Fuck, Ali."

"That's what we're doing." He smiles. "I don't think I'll ever tire of you. I don't know what to do."

That makes the two of us. To muffle his words and my rattled brain, I bend down and kiss him again.

It feels so damn good with Ali deep inside of me. I won't need too much more stimulation to come again. Neither will he. He pushes himself up to meet me. All I can hear is our laboured breaths, and the slapping of our flesh together. Ali soon tenses and thrusts upwards into me again and again with full force, driving the couch across the floor, until he's spent.

I move off him, and wrap my hand around myself. Ali's zoned-out eyes are utterly absorbed by me as I jerk off; his concentration consumes every inch of me when I give in to pleasuring myself and I come all over his abs.

Ali's grin is precious. "Come here."

We ignore the sticky mess between us. I reach down and let myself be hugged this time while I calm down from the intensity of sex. As I do that, Ali idly strokes my hair and kisses the top of my head. "You're incredible."

I can say the same about him. Ali and I together feel effortless. At that moment, I wish I were still being a professional escort because changing our relationship would complicate things too much. It's something I'm afraid to confront. What if it doesn't work out, whatever 'it' is? What if I hurt him, like I did Sasha? Trust. I don't think I have enough of it left in me.

I don't know how long we have lain there, as my eyes feel increasingly heavy.

Ali whispers, "Hey, let's have a shower and go to bed."

My legs feel like jelly but he gives me a hand and pulls me up. He turns off the film, our effort to watch a kiddie movie having been long abandoned. Instead, we take an extended shower. Unlike the meagre lukewarm jet at home that passes for a shower, Ali's is bliss. He soaps me up and washes me with a flannel. The gentleness he's showing me will kill me. My weariness disappears under his ministrations.

We crawl into bed naked, our skin still warm from the hot water. Ali holds me from behind as we lie like two spoons. He kisses my neck and I relax against his larger body. After a while, I turn around and we start kissing. It's the kind of lazy, tender kisses that make my heart flutter. I don't know why Ali has made me love snogging so much because I'd always associated kisses with sex, and they were normally pretty urgent and desperate. It's late but neither of us seem to care as we cuddle and kiss half of the night away.

It feels good to see the awe on Ali's face, whether he's a client or not. I keep reminding myself it's my downtime and I am spending it the way I like.

Ali plays with my hair and asks quietly, "Do you stay with any other…uh…do you call us clients?"

I have my eyes closed but now I squint in the dusk of the room to watch Ali's face. "No, not really. I told you I'd got the rest of the night off."

"Thank you."

I am exhausted, so I only reply lazily, "What for?"

He kisses me again. "For coming back and sleeping with me like this."

I am never introspective about the decisions I make. I may have broken my principle but it feels good to be wanted by Ali.

I'm so exhausted that I soon fall into a slumber. I enjoy a rare night of restful sleep and wake to find an empty space beside me in bed. The smell of fresh coffee tells me where Ali is. I inhale his leftover scent on the pillow; I can't help but smile. Reluctantly I drag myself up. I have a quick wash in the bathroom. Downstairs,

I find him sitting at the dining table already finishing his toasts and coffee and browsing a laptop by the side.

He offers, "Breakfast? I've got juice, bagels and coffee. Or you can have some fruit." His grin is broad. I always dislike mornings, which is convenient, since I rarely have to work too much before the afternoon. But today, his beam wakes me up nicely.

"Nah, I'm not a morning person. A coffee would be good, though."

"Help yourself. Coffee's in the pot." He taps something on his keyboard with one hand. I like the way he works and eats breakfast at the same time, looking serious. He's hot like that.

I fill a mug with coffee and take it out to the back garden to have a smoke. Ali comes out to keep me company but he is obviously dressed for the office, wearing a dark shirt and tailored trousers. His hair is combed and he smells freshly showered. This feels like a regular occurrence, as if we are lovers sharing a coffee before heading out for a day's work. That's what I imagine anyway because I've not had the experience of an 'ordinary' life.

Ali looks at the time on his mobile and frowns. "I've got to go. You can take your time. Just shut the door behind you." I'm reminded of his responsible job and how that's what most people get up in the morning for. A job, regular hours. Nice home to come back to. A boyfriend. *Fuck. Don't even think about it, Liam Murphy.* I get on with Ali and he'd let me stay with him last night, but I worry about expecting too much and getting disappointed.

I hurriedly finish my cigarette and drink the last of the coffee. "No, no. I'll walk out with you." I don't feel comfortable being in his house without him, even though he trusts me.

We leave the house together, and it's strange to walk in the oblique rays of the morning sun, as I don't usually spend time with him during the day. He smiles at me and I give in to my urge to hold his hand. We walk with our hands together and fingers entwined.

We stop in front of his Tube station. It's busy with morning commuters streaming past us, hurrying to work. At that moment, though, I see only him. The hustle and bustle of the Angel Tube fades away in the background. He hugs me and kisses me goodbye.

"Thanks again for last night," he whispers for my ears only.

I watch him disappear into the station, his powerful body moving fluidly in the crowd. I wish I were with him, going to work, doing ordinary things like commuting.

No matter how much I've loved staying with Ali, I tell myself not to repeat this. I can't get used to being intimate with a john like that, even if he is special; Ali is not like a hookup or just one of the clients. Whatever I'm feeling is too confusing.

I walk home slowly, enjoying the bright sunshine. My feet crunch the leaves on the ground. The melancholy always returns and eats me from the inside out. Every day I feel that ache acutely except when I see Ali. He always makes me forget. In between his appointments, work drags, and I begin to feel restless with my life.

CHAPTER 6

'VE GOT AN evening off. I am tired from an afternoon appointment with one of my regulars who tends to treat me a bit like a sex doll, making me uncomfortable even though I don't think he means to. He must subconsciously believe that I don't feel pain because I'm in sex work. He's otherwise quite a sweet elderly gentleman and he tips well, so I can't complain too much. When I get home, I play my flute while all the guys are out. Then I fix myself a cheese sandwich and tea. I've just made a bomb when Chris comes back.

Chris comes to sit next to me on the sofa and plants a brutal kiss on my lips. He gives me a devilish grin. "What's up, man? You've been moping around the joint lately." He lights a cigarette and watches me with his beautiful eyes.

"I think you're quite mistaken. Nothing's up with me, C." I try to deflect. "How's your love life?" With Chris, it's probably a mistake to ask such a thing.

"I wouldn't know what you're talking about." He sucks in a bellyful of smoke and exhales. "And yours, my Irish princess?"

I laugh at his term of endearment. "Fuck right off. I wouldn't know either."

Chris finishes his cigarette and helps himself to my bomb and takes a toke. "Some days I see a goofy smile on your face when you come back from work."

The man is sharp. I give him that but I am not gonna admit to my feelings for Ali. I'd behave like a teenage girl having a crush on someone unattainable and I'd seem foolish to Chris. "Nah, you must be mistaken."

Chris shakes his head and he focuses his gaze on me, as if he's trying to access my soul. "If you say so, but man, I've been fucking people for a living for eight years, on and off. I know what I see." He goes to the kitchen and comes back with two bottles of beer. After a few gulps of the lager, he asks again, "Who is he?"

Busted. "I don't know if it's anything. He's really nice and considerate." I *do* sound like a twelve-year-old.

"A client, right?" Chris frowns.

I nod. "Yeah, it's totally stupid. He's forty-five, hot and successful. I'm what? A fucking prostitute, a young kid and a nobody. It's a cliché. I should forget about it." I'm not a young and misunderstood gay escort waiting to be saved by the rich white knight.

Chris continues smoking. He's got more sense than to tell me that it's all going to be okay. Life is not one big fucking fairy tale. We are both too realistic to think that. Chris is also too jaded to give advice or suggestions when it comes to a matter of the heart. So, he remains silent for a while.

Finally, he leans in and kisses the side of my head. "It's not a cliché if you feel it. Just be careful, okay?"

"I will."

Chris takes his time and rolls a joint. We pass it between us. "What's his name?"

"Ali, short for Alastair. Why?"

"Ali. I like that. A name that can be male or female, like mine. Is he queer?" Like Chris.

"No, just gay." I smile at him. "How ordinary."

Chris laughs. "Okay. If he fucking hurts you, I'm sending in the Cavalry. Do you know his second name?"

"Nope." I shake my head and chuckle at Chris's protectiveness. It's cute. Even though he's the one who helped me when I came out of rehab, I don't want to be dependent on him and have him worry about me like a big brother. "I'm a big boy. I can deal."

Chris rolls his eyes but otherwise doesn't reply.

We sit, sipping our beers and smoking. After a while, he tells me as casually as he can, "I bumped into Sasha the other day."

Shit, I nearly choke on my beer. "How's he doing?" I still can't shake that ache in me whenever his name is mentioned.

Chris regards me closely. "He's going to college and he's in love with someone else, but you know about that."

Yeah, I sure do, remembering how I'd spied on them, just to make sure that he was well. I sigh. "That's good."

It's a blessing that someone treats him right. He deserves it. Sasha's the most damaged kid I know from my homeless days and I am probably aware of only the tip of the iceberg because he's also really guarded. He was on the road to total self-destruction when he met his current boyfriend. What can I say? I'm not boyfriend material. I should have seen it coming and helped him but I failed him.

Chris drinks his beer and shakes his head. "Funny cuz he asks me the same question. 'How's Liam doing?' Every fucking time."

I cock my head. After everything we'd been through and how I'd treated him, he still cares about me. "And your answer?"

"You're still an asshole! Seriously, man. I gave you his number. If you wanna know, my radical suggestion is for you to call Sasha and speak to him yourself." Chris blows smoke in my face and then he turns serious for a second. "I told him you're off drugs and you're doing well. He's happy for you."

I smile. Chris has somehow become a bit of a go-between for Sasha and me. The only direct contact I had with Sasha should make it to the Guinness Book of Records for the longest text message in history because I poured my heart out at length and apologised for hurting him. I couldn't face him but my message was heartfelt. Sasha replied with a single word: okay. It was enough of a consolation. I'm comforted by the fact that he has forgiven me and cares enough to ask how I am. Still, I wonder if I can turn things around like he has. For the past year, I have only existed to go through the motions. I can perhaps save up to go back to college to study music. A pipe dream will give me a goal in life.

Watching Chris reminds me of how I was when I was first released from the drug programme.

I found Chris and asked for help from him. The main reason I didn't return to drugs was the absolute indignity of being treated like scum in the hospital, of experiencing the panic, confusion and agony in the rehab. Every time I've been tempted, I remind myself how painful giving up was. It isn't something I want to repeat. Yet, every day I still fear I've become the broken man from the homeless shelter or I'll make myself a noose and hang it from a high beam.

Only a survival instinct pushes me to continue. The best I can manage is to have a little room to call 'home', and selling my body is still an improvement.

I must have sighed audibly.

"What?" Chris gazes at me.

"Just thinking about how I came to you and you helped me move in here." I light another cigarette as we talk.

Chris leans against the back of the sofa. "I remember. You were looking better than I'd seen you before you OD'd but you still scared me."

That surprises me. I hadn't sensed that I was frightening anyone, let alone Chris who was usually unflappable. "How?"

Chris starts rolling another joint and he steals glances at me. "You were quiet. Like something had broken inside of you. You used to be so animated, man."

Animated? I had tried to hide how I thought so little of myself, how I couldn't let myself trust another person again because I'd got nothing to give. My heart was broken and the pieces were scattered in Ireland and on the streets of London.

I chuckle to hide my real emotions. "I was probably on crack and fucking high as a kite most of the time."

Chris joins me in laughing. "Yeah, you were. Liam, you really were such a twat, and fucking dumb as a rock to take drugs the way you did." Chris doesn't touch the hard stuff. That's why he can lecture me about using it. Anyway, he's right about me being stupid. I can only agree with him.

"Sasha told me he could see you being happy, if you'd just believe in yourself."

I'd be happy if I could believe in myself.

Chris has been watching me as I ponder about my sorry life, and now he ruffles my hair and smokes his joint. Then he seems deep in thought again. "What do you think is the worst thing that can happen to an escort?"

"A skanky john with a gigantic dick?" I venture.

He snorts. "There's that." He pauses for thought. "The other day, I was hammering into this guy, yeah? And all the time I was compiling a shopping list for the supermarket on my way home."

He cracks me up. Yeah, I know what he means.

Chris looks serious, though, as his brows knot together. "Have you ever imagined finding a soul mate, the one?"

"Uh?" I consider the question and I'm truly surprised that Chris even thinks about that. He changes his boyfriends and girlfriends every few weeks, and gives no indication he ever wants to be serious with any of them.

"A soul mate?" When I was with my boyfriends, I thought I had found him. I'm now too jaded to think that. I have no answer for Chris.

I don't want to feel nothing anymore, though. Even when I was wasted on drugs, I wouldn't allow myself to be completely numb. It's probably why I can't ignore Ali while I try hard not to lose my head over him. I don't think I'm good enough for him. I'm still afraid that I'll get hurt if I let myself trust someone again.

~~~

I rarely do calls to hotels. The client is a Canadian businessman who happens to be in the city, and he wants a little action before going to his meetings. It feels very strange indeed to be working in the morning in an expensive hotel room in central London. I can count the number of times I've stayed in a hotel or guesthouse with one hand, so this is pretty neat.

Afterwards, he tells me I can take a rest and have a wash in his room, while he goes out to his business meeting. I have a long wash and enjoy the jet of hot water. It beats the sorry excuse of a shower at home. I should head home but it's lunchtime, so I text Ali who works close by.

– *You free?*

He texts back almost straightaway. *Where are you?*

– *Near your work.*

Meet for drink?

– *Yup.*

I arrive at the coffee shop in Soho that Ali has suggested and he's already sitting there reading something on his tablet. There's a small frown on his forehead. I love how the sunlight streams through the window and crowns him. I lean in and give him a quick kiss on the cheek, surprising him.

Ali looks up and smiles. "Sit down." He gestures to the metal chair next to him. I take it.

"I've asked a colleague to join us, if it's okay? Sue's a good friend."

Of course, I've never met any of Ali's friends. I'm anxious in new social situations but I am quite good at masking my nerves. "I guess."

The small café is pretty packed; the hip lunchtime crowd from nearby offices gathers around small tables, taking a brief break from their busy jobs. The sense of being out of place circuits through me.

Ali stops my second thoughts about having lunch with him. "Do you want some lunch? I'd recommend the paninis here." He takes a sip of his coffee. "I'm about to order."

"Okay. I'll have the same as you and a cappuccino." I give him a twenty.

"No, no. I've got it." He passes the note back to me and stands up to head to the counter. Ali always tries to pay for food and drinks when we're out.

"Come on. It's my turn. I texted you first. So, I've invited you to lunch. I'm buying." I'm not a charity case. Reluctantly, Ali accepts the money that I press in his hand.

When he returns to our table with two paninis and the coffee for me, I've been scanning Grindr. I show him this hot guy I've been flirting with. "Look at that nice smile. Thirty-two. He seems fit."

Ali grabs my phone and reads my chat on the app. "Are you? Do you want to hook up with him?" He frowns.

I have found extra jobs through the app, but it's quite rare. I sometimes sign on when it's a slow week and hope to get lucky. "No, I don't use it that way. I mean I don't search for hookups much. Not anymore." I watch Ali's face, wondering whether I need to explain more.

"Why..." Ali starts, but he doesn't finish his question. Why would an escort need to have more sex in his spare time? I guess I could, but a quick wank is usually more than enough to take care of my needs. The last thing I want outside of work is spending more time trying to negotiate and to get another guy off. It's also why Chris is a pretty decent fuck buddy because we both know what we want from a sexual encounter. Flirting can be fun, though, when I have the inclination.

I take a bite of my panini with mozzarella and tomatoes. It's tasty, even though I still think a toasted cheese and tomato sandwich shouldn't cost so much. I suppose it's central London.

Food here is meant to be for the hipster workers who are happy to pay the high price.

"You should definitely sign up, Ali." I speak with my mouth half full.

Ali needs to sample the scene. He only realised he was gay when he was nearly forty and he loved his wife too much to do anything about it. But now, he's got to start somewhere if he wants a relationship.

Ali shakes his head. "I don't know." He leans over me to look at my chat again. "What's your profile like?"

I show it to him. The photo's quite revealing without being pornographic.

Ali glances at me sidelong. In the photo, I wear no top and you can almost see my pubes, as I am clad in a small pair of briefs. It comes from a batch that Chris did for my profile on the escort agency's web page. But Ali doesn't comment on the semi-naked me in the image.

Instead, he averts his eyes from the mobile and asks, "Anyway, what're you up to in town?"

I think about it but I don't want to lie to Ali. "I was on a job."

"Oh." Ali's eyes dull for a second. He turns quiet and doesn't prolong the subject.

For the first time, I feel something that resembles guilt when it comes to Ali, as though I'm betraying a boyfriend if I work. I have begun to think of him when I'm with other guys, comparing them to sex with Ali. I need to put my sexual encounters in separate categories. Great sex with Ali, work sex and…not much else.

I do the same with relationships:
Friends=a few who're mostly flatmates
Good friend and lover? Ali, who's also a client
Boyfriend=unlikely.

Unsure. It's a scary thought because I have to change my life to go that one step further. Will I do it for someone like Ali? I should...

As I ponder about my life, an awkwardness hangs between us. We eat our lunch and drink coffee. Soon, Ali's friend arrives, breaking the silence. Sue's a woman in her thirties. She wears a dress with bright geometric patterns and appears well-groomed.

Ali introduces us. I can see her checking me out. Ali takes my hand in his under the table as silent support to make sure I'm comfortable with the situation.

After buying a salad and re-joining us, Sue smiles faintly, her eyes curious. She strikes me as a straight-talking woman and I'm proved right.

"Are you guys, like, dating?" she asks as she starts forking some leaves and putting them into her mouth.

"Yes," Ali says.

"No."

We answer simultaneously. Shit. Under the table, I detach my hand from Ali's.

Sue watches us, especially Ali's face, and frowns. "Is there something I should know?" She directs her question to Ali.

He puts down his sandwich. "It's...we've not known each other for long."

I let him come up with an excuse with his friend, but he's tongue-tied. I'm sure she's an intelligent woman who will now think I'm a stupid twat. Ali wants us to be more but I'm a freak who won't commit. For Ali's sake, I hope that she can't guess the other half of the reason for my faux pas. Considerate and open as Ali is, I'm not going to out him as someone who uses an escort service in front of his colleagues.

I finish my coffee but my appetite has gone. I want to leave so I don't embarrass Ali further in front of his friend.

Eventually, it's Ali who salvages the situation. "Clearly, we need to talk about this." He gazes at me and grins. I smile back, my attempt to show solidarity.

Sue laughs at the end. "Ooookay. You're at that stage, right? I get it."

Ali and I nod at the same time, grateful for her interpretation. Sue smiles. "You're kinda cute like that!"

Cute? Ali's tension eases. I just want to escape. Sensing my nervousness, he grabs my hand back under the table. I stare down. How can I be with anyone like Ali, if I can't even deal with one of his friends, sharing a perfectly ordinary lunch?

As we silently return to our food, I feel Ali's gaze on me again. I meet his and plead for his forgiveness. I can't read his expression for a second, but then his grin widens to make me feel better.

"Ah, there's Michael." Sue looks towards a slim guy in a shirt and tie, who has just entered the café. He moves to the counter to order. "I'll tell him to come sit with us." She stands up and approaches him.

Taking advantage of the gap, Ali asks me, "You okay?"

I nod. "Yeah. I mean, I didn't know what you wanted me to say to your colleague. I'm sorry."

"It's fine. Sue's a good friend. I'd have told her about you. She'd understand—" Ali's cut short as Sue and this Michael return to the table.

Michael grabs a chair and sits down opposite me, on the other side of Ali. *Fuckety fuck.* My heart thumps against my ribcage, as though I've been running. I'd had an appointment with this guy, minus the serious-looking glasses. I'm good with faces, even if I can't remember his name. I don't think It was Michael. I suppose he might have given me a false name. It doesn't matter anyhow. But this. I don't want to make things awkward for Ali in front of his colleagues any more than necessary.

"Michael's our corporate lawyer." Sue introduces us, "This is Ali's friend, Liam."

I manage to paste a smile on my face, or, I hope it's a smile, because I'm filled with dread inside. My stomach contents threaten to come back up.

"Liam?" Ali seems to have been calling me. I don't know how long I've been ogling at no one in particular.

Michael stares at me, then at Ali.

"What's wrong?" Ali asks.

I put my napkin down and stand up. "I've got to go. Sorry. It's nice meeting you." When my eyes fall on Michael again, his glare chills me to the bone.

I don't know how I manage to walk out without feeling my legs. Ali follows me. Outside, he grabs my arm and turns me around. I see the concern on his face.

"What's the matter?" he demands again.

"Nothing." Behind him, Michael has now come out. *Please, just leave me alone.*

Michael's voice is low. "Ali, I suggested the escort agency for anonymous hookups. I didn't expect you to bring a sex worker to lunch." So, he's annoyed that he may be outed as someone who uses escorts.

I can see the revelation on Ali's face. He's realised that Michael has bought my services before, but he recovers quickly. "Liam's a friend, Michael. I was having lunch with a friend. It's not a problem, is it?"

Michael's gaze remains on me. Sue has now emerged from the coffee shop too, and she appears totally confused.

I turn to go. Ali leaves the self-conscious and annoyed Michael to have another attempt at talking to me. When we are out of Michael's ear shot, I stop and face Ali.

"Liam, I know you sleep with other men. I can deal. Will you tell me how you feel?" Ali's patience is out of this world.

I try to deal with my tangled thoughts but fail. "I don't feel... Michael was a client. You'd already worked that out. I didn't want to embarrass you in front of your colleagues. Anyway…let's not do this here. We'll talk on Thursday, okay?"

I look back over Ali's shoulder to glimpse that Michael is still watching us warily.

Ali attempts to respond. "I'm not ashamed of you…"

"Your colleague is." More quietly, I try to explain as if repeating my terms and conditions to him, "I don't only 'sleep with men'. I fuck them for money. It's not the same thing at all."

Ali is paralysed from those words. *The truth.* I make my escape. We need to talk.

PART THREE
HIS DOWNFALL

CHAPTER 7

ALI HAS SENT me a text. *I'm not embarrassed.*

I stare at it all day. I know that, but it doesn't mean we can be equals. Not in the eyes of most people. It was certainly not all right with Michael. I am not that naïve. They're part of the Soho creative set. I'm okay with what I do but it doesn't mean I fit into their gang. Ali should be careful with his reputation at work.

I even expected him to stop asking for me after the clusterfuck of a lunch encounter. But Ali makes arrangements to see me the following Thursday as usual. In fact, he requests an overnight appointment and he wants us to go out for a meal.

We'll be talking, right? I'm not good at that, at confronting and verbalising my emotions. I stand outside the restaurant, nervously smoking. When I can't put it off anymore, I stub out the fag and go inside.

Sitting in the posh Chinese restaurant in central London, I feel self-conscious. Okay, I put on my best shirt and an expensive pair of jeans but it's still weird. Even when I was living at home, Mum and Dad rarely took us to restaurants. We had a small family-run farm and little money. It would cost too much to feed the five of us kids in a restaurant.

The red and black décor of this place is classy and Ali looks gorgeous tonight in his dress shirt.

"What's the occasion? Why can't we have a usual appointment in your house?" I feel anxious as hell. I'd much prefer that we simply fucked our brains out.

Ali narrows his eyes, but before he can answer, a waitress brings the menus.

"What would you like?" he asks, trying to busy himself with reading through the menu.

I try not to faint at the prices. What the fuck! And I don't understand half of the items on it, as though they're written in Chinese. "Why don't you choose for us?"

Ali orders when the waitress returns. I'm so nervous I haven't heard what he's said to her. We remain quiet until the starters arrive. I pick up the battered prawns. They'd have tasted heavenly if the circumstances were different.

I clear my throat. "Ali, I don't want a relationship with a sugar daddy."

Ali puts his chopsticks down and sighs. "I don't treat you like you're a play thing, do I?"

"No, but…" I try to reason. "You're too good for me, Ali. Your colleague clearly thought so." I put down my fork and hide my clammy hands between my thighs.

"Michael was the one who suggested the escort agency to me," Ali opens. I heard Michael say that at the café too. I remembered what he was like with me. Vanilla sex, I seem to recall. Rich, professional guy who expects good service. Nothing more, nothing less.

I stare at my plate of food, my meagre appetite gone. "It's fine, Ali. I was only worried about your reputation at work. It doesn't matter to me. I told you. I am not ashamed of what I do. But I don't want you to know that I've fucked your colleague." I wasn't embarrassed before I met Ali, but now he's gone and changed me.

Ali's retort is quick. "Why's that?"

"Because…" I'm scared of falling for someone only to be told later that I'm not good enough. "I'm poor and this is what I do to make a living. You should find a guy who's more together, and who doesn't have a history of drug addiction and all the rest of it!" I get it all out. I'm shaking inside, emotions bubbling that I can barely contain.

"I'm not embarrassed by you. By us." He repeats his text. "You asked me not to ever feel sorry for you. So, I don't care that you don't have money and you have a troubled past."

I dry laugh. "You may not but I'm not made for polite society, Ali."

He shakes his head. "Fuck that. It's time you stop feeling sorry for yourself."

I stare at him. Is that how he sees me? That I feel sorry for myself.

"I talked to Michael once he got over his shock. He was more worried about *his* name."

"I don't out my johns, ever. You can tell him not to worry about it." I swallow a gulp of my wine to steady myself. "What else did Michael say?"

Ali stares at me while he hesitates. "I'm not interested in what Michael thinks."

There's obviously more to it. I demand again, "What did he say?"

He exhales. "Just that you're not good enough for me...and you're too young."

It hurts but I have to agree. "He's clearly right."

Ali frowns.

"There's more. Ali, tell me." I can read everything on his face. He hasn't got a dishonest bone in his body.

"I don't care what Michael thinks." Yes, he's already told me that, but I want to know what's bugging him.

"You bloody should. Come on. Let's hear it."

He shakes his head. "He thinks you may be after my money."

I stare at Ali. "I *am* after your money. You pay me, don't you?"

"Not like that. I know who you are."

"Do you?" I'm up to the challenge now. I need to end this, whatever this is. I can't commit to someone so perfectly sweet. Damn it. "Okay. I don't want your money the way your friend suggests but I'm not some tart with a heart, either. And I don't want a sugar daddy or need someone to save me. So, in a way, I don't need you." I get it all out, regardless of whether all of it is true.

Ali balls his hand on the table. "I know you're none of those things. And I'm not a lonely old man preying on a young guy. I

have friends and I like being alone. I don't want to rescue anyone."
He gazes at me, pain already infusing the tears that threaten to
fall.

"Then, what do you want from me?" The heaviness I feel
inside is suffocating me. If he breaks down, I think I'm also going
to burst open with emotions.

Luckily the waitress comes and distracts us with the chicken
and rice we've ordered for our main course. I sip my wine. The
food smells heavenly delicious but I've stopped feeling hungry.

We force ourselves to eat for a few minutes.

"For what it's worth, Sue thinks you're adorable, though she's
confused about what went on with Michael."

"What did you tell her?" I ask.

Ali sighs again. "Michael didn't want her to know, so I only
said that you'd hooked up with him. A one-night stand. Small
town, et cetera. That's why it was awkward. I wouldn't have told
her you're an escort without making sure you're happy for her to
know."

I don't like the fact that Ali had to lie for me but I guess it
couldn't be helped. I sip my wine. "You do what's most important
for you, Ali. Don't worry about me."

"Is it so bad that I worry about you?"

I stir the rice in my bowl but I've hardly eaten any. "I appreciate
your concern, but I've been taking care of myself for a long time,
Ali. I don't need you to fret over me."

He narrows his eyes and drinks the wine. His voice is croaky,
as if he's about to cry. "I care about you, and maybe I also want
you to worry about me."

I try to understand what he means but my brain's not in gear.
I've always been told by my family and my homeless friends that
I'm too fucked up. I can't see how I can help him. I'm afraid of
hurting, which seems to come with being intimate with someone.
So, the best thing I can do is not to go down that road in the first
place. *Too fucking late.*

I spoon more rice into my bowl, just to have something to do
with my hands.

When we've both tried but failed to finish the main dish, he gives me a card. I examine the envelope. I can't help but frown at it.

"I didn't ask you out so we could argue. I wanted us to have dinner for a reason." He rubs his nose bridge. He still appears shy in front of me. "I don't know when your birthday is…was. It must be around now, isn't it? Because of your star sign. Here's a small thing."

When I look at Ali's eyes, they seem particularly bright under the red light of the fake chandeliers in the restaurant. I can't believe the bugger even remembered I had a birthday.

I finger the edge of the envelope. "It was last week. I gave myself a day off and bought some dope."

"Why didn't you tell me? If not with me, you should celebrate with your friends."

I exhale a heavy breath. "Last year, when I turned twenty-one, I'd only just given up drugs and started selling myself. It was one of the lowest points of my life. I've not celebrated my birthdays since coming to London. What homeless person celebrates another year of nothing?"

Ali rubs his face. "Oh, Liam. You're not homeless now."

I stare at what must be a birthday card.

"Why don't you open it?" he suggests gently.

I do, and try to hide my face from Ali, as my emotions may be too raw. I don't want attachment. *Do not get fucking emotionally involved*, I repeat to myself. Still, I am happy and frightened at the same time. My fingers are not cooperating as I attempt to rip open the envelope. Inside, the rather plain card is his elegant and neat writing that says, 'Happy 22nd, Liam'. That was all, but I could have broken down in tears.

I can't let him see me cry so I try hard to stop myself. Only my big sis sent me a text but Ali has gone to all this trouble for my birthday? There's another small envelope inside. It contains a gift card for a music shop off Charing Cross Road.

"So you can buy some scores for the flute," he says. "I wouldn't know what else you might want."

Fuck's sake. It is a perfect present. The man is killing me with wining and dining and gifts. This is getting out of hand. My first encounter with his colleagues is proof of what a fuck-up I am. I'll only ruin anything with this sweet man.

I thank Ali and kiss him, not caring that we are in the middle of a busy restaurant. We grow quiet again. We don't want desserts but I ask for a coffee and I am dying for a cigarette. Ali orders a jasmine tea. I can't quell the unease in my stomach.

Before we get back to the earlier conversation, I clear my throat and tentatively suggest, "Ali, why don't you try to meet one of your colleagues' guys? You know, the ones they set you up with." We have been through this a few times when we talked about Ali dating again.

His eyes widen, the emerald colour making me nostalgic for the Irish Isle.

"Liam." I can see his brain working, as he gazes at me directly. "Are you really that insensitive?"

Yes, I am. I force myself to be. For the job, for sanity. But I say nothing.

Ali heaves a sigh again. I don't like it. I don't want to be the one that frustrates him. After a while, he utters, "I've told you casual hookups are not for me."

"Fuck's sake, man." I tap my fingers on the table for something to do. "Who are you having dinner with right now? I am by definition a casual fuck and always will be."

He squeezes his hands together. He had taken his wedding band off a few weeks earlier. I wasn't sure what it meant. *She's been gone a year*, I imagined.

His cheeks colour when he verbalises his feelings. "I think I understand you a little. You may feel differently but…I really like being with you. I want to find out more about you. We don't have to make any promises to each other. Not now. I'm sorry I'm over twice your age and you probably think of me as an old cradle robber." He rubs his neck as he speaks.

I try to keep my voice down. "Damn it, Ali. It's not about what I think. You're serious about this? I don't know what mad idea you have about us. You know what I do for a living. We have sex because you pay for it. Nothing more. I can't be a permanent thing. You got it?"

Ali deflates; his shoulders sag. "I'm sorry." He picks up his tea and has a sip.

"Ali, I couldn't even have a perfectly innocent lunch with your friends. Why would you want to be with me?"

He shakes his head. "There's nothing wrong with you meeting my friends. Michael overreacted but he'd come around, too. I'm not good at hiding my feelings. I know I want us to be more than, you know, sex." He drops his voice.

It's better in the long run that I hurt him now. "Ali. You're a great guy," I attempt to reason. "You're good-looking, sorted. A cool job, a great house. I know you have some regrets with your wife. But, you'll find a good man soon, someone who loves you. I know it."

Someone who deserves to be with Ali. Jaysus. I sound like a bloody agony aunt albeit not a very eloquent one.

He struggles to smile. "Is that your way of letting me down gently?"

Fuck, the stupid fuck. "No, I don't get to let you down. You understand? You book me, I'll come, but I am not what you want long term."

I don't even mind losing a client. I have enough regulars now. It bothers me to think I won't get to spend time with him every week but what the fuck is someone like Ali doing with me? We finish our drinks in silence, an awkwardness growing between us. He gets the bill. When we are in the car, he gives me two hundred pounds.

"I think I'll drive you home." His voice is low and uncertain.

Fine. I direct him to a few doors down from my bedsit near the Arsenal football ground in North London. I am not prepared to reveal where I live, not even to Ali.

He kisses me softly on the lips. With unshed tears in his eyes once again, he gazes at me, and touches my hair. "Thank you for everything, Liam. Goodbye."

"Yeah. Bye, Ali." I refuse to look at him as I quickly get out of the car.

I slam the car door shut and run away. If I look back, I may lose my resolve and beg to take back everything I've said tonight.

Tears threaten to fall all the way back to my room. Once I shut myself away, I cry and I can't control the tears. Over the years, I've cried over being told what a worthless freak I was by my dad, bawled when Cillian cheated on me, wept and howled when I struggled with withdrawal, screamed for my stupidity when I hurt Sasha. These tears are for a relationship that I'm afraid to have.

Why did you have to go and make me feel like this? I ask silently, over and over, but Ali isn't here and I'm not going to see him. I bang my fist against the hard wall, anything to distract me from whatever else I feel.

I don't know how long I've been in a daze in my room but the tears have dried. A couple of stubs from the joints I've smoked lay idly in the ashtray.

I go into the bathroom, wash my face to get rid of the salt under my eyes and have a shower.

Dmitri is watching TV alone when I emerge from the bathroom, a violent film by the look of it. *Fuck.* I need to go into my room and avoid him but I don't.

"D, have you got any crack?" I ask before I can talk myself out of it.

He looks up with mild surprise. "Only a few rocks." His eyes search my face. "Are you sure?" Even Dmitri is questioning a recovering addict and whether I should buy from him. I don't know anymore. I need to stop thinking for a while.

"Yeah, I'm sure. I want three. How much you want?" I reply.

"Just give me thirty." Dmitri gets up and goes to retrieve the drug from his room.

I shout after him, "Let me borrow your pipe." He raises his hand in acknowledgement.

CHAPTER 8

THE RUSH THAT the crack brings is euphoric. For a while at least. I know I'm making a big fucking mistake. Realising what I've done, I promise myself the three rocks are all I'm going to take. Then I'll be all right again. Breaking promises is easy. Far too easy, and I hate myself even more. If I can't even trust myself, what good am I to anybody else? Well, yeah. That confirms everything I've known about me. Liam Murphy, the waster of a son and poor choice for a lover.

Giving in. Hating myself. Repeat.

When the good feeling floods my sensory system, it's as if I haven't ever given up. But of course the crash landing in between the crack pipes gets more and more depressing, and more and more urgent.

I fucking hate myself for falling back on it.

And I miss Ali terribly. The stupid bugger. I even miss 'making love' as he calls it because the days drag in between appointments with johns who remind me how *not* everyone is like Ali.

Taking drugs soon consumes me during every waking hour.

I've lost track of how much crack I'm smoking, but I try to hide it from Chris and my clients. No one wants to fuck a drugged-up whore. I must be using quite a lot because the money I earn seems to disappear quickly. I'm working more; some days I desperately try to drum up business.

I badly want to talk to Ali again. Instead, I keep to myself in my room. I sleep with Chris occasionally when we are both doped up and drunk or bored. You may think two professional escorts having sex means a great fuck. Hell, no. When we are not performing, we're actually bloody lazy and sex is more about physical needs than anything else. So, we are usually sloppy like two teenagers not knowing what they are doing. That's pure irony.

I've just fucked Chris after he sucked me off. It was a very accomplished blow job for a change. The man's gorgeous and a champ at giving head.

We lie down next to each other. Chris lights a cigarette.

"What happened to your guy?" he casually asks.

I know straightaway who he means. "He doesn't book me anymore."

Chris turns his head, props himself up on his elbow and scowls at me, no doubt debating whether to ask me more. He must have guessed the reason for why I stopped seeing Ali, though. "I told you I'd fucking waste him if he hurt you."

I smile without feeling any joy. "I like the tough Chris. You don't look the type."

He tuts. "I'm not a type. Well, did he? Hurt you?"

I shrug to hide what I'm really thinking, that it fucking hurts like hell. But it's not Ali's fault. It's entirely mine, and self-loathing is a sentiment that I know too well. "No. If anything, I ended it." Not that there was a proper beginning, so I don't know which 'end' I'm really referring to. And I've broken Ali's heart, for sure. Mine is also breaking even though I'm forcing myself to forget about it.

Chris seems to have decided not to push me for more details. There's no fucking point discussing spilled milk. He flutters his long eyelashes at me. "You wanna stay the night? It's good for a broken heart."

I shake my head at his insight. Some human contact is better than nothing. A cuddle is what I need and I like Chris's lithe body. But I have the aches, so I push up. Dmitri sold me a couple of rocks this afternoon. "I need to get something from my room. I'll be right back." I put my pants on and cross over to my room.

Once there, I retrieve the rocks from their little plastic bag. I prepare the pipe with one of them, and I'm about to heat it when

Chris opens the door. He stands in his very small briefs and stares down at me with a massive frown.

"Fuck, man. I knew something was up." Chris grabs my pipe. "What the fuck do you do that for?"

If only I knew the answer. I thought I'd kept my drug use under control but it had spiralled. I try to pull the pipe back from Chris, though. "Give it back."

Chris eventually releases it from his grip with a heavy sigh. "I'm going to kill Dmitri."

I'm not going to smoke in front of Chris but I'm too irritated and annoyed. "It's not his fucking fault, okay?" I add, "I know what I'm doing."

"The hell you do." His scowl deepens. "I remember what you were like fresh out of rehab. You're gonna waste all that? For what?"

I only feel annoyed, mostly with myself. I also don't want to think, to analyse, to miss the one person who keeps coming into my consciousness. I wonder what Ali has been up to all the time. Would he finally try dating or retreat back to his own little world? Perhaps he would find another escort to replace me. Fuck, that thought stings. What is wrong with me? I was the one to 'break it off', if you could call it that.

"Shut the fuck up." I starts to light my pipe. "Go back to your room, Chris. Let me do this, but I promise it's my last." *That stupid promise again. No, you should never trust a drug addict.*

I push Chris out of my room.

He half-turns to me. "I'm still going to kill Dmitri."

It's not Dmitri's doing. That's one thing I know about addiction. No one but no one is responsible except the person who decides to take drugs. If I hadn't turned to Dmitri, I would have gone to someone else, another pusher, and London's not short of them.

Afterwards, I return to Chris's room and push him onto the bed. Hovering over him and making my intention quite clear, I grin. "What is it with you tonight? Threatening to kill Ali, then

Dmitri. Have you turned into some kind of superhero all of a sudden?" Now that I've had my hit, I am all confident and sexy again.

"Twat." He smiles at last. "Come and fuck me good, Wilheim."

I laugh. "So romantic, aren't you?"

"No, I have absolutely no clue what the fuck you're talking about." Chris reaches out to take my underwear down in one sweep.

~~~

Saturday night and I've already had two clients. I should be feeling pretty trashed. But after a couple of pipes, I won't be sleeping for a while. With the receding buzz, I head down to the clubs in Vauxhall.

The guy's hot, if appearing way too drunk; his pupils are dilated and sweat has beaded on his forehead. I wonder if he's as coked up as I am. He leans close to me when I'm standing with a bottle of beer, his erection pressed against mine. I can see his blue eyes and pretty smile, and smell alcohol on his breath. I'm horny. Especially so after the crack.

The lights in the dark club are beginning to give me a migraine but I don't want to leave. I don't want to think either.

He shouts in my ear over the blaring music. "I'm Marco. You're gorgeous, man." His hands circle my waist and pull me close. Jimmy Somerville is singing 'Smalltown Boy'. Really? And why is my life like that of the boy in the song and so fucking eighties? The decade was before my time.

I put my almost finished bottle of beer down. "My name's Liam. You want to get off?" I nod towards the bathroom. I start walking and he grabs my arse and follows. Damn, the man can't keep his hands off me. Once we are in the stinky toilet stall, he slams the seat down, and presses me against the graffiti-filled wall.

His kisses are rough and sloppy and I don't like the taste of alcohol on his tongue. It doesn't stop me going along with it, though. At this point, I'm as wasted as he's drunk. We both reach for each other's trousers, impatiently unzipping and freeing our erect cocks. When he leans back, he appraises me with his deep eyes and grins, liking what he sees. I wonder if he's Italian or some other Latin type, with a name like Marco. But then, it may even be a false name. After all, I don't expect to see him again after this little tryst.

"I think you're the most attractive Irishman I've ever met," he slurs.

"Fuck that." I laugh regardless. "Just take care of this, yeah?" I gesture to my groin.

He moves his mouth down my chin, neck, and his right hand works my dick, smearing pre-cum around my crown. He burrows under my T-shirt, so his tongue circles my nipples, sending electric currents through me. Fuck, it feels good to be the one getting all the attention.

After I've come down his throat, I give him a hand job and try to send him on his way. He follows me back onto the dance floor and tries to talk to me, inviting me to go back to his place, wherever it is. Eventually, I stagger through the dancing crowd and manage to escape the club.

All I can smell is the pavements as I make my way home. And it reminds me of begging, of desperation and hurt. I want to forget Ali but I can't. The blow job in the toilet did nothing to quell my desire to call Ali and to tell him I want him. But I won't. He is better off without me.

My head's full of jumbled thoughts as I hurry home so I can have a smoke. *Fuck. I'm a mess.* I so despise myself as my addiction engulfs me once more. I can't see any escape.

~~~

I wish I could see some light at the end of the dark tunnel I've put myself in. I am not doing well and the only way I know how to cope with everything is through smoking crack.

When I come out of the shower, I go into our lounge and roll a joint with the strong skunk Dmitri manages to source. Fuck. That, together with the pipe I had earlier, sorts some of the tension out. Chris plonks himself down next to me, the whole sofa shakes and sags. The cheap furniture in this place.

"What's up, man?" He has his own gear, probably bought from our Russian flatmate too. I shrug. I don't need to tell Chris the extent of shit I'm in because he's shrewd. Chris and I don't talk a great deal since we tend to work at odd times of the day, even though Chris has been a good friend and we understand each other. He regards me for a few seconds. I know what he sees.

Chris is shaking me. "How much have you been smoking, Liam? You look like shit."

Yeah, I do. I've let myself go, forgetting to exercise, to eat. Insomnia plagues my nights. I'm already coming down and feeling nauseous.

I am staring at Chris and speechless when Dmitri walks through the front door.

Next thing I know, Chris is having a go at Dmitri. I sit with my eyes closed and sink into the sofa, listening to the two of them talking about me as if I were not there. My heart is once again filled with dread and hopelessness. *What's the fucking point? Why do they even care?*

"Do you have to supply him? You're turning him into a crack whore!" Chris doesn't mince his words once he gets going. He's raised his voice and their bickering is hurting my brain. I try to shield my ears with shaky hands but it's not working. They sound even louder.

Dmitri's drawl is hoarse with that strong Russian accent. "He's already a prostitute. Someone else will sell to him if I don't." These flatmates understand me, and they know the world I inhabit. It's often not pretty and getting darker by the day.

"You're still a fucking idiot." Chris shouts at the Russian.

Chris and Dmitri continue arguing. It feels like an intervention all of a sudden but it's doing nothing to help me. Only I could stop myself using. Anger, irritation and anxiety flood my head.

"Don't shout." I keep my voice down as it's the only control I have at this point. Chris and Dmitri stare at me, two pairs of eyes wide with contrasting shades. "You don't need to stand up for me. I'll do something about it. Soon, I promise," I address Chris, pleading, my hands fidgeting.

"The hell you will." Chris shakes his head, staring at my useless body.

"If I stop selling to him, he'll go to the fucking little shit down the road," Dmitri adds and he's right.

I gaze at Chris and can't help but feel annoyed even though I know he's trying to help. That's what crack does to me. "Why do you care?"

"Yeah, you're not even his boyfriend, man," Dmitri drawls.

Chris crosses his arms in front of his chest. "Do I have to be your boyfriend to care, Liam? You saw Sasha when he nearly died. You went through the scare and the detox yourself. I fucking dragged you out of the gutter when you first came out of rehab."

I feel a major migraine coming on, so I squint at the sharp light in the room and hold my hands up, as if I'm surrendering to his logic. "I know. I know."

Chris's voice lowers. "My mum...she had drug problems."

He doesn't elaborate. Chris has never talked about his family. I didn't even know he had a mum.

Dmitri shakes his head, regards me and Chris one more time and retreats to his room.

Chris sits next to me and hugs me. "Babe, you're like a fucking rag doll." He must be referring to my physical decline.

Tears threaten to fall from my eyes but I push him away, refusing to show that I'm once again completely out of control.

~~~

I should ignore the buzz of my phone. The last client took ages to come and I'm shattered. I just managed to fall asleep. The time on my mobile indicates it's already gone half past two.

I stare at the name against the sharp back light: my sister Marie.

She wouldn't have called at half past bloody two. Knowing something terrible must have happened back home, I reluctantly press the green button. "Marie. Why have you called? Is something wrong?"

"It's Dad. He's had a major stroke. You gotta come home."

My heart sinks. I don't know if I can face my family after all this time and see Dad. Despite the fact that I'd felt ostracised, I loved them. In some ways, I want to see my mum and my sisters and younger brother. I have missed that connection. Being all alone in the world has driven me to all the desperate acts of the past few years. That's why it makes facing them now terrifying. I've let them down and let myself down.

And the practicality. Fuck, how much money have I got? Can I even afford the trip? My careful control is slipping away fast.

My voice sounds as rough as I feel. "Yeah, I'll be there as soon as I can."

~~~

I've nearly forgotten how the quietude in Cork can be unnerving to those not used to it; it strikes me as unfamiliar now, after getting used to the buzz of London. The small airport is like a ghost town compared to Heathrow. The immigration officer glances at my green passport with the Irish harp on the front and doesn't even open it before letting me through. I didn't bother to look for my identity card.

The sound of my heels on the wood floor foregrounds my worries for the visit.

No one bothers me at customs. I was a stupid cunt for bringing a very small amount of hash in my suitcase but I couldn't see myself living a few days without anything. I would have killed someone with the withdrawal. I saw myself in the mirror on the plane over; my eyes were bloodshot from the lack of sleep and everything else. I'm reed thin and my hair is far too long. My facial features are quite sharp anyway and right now they've taken on my desperation. I'm dying for something to calm my nerves.

Marie and Niamh are patiently waiting in the bright arrival hall, among other people welcoming their friends and families. They stand out from the crowd. My family has always had the good looks in a rustic kind of way. Niamh has matured and she's only an inch or two shorter than me now. I hug them both.

Marie presents her baby in a sling. "Little Paddy. Meet your uncle." His fat face and rosy cheeks melt my heart right away. He definitely has the family genes.

I let him wrap his fat sausage fingers around mine and he smiles. At least, I think he does. Wish everyone could look at me with those bright eyes. I wish I could regain that innocence.

"Sorry I haven't told you I've got this little man. I've been meaning to give you a call sometime. It just got too hectic at home. You know how it is."

I lean down and kiss the baby boy's rosy cheek. "No. It's a nice surprise. It's much better to meet the latest addition in person. Isn't that right, Patrick?" I stroke the soft skin of his face. I am happy for Marie to have her second child, but all this only reminds me of what a fuck-up I am. I'm once again losing my battle against drugs and the depression between the highs is getting harder and harder to ignore.

I force myself to engage with the conversation. "Where's Sarah?" I've not met my niece either. I think she's about three years old.

"She's with her dad." Marie nudges my elbow. "Come on, let's get home."

The chill of the Irish Sea coast is unmistakable. The evening air feels damp but it's not been raining. I pull up the collar of my jacket even though it's doing nothing to protect me against the anxiety, the craving, and the flood of mixed feelings about seeing my family again. Just an expression of acceptance of me, for who I am, would be sufficient. *It's not too much to ask.* I follow my two sisters to their car, carrying my small bag over my shoulder.

In the drive up to Bantry, Niamh makes small talk. She's seventeen and planning to go to the local university next year to study commerce.

"What's it like in London? What've you been doing?" Here comes the dreaded question.

"This and that. Nothing really exciting." I desperately need something to help me through this, right fucking now. Shame fills me. I feel once again like the failure and disappointment that they expect me to be and I haven't seen my parents and older brother yet.

Marie half-turns. "You are so skinny and pale, Liam. Hope you're looking after yourself."

No, I'm not, but I only mumble, "Yeah, I'm fine." My eyes are drawn to the scenery flying past. Through the reflection on the window, I can see my face. Yet I'm looking at a young man's face that doesn't belong to me anymore. He's just another lost soul unable to help himself. I bite my lip to stop the shudder I feel.

The rest of the journey passes mostly in silence. Paddy has already gone to sleep in his car seat. "We're going directly to the hospital. Ma's expecting us," Marie tells me, while manipulating the car with ease. Talk about in at the deep end.

The hospital smells of disinfectant and death. Dad's room is utilitarian: white sheet, beige curtain; machines and instruments issue a low hum.

I don't exactly expect a welcome-home party but my other siblings are all present: the oldest, Patrick, and my younger brother, Finn. Patrick takes one look at me, stands up and leaves the room. I stare at his back as he exits, only to be surprised by Finn, when he comes forward and pulls me into a hug. Four years is a long time, and he's grown taller and broader. He's already in his second year at university, studying chemistry, as I recall.

I have Mum's colouring. She looks older; her dark hair streaks with white and silver. Her face is puffy with worry. "Oh, Liam, m'lad." With shaky arms, she pulls me into a hug, too. The once-familiar floral scent surrounds me again. She gazes at me, her face revealing profound sadness and loss. Whether she grieves for Dad's impending death or my abandonment, I'm not sure. I wish I could protect her. I've let her down. A good son would have been here helping her, taking care of her.

"Ma." I want to cry but I'm determined not to. I shouldn't feel I owe my family anything. Still, I don't like to see Ma upset. I've failed them. I'm not deserving of their love.

She pushes me towards the bed and whispers, "Your dad's not doing well, son. The doctors said these few days." Her eyes glisten with unshed tears once more.

"I know." I pull her into a hug. I'm more worried about Mum than my dad. Marie already told me he was on his last legs. The hospital can do little for him. The stroke was bad but his rapid decline is also due to years of heavy drinking and smoking. Drinking which sometimes resulted in physical violence against the rest of us, experiences that plagued my childhood. A slap here, a belt there. A clip around the ears. I was the son who disappointed him most and I used to get it worse than my brothers and sisters. Facing my dying father, I want to cower and duck, and hide behind something, like I'd done before I was big enough to fight back. I was about thirteen or fourteen when I'd started to stand up to him. But inside, I feel I haven't grown out of that fear at all even though I pretend I have.

I force myself to face my dad.

His eyes are closed, and his face is sallow and drawn. One side of his face has been affected by the stroke. There's no doubt that what I'm seeing is the picture of a dying man. My chest tightens. Despite everything, I know I want to love him. That's why it hurts so much when all I feel in return is rejection.

"Martin. It's Liam. He's come back to see you. It's great, isn't it?" Mum takes his hand into hers and says softly.

I sit down by the bed and take his other hand. He can't talk anymore and can't move.

"Dad. It's me."

He opens his eyes and moves his head to face me, a glimmer of recognition in his eyes.

I wasn't prepared to meet the disgust shown on his face. He blinks and makes some incomprehensible grunts and removes his hand from mine. I'm stunned, as though he's slapped me again.

He clearly has no wish to see me and he's annoyed by my presence. At this moment in time, I wish I could say that it hurts, but I only feel numb. Mum tries to reconcile us. She places her palm on his shoulder and gently pats him to calm him down.

"Are you glad all the kids are back, eh? Liam's come from London 'specially to see you."

Dad stares at me with eyes that are cloudy and yellowed. He then closes them, as if he wants to block me out.

I stand up and move away from the bed, from my dying father. Out in the corridor, I sit on a plastic chair and bury my head in my hands. *How dare he? How the fuck does he make me feel so bad about myself with not a damn word?* Back home, I'm still the worthless, perverted son that my parents only manage to tolerate.

Finn comes to sit down next to me. I last saw him when he was fifteen and he was embarrassed by his gay brother, despite the fact that I pretty much single-handedly brought him and Niamh up when my parents and Patrick were too busy with the farm work.

"I'm sorry. Dad's just stubborn." He tries to defend him after all these years.

"I don't care anymore," I reply. Wish there were more I could say on the subject, but really it is too late for me and my dad.

CHAPTER 9

Patrick will take over the farm. You know we don't make that much these days. We can't compete with the big boys and the Europeans, but, if we have a good year, we can give each of you some money. Finn and Niamh get their education paid for out of our savings. So, it's a fair deal." Mum looks at each of us in turn. We're sitting around the big kitchen table. Our farmhouse hasn't changed much, but I bet it feels empty and lonely to my mum after all of us—the kids—have moved out. Even Patrick, the eldest, has bought another small cottage in the village down the road.

Patrick stares at me, then addresses Ma. "When he left home, Dad said he considered Liam disowned. It's not changed just because he deigns to turn up."

"Paddy!" Marie exclaims.

Mum glares at him and sighs. "Is that really necessary?"

"He needs to hear it." Patrick's sharp gaze bores through me. "He and Cillian both are aberrations."

Marie draws a deep breath and shakes her head.

"I haven't seen Cillian in four years." I shoot daggers back at Patrick. "For the record, I don't give a shit. As far as I'm concerned, he can shove the farm up his arse." I've never expected anything from the family estate, so I'm not going to start now. I'm poor but I don't beg. I don't want handouts from my family.

Mum's backhand is entirely justified but saying it out loud makes me feel better. My left cheek stings. Marie and Finn gasp. Niamh starts to sob. It's not like this is the first time I've been hit by a parent, although it had always been my dad rather than

Mum. I didn't even think it was anything illegal to be physically disciplined when I was growing up. Out of the five of us, I was the one that enraged my dad most.

Paddy attacks me again. "Better than taking it up your arse." *Right. If only he knew.*

"Patrick, enough." Mum's tears are ready to fall again. She's physically shaken by the argument. "He's still your brother. Your father's property will be mine. I make the decisions now."

Patrick opens his mouth to say something but thinks better of it.

I stand and push the chair back with a loud squeak, getting ready to leave. Marie looks as though she wants to come with me. Niamh has her head down to hide her tears. I hate myself for always being the one who causes arguments.

In the end, Finn runs after me as I head towards the small piece of green at the end of the back path of our farm. It's a place full of childhood memory.

Finn silently walks alongside me. It takes about fifteen minutes' stroll to reach the clearing, almost unknown to anyone other than Finn, Niamh and me. We came here and messed about all the time when we were kids. I pull out a cigarette and start smoking.

The sky is threatening rain but it only reminds me of my childhood. The smell of grass and wet soil fills my nostrils. My pain sails along the light breeze and makes me shiver.

When we reach the clearing, we sit down on the slightly moist ground. I roll a joint. Finn considers me sidelong.

"You want some?" I ask, not knowing anything about my younger brother as an adult. I also discreetly survey him. He looks straight-laced enough in a pale checked shirt and jeans. Among my siblings, Finn looks most like me, except his face is more angular, harsher.

"No, thanks."

"Not into drugs, huh?" I tease.

"Not really. You?"

I want to laugh and tell my bright-eyed brother about my life in London, but I don't. My family already think that I betray them just by leaving. Why give them the satisfaction of my life story that confirms I've been up to no good in London? Instead, I suck in a bellyful of hash and try to relax.

After a while, Finn turns to me. "Sorry. I was a dumb kid. I didn't appreciate you. I've got gay friends at uni now and everything."

I take another toke. The cannabis is not enough these days but it will do for now. "Oh, so it makes it okay, doesn't it? Fuck you."

He responds, "I was a teenager. It was a big deal to be bullied because of your brother."

I'm not really angry with Finn. He was just a kid. And children don't want to be singled out by their school friends for whatever reason. Who could blame him, indeed? I'm only annoyed with my parents and Patrick.

"No problems." I relight the joint. "Let's not talk about it."

"Anyway, what are you doing in London? Do you have a boyfriend?" He watches me. "I've bumped into Cillian a few times. I know you guys are not together anymore."

"We broke up in Dublin." I squeeze my eyes shut, squinting at the oblique sun which has been ever so desperate to shine through the clouds. "I'm not doing very well, to be honest, but I'll survive. No boyfriend either."

"That's a shame." I wonder if he means Cillian, my sorry life or the fact that I have no boyfriend. Of course, all of them are my own fault. I can't exactly tell him what I do for a living. Despite all my effort to stay afloat, to not be a loser, I'm still the shameful little secret that my family believe me to be.

"You know you guys can get married in Ireland now. I voted for marriage equality," he tells me, with more pride than me.

"We, uh?" I know about the referendum. "Well, it looks as though Dad and Paddy never got the memo."

Finn sighs. "Yeah, the older generation. It's not so bad in the cities. Will you ever come back to Ireland to live?"

I look to the sky and inhale the grassy smell in the air. "Nah. I don't think so."

To change the subject, I ask, "Well. How's college?" We move onto safer territory. I am truly proud of him to have gone to university. He's the first one in our family. And now Niamh is about to do the same.

I wish there were more I could be proud of myself. Something that makes me worthy enough for Ali and makes me deserving of his attention. It's been nearly three months. I guess he's not going to come chasing after me.

Finn tells me a bit about his life at university and it sounds great. At the end, he pulls me into a man hug. "Good to see you, brother. I know it's not easy for you to come back here but I'm glad you did."

I gaze at him. It's as if I'm looking at a less fucked-up version of my younger self. I smile. "I'm happy to see you too. Keep up the good work, yeah? When I'm more sorted, you need to come to visit me in London, okay?"

He smiles brilliantly. "I'd love to."

I mean it, though I haven't considered how I'm going to sort myself out exactly. Getting clean again will be a good start.

~~~

I return to the hospital to see my dad and find him sleeping. I guess it's goodbye. I'm getting a late flight back to London today. I sit by the bed and observe him, the lines on his face, the once-powerful arms and hands. He'd worked so hard to raise the family. I'm not ungrateful but I also remember the disappointment in his eyes. He'd wanted Patrick and me to take over the farm, and instead he got a gay son who was interested in music. I hated how I'd frustrated him. He'd drag us along to Gaelic football every weekend and gradually I'd escape. I'd run away to hang out with Cillian or hide away somewhere. I could not be part of this community or my father's child because I didn't like the GAA.

Seeing that drawn face, I try to remember whether he'd ever appeared happy, just content that we were all okay. I think about how I'll never have a conversation with him again. I'll never make peace with my dad.

Goodbye, Dad. I'm sorry I fought with you. I tried to be the son you wanted but it didn't work. Don't hate me.

My fingers touch the once-strong hands. They're cool and skeletal now, but I remember their strength. I know how rough and callus they are and how they used to feel. They're so fragile now against my fingertips.

I sit there staring at him. I don't know how long I've been like that in the room with the low hum of the medical devices. A hand gently touches my shoulder. I look up, realising my face is wet with tears.

My mum looks closely at me. Her eyes are also red from crying.

I stand up.

She pulls me into a tight hug. I'm half a head taller than her. I cup her head and rest her face against my shoulder. We stand like that for a while without words that may express how we feel.

"Let's get a drink, son. There's a small courtyard on the ground floor," Mum suggests.

We walk to the cafeteria, then take the two cups of tea to a table outside. I light a cigarette.

Mum frowns. "Those things will kill you. Even Paddy's given up recently."

I cock my head to consider my mum. She's worrying about me and a cancer stick. Lucky she doesn't know about my drug addiction. My cravings have been killing me. I can hardly concentrate on anything since coming back.

"I'm sorry."

My mum's mouth opens a little in surprise. "What for?"

I don't even know what for. For disappointing them, for not looking after the family, for resorting to begging and selling myself. I'm sure they'd be less than proud if they'd known. I can't say any of it. "I should stay here and help, I suppose." Like a good son.

She shakes her head. "You wouldn't be happy if you did that."

I gaze at her face. The once-young features are gathering many lines. "But I'm not happy now." I suck on the cigarette.

"Why not?" She frowns. "Did something happen with Cillian? Your dad didn't like the boy. I don't know. You were so smitten with him."

I'm surprised. "You discussed me? And talked about Cillian?"

Mum sighs. "Yes, in a fashion. We didn't think what you did was right. It's not the way we were brought up. I had to follow your dad. I'm married to him."

Anger surges inside of me. "He hates me."

"He was proud of your music and that you were good with your school work. He just thinks you're too cocky for your own good. He couldn't understand you and that frustrated him."

It's all an act. I feel so bad about myself sometimes that all I can do is to pretend I'm someone else, someone confident.

"I couldn't help falling in love with the wrong person. You made me feel worthless." I want to stamp my feet like an impetuous child.

"I'm sorry." Her voice croaks. "We just can't accept..." She watches me with her red-rimmed eyes.

"You can't even say the word." I blurt out. "I'm gay, Mum. I. Am. Gay." There. I come out ten years too late. Angry and elated tears pour out of my eyes.

"I know. And I understand why you ran away. You needed to be true to yourself. I just knew love between eighteen-year-olds wouldn't last. And you're too fragile. It'd break your heart. But what could I do? I had to be on your dad's side."

I swallow and try to control my emotions. I'm fragile but I have to be true to myself.

"He did. Cillian broke my heart. And all these years, I've thought of myself as a disappointment. I believed that's why I couldn't hold on to someone. I'm afraid no one will ever want me." I look away to wipe at my tears.

"Oh, Liam! You're too young to think that. Haven't you met anyone who's good to you?"

I put him off, pretending that I wasn't interested. My dad made me feel like I wasn't good enough. I must have spoken my thoughts out loud.

Mum sighs again. "He's not going to be around much longer. Don't hate him."

"I don't. I hate myself." I grind out the cigarette underfoot as more tears fall down my face.

"Oh, Liam. You're a lovely person. Why would you do that to yourself? There must be some people like you in London."

People like me. Ali.

"There'll be a nice young man for my Liam." She comments, as if to convince herself.

I'm choking on my tears. She has no idea how difficult it is to change from believing I'm fucked up to allowing myself to be loved.

Finally, I can only apologise. "Sorry, Mum. I won't be at the funeral. I said goodbye to Dad earlier."

She starts to sob, too. "I know. It's probably for the best. Some of your uncles, Patrick…" She doesn't need to finish the sentence because I know it may be awkward. I'll embarrass some of the relatives. We sit, holding onto each other for a long time.

Later, we return to the farm. I've had a joint but I still feel pretty agitated. I force myself to behave. Finn, Marie and the kids are staying in the cottage too. I've taken baby Paddy and Sarah off Marie to give her a break. Sarah's a ball of energy and she makes me laugh. I've been trying to draw with her but she keeps sneaking off after only a few minutes, too excited to sit still for any amount of time. Marie's definitely got her hands full with this one.

I have Paddy strapped in a sling. I've just sung Brahms' Lullaby to him and he's gone to sleep. At least I hope he is and not doing pee-pee or poo-poo on my good T-shirt.

I just had a coffee and some toast for lunch. Irish television plays in the background. I've put Paddy down, and he's sleeping in his rocking cot that I use my foot to operate. Sarah is back drawing on the coffee table and making a big mess. I wish I could watch the kids grow up, but I'm an escort living from hand to mouth, with a drug habit. I'm not exactly an inspiring role model. I promise myself to remember their birthdays and Christmas, though, and send cards and presents when I can.

The cheerful female TV presenter has caught my attention.

We have a special guest today. Returning to the National Theatre this season, our loveliest, most glamorous...Dara O'Shea.

I stare wide-eyed at the television. The red-haired actress is wearing an embroidered ruby dress, which suits her beautifully. I assess her to see if I can recognise Ali's features. He doesn't have the flaming hair but everything else is familiar: the sharp planes on his face and distinctive green eyes. I miss him so much it hurts.

I look around at my family who are completely oblivious to my inner turmoil. It's as though loneliness can seep into my bones and eat at me even when I'm surrounded by people.

Presenter: *Dara is sixty-five this year!*

O'Shea waits for the studio audience to gasp and clap, glancing at them all, possessing the stage. Then, she smiles majestically at the camera and the imagined audience at home.

Presenter: *How do you keep your skin so smooth? You have to share your beauty secrets with all your female fans.* She chuckles.

O'Shea beams: *Oh, you know. I'm young at heart.*

The studio audience laughs.

Presenter: *No plans to retire at all, then? You've been successful on television and the stage for over forty years, right?*

O'Shea giggles: *I love my job. I've been a drama queen for forty-five years. I'm not giving up anytime soon.*

More laughter that sounds forced, as if the presenter and audiences are mocking me for the mess I'm in.

Presenter: *But there must have been some regrets.*

Ali's mum quiets, tears shimmering in her eyes. Damn, she's a good actress.

O'Shea: *Well, you know. I didn't have time for my family.* The audience collectively sighs.

What the hell? My chest aches for Ali but it must be how showbiz is. She's giving the viewers and the broadcaster exactly what they want to hear. The poor actress sacrificing her home life for a successful career. I picture young Ali on his own, never having the luxury of being cared for by a loving, doting parent. I can't bear any more of the untruths that come out of O'Shea's mouth. Her interview leaves me aghast that a woman who has abandoned her son when he was a child can walk around as though nothing has happened. Looking at her face reminds me of Ali all too painfully.

I've been totally disturbed by her TV appearance when Marie tries to call me. "You okay, Liam?" She's probably been saying my name for a while.

I wish I could tell my family about Ali but they wouldn't understand. I certainly can't say anything about being paid for sex.

"Liam, you all right?" Marie sounds concerned.

"Yeah." I try to focus again. Speaking with my mum and seeing Ali's mother on television has rattled me. "You okay to look after the kids now? I think I'll just go and pack." I want to get back to my room though it's not for arranging my luggage. I have brought nothing that warrants it. I can just dump everything back in the bag. But I need some time to myself.

"Okay." She checks on the baby.

I stand up.

Marie looks around the sitting room. Niamh is playing on her mobile in the far armchair. Marie stands too and with a frown, she stops me in my tracks. "Liam."

I look intently at her. "Yeah?"

"What's going on in London? You're so miserable. It's not right."

I consider how to answer her but fail. I can't offload my fuck-ups here, not to Marie. "I'm all right. Really. Don't worry about me, sis." It's an obvious lie.

She shakes her head. "If you need anything, anything at all, you'll call me, won't you? Or come and stay with me. Okay?"

I nod. "Okay."

"Promise?"

I smile through threatening tears and hold up my pinkie. "Yeah, I do." She doesn't know that my promises come cheap. It's good to know some of my family members give a shit. I will make more of an effort in future to stay in touch.

Seeing that she's satisfied, I continue to my childhood bedroom, which I've been sharing with Finn again in the last couple of days. It still has some football posters that Finn had put up, and books, magazines and action figures from our childhood. I have a few trophies for musical performances, competitions and so forth. My eyes are drawn to the span of green outside. The emerald colour of his eyes.

I pick up my phone and dial, as though I've been hypnotised.

After numerous rings, I'm about to give up when Ali picks up, a little breathlessly. I look at the time. He must have been still at work. "Liam?"

I like the fact that he has kept my contact on his phone. "Yeah." Before I can regret calling and simply put the phone down, I burst out, "I miss you."

He takes a sharp breath and exhales. "I miss you too."

"That's all. I don't want anything." I'm going to ring off. It's a stupid thing to phone him on impulse. He's clearly doing okay without me.

"No, wait. Wait." I hear him move, his clothes rustling. "Where are you? You sound upset." How can he tell?

"I'm in Cork with my family." I light a cigarette. Finn will have to deal with the smell. "My dad's dying."

"Oh, I'm sorry." Ali's voice soothes me. How does he do that? "Do you want me to come over? How long are you staying out there?"

"Come? You'll come all the way here if I ask you?" I inhale deeply.

"Yes, of course. If you need me to." Oh, fuck. Really? I'm too stunned to reply.

He sighs again. "Liam, you didn't really tell me but you ran away from Ireland, right? Perhaps you didn't get on with your family. You don't need to do this alone. I'll come. To be with you."

Tears fall down my cheeks silently. I'm glad he can't see me.

"I'll be back in London tonight." I try to steady my voice. I don't know what the hell I'm doing anymore. "I'm fine. I shouldn't have bothered you. Thanks, but I'm a train wreck. Forget it."

I end the call before Ali can reply. He tries to ring back a few times but when I won't answer, he stops eventually.

CHAPTER 10

Iᴛ's ʟᴀᴛᴇ ᴀɴᴅ I'm seriously withdrawn. My body has been screaming, roaring for relief. I try to sleep, leaning against the cold pane of the Perspex on the train back to central London. Greenery soon turns into ugly blocks of flats and walls covered by graffiti. I can't make it to my flat. I don't want to arrive home to find Dmitri absent and I'm left without any crack. Instead, I get off the Tube in central London and pay a visit to my old dealer who's surprised to see me but happily sells me five rocks and a small pipe. That's the last of the cash on me.

I see on my phone that Ali has tried to call me again.

I smoke some as soon as I get back to my small room. No one's around. I play my flute until my mouth goes numb and my finger pads hurt. I can try telling myself that the coke's good for staying awake and being high enough to practise for hours. But I know I don't do crack for my music.

My phone battery is dead. It doesn't matter because I shouldn't have phoned Ali. And now he's worried about me and keeps calling. I'm a dumb fuck.

The morning comes soon enough.

Marie's phone call brings the expected news. I stare at my hands and remember my dad's and how I trusted them when I was a kid until I learned that they could turn into fists. And words could hurt even more than the bruises.

I must have spaced out for a long time. When I come to, I realise I need to find a few tricks. Instead, my confused mind drives me out to central London with my flute. I recognise my mistake as I'm walking down Shaftsbury Avenue. It's my old stomping ground. *Oh, yes, rent.* I'm going to be kicked out of the flat if I don't make some money soon. I put my hands in my trouser pockets to keep warm where I can feel the rocks of crack in their individual small packets.

Where's my phone, though? In a rush to come out, I've left my mobile. How the fuck am I going to connect with the agency and my regulars? I should head back but my legs take me in the opposite direction.

I walk south and I'm soon on Lambeth Bridge where I stop and contemplate the landscape, gazing at the dirty Thames below. It's irrational, but I yearn for the freedom of the streets right now. No more sex for cash. I can survive, or can I?

The inky water flows past and for a few minutes, I contemplate what'll happen if I jump. High. Low. Swinging moods as if I'm travelling the high seas. The water is beautiful with the floating reflections of the light. It draws me in. If anyone will miss me at all. Will they even look for me? No one will know I'm down the bottom of the river, anyway. So, I'll become part of the sea, consumed and swallowed by nature. *It's not a bad way to go.*

Behind me, a couple of kids run past. I hear their laughter.

I shake my head. *Come on.* There's crack in my pocket. I start heading south of the river, as though an alternative destiny awaits me.

I'm surprised the squat is still there. The stale smell tells me it's not been used for a while. Some unknown remnants of other squatters have been left and scattered, though. The air is filled with a combined odour of piss and decay. It wouldn't have mattered if others came. I need somewhere familiar tonight. I sit on the floor and dig out a rock from my pocket.

I don't know how long I've been in the old storage unit. The rumbling of the train overhead seems nonstop. Eventually, I make my way back to my bedsit. I need to find work. My head hurts and all the colours around me seem to come at me, bursting the sensors in my brain. The journey back is relentless. With shaky hands, I open the door to the flat. It doesn't feel right. Nothing does. Not anymore.

With my phone charged and back on, I check and read the few bookings and messages which came in when I'd been in Ireland and there are a couple more missed calls and a text from Ali, asking me if I'm back and whether I'm all right.

I'm still wasted from the amount of coke I smoked back in the squat. I can't think straight, so I have a cigarette in the lounge.

Chris emerges from his room and plonks himself down next to me. "Where've you been?" His frown deepens as he scrutinises me.

I tell him about my dad and being back at home. I miss out the part about staying in the squat and binging on crack.

I sense Chris is about to give me a sermon. But he doesn't do that. He must be really worried about me. His eyes search my face for some sign of sanity.

Then the doorbell rings.

"Oh, shit. The landlord's coming for the rent." Chris returns to his room for his rent money. Cash only. None of us in the flat are in steady employment with regular salaries getting paid into bank accounts and other legal shit.

I rush into my bedroom to check on my finances. Fuck. All it takes is my lapse in control and I'm going to be out on the fucking street. I find my stash of saved cash, which has dwindled to two hundred and I've not made anything for a week while I'd been in Ireland and the squat.

Chris knocks on my door. "Gonna let him in." He can see the worry on my face. "What's up? You okay?"

"No. I don't have enough."

I needn't say more. Chris is calm. "Go to my room. I'll tell him you're out. I've got mine, and Dmitri and Alberto have left theirs. I can stall him."

I do, and listen to the muffled conversation between the two men through the door. The landlord's not happy. After he leaves, Chris comes back into his room.

Chris holds me and looks into my eyes. "Liam, can I do something?"

"No, I'll be all right. I'll have the cash when he comes back." I try to smile. I can't let Chris worry about me. Not again. He's already helped me plenty. I stand to leave the flat.

~~~

In the sunshine, I reach for my phone in my pocket to see what date it is. Not that it matters much these days. I've forgotten my mobile again. I've left it in the flat, plugged in to charge. My head spins. I can find a cheap phone and some tricks tomorrow. I should sleep first. I start walking and I'm soon back in familiar territory.

I really hate it when people stare at me. *Remember, you're the one who's paranoid.* I feel as though they can read my every thought and they know I'm an escort without means of communication and about to be homeless again. Back on the street with nothing to my name.

My intention is to get back on track but I fail. With the two hundred quid in my pocket, I hide in the squat, using crack from the dealer.

I haven't slept for a few days. My drugged-up dreams are jumbled. I see the sallow face of my dying father and hear noises that sound like a mixture of wind and snippets of conversation. I am running, the passing landscape incessantly reminding me of Ireland but the strong gust blows in my face, dragging me back. I wake up, sweating and hyperventilating.

I smoke what's in the crack pipe. I must have gone out at some point and done something I shouldn't. Oh, yes. I turned up at the flat of one of my regulars and he let me in. He paid me and we had sex, but he was not happy. Later, I found a cheap phone and SIM and I'm back in business.

I can't recall how long I've been holed up here in the storage unit. One more rock and I'm going to sort my life out. *Fuck's sake, Liam. It's an addiction. You'll want more and more and you know it.*

Do something about it. *I dare you.*

I stand by the water flowing along the river. I throw my cheap mobile and the last rock into it, and watch them disappear.

I remember climbing over the fence of the bridge and dangling my legs, thinking about the jump yet again. *Believe in myself and I may be happy.* I howl abuse at the passing boats. I turn and see the horror on the pedestrians' faces. All my muscles ache. Two men yank me back down and curse me for being stupid. I sit on the floor, my body trembling as they shake me and ask me what I'm thinking, whether I need a hospital. I stare at them with wide eyes.

Eventually, I drag myself back to the squat. I'm utterly exhausted. Wakefulness intersperses with vivid dreams. Of Ireland, Dublin and the dirty streets.

~~~

Someone pushes the door open to let a shaft of sunlight through, along with the morning air. I'm sitting with my knees drawn up and my arms around them, making myself small and safe, except it's never safe in the squat. I can't remember how not to be wary.

"Liam?" It may be Ali's voice. Why would he be here? I must have been confused and suffering a hallucination. I squint to see. The hazy light illuminates specks of dust as they dance along the shaft of a sunbeam. But who?

"Liam?" he repeats.

I look up to be met by his green eyes, which are infused with a grey tint today.

"What are you doing here?" My own voice sounds distant, croaky, as if I'm under water. "Why can't you leave me alone?" My vision is blurred with the flood of tears.

He says, resolutely, "I can't and I won't."

He takes off his jacket and wraps me in it, transferring his body heat to me. Then he embraces me in his arms, observing me in this calming way that is so uniquely Ali. "What happened to your face?"

I grimace. I don't have a fucking clue. I often knock into things when I'm on drugs. So, who knows? I glance around the spartan squat. "I must have bumped into the bed frame here."

Ali doesn't laugh. His eyes narrow and he purses his lips but he doesn't call me out on it. "Glad to see your humour's intact."

His arm encircles my left shoulder, and now that we are so close, I'm forced to face him.

I turn but I can't see him through my tears. Ali's here. He hasn't given up on me.

"How did you find me?" The glare of the sunlight is bothering me.

"Chris phoned me. How could you leave your mobile? He's been worried sick since you disappeared."

I force myself to focus, to think. What happened? I dodged the landlord, then ran out of the flat. What did I do next? Why is Ali here again? Right, I had a binge and I was so high. Then there was a crash and I was at rock bottom. The bridge. That sounds familiar.

I've gone without crack since I sat on the edge of the bridge and I disposed of my last rock.

Now I'm craving and I can't fucking concentrate on anything. But I point to some marks on the wall as if that answers Ali's concerns. "See, Ali. Look. My own blood on the wall. It's from before. Maybe I should have fucking died when I'd stayed here and I OD'd. It'd have been better that way."

"No, it wouldn't. Definitely not." Ali frowns. He grabs hold of my shoulders and shakes them. "You're totally wrong. I care about you." He pulls me close again with some force and hugs me.

Our faces are so close. I can smell his faint scent, familiar despite everything.

"You've lost so much weight," he says.

I've fucked up. I couldn't accept that someone would care. The fact that the person is Ali should have given me joy, but I'm only filled with dread that I'm not a great match for such a perfect man. My voice, when I start to talk, doesn't seem to belong to me anymore. "I'm sorry." I don't want Chris and Ali to worry about me. I thought I'd find a way out of this by myself.

"Liam, I see you, all right? Parts of you that you've tried to hide from me, from yourself. I remember your face. The first time you stayed after we had sex and you sat in the garden smoking. I couldn't bear the loneliness, the pain and every fucked-up emotion on your face. I wanted to hug you then. You seemed too young for all of it. I wanted to take you back to the time before you began thinking you were not good enough for this world. I'm still here. I'm going to do that from now on. Will you let me?"

"I'll be fine." Ali's chest feels good, though. I love the lemony fragrance on his shirt.

He pats the back of my head lightly. "You don't have to be fine. When you're not okay, I'll be there to catch you. All right?"

When I'm too stunned to reply, he continues, "It's okay. I'm here now. We are. Do you know who brought me to find you?"

I pull off a little, so I can see his face. I feel paranoid for a split second that the police are around. Like that time they'd come to take me to the police station to help them find the gangsters who'd been terrorising Sasha.

I shake my head violently and try to think. "No one knows this place…" It's been two years since I stayed here. I'd have thought the gentrification all over London would get rid of squats like this.

"Uh…Sasha? How has he…?" My brain gets into gear finally. He's the only one who would have known my last squat. But why would he bring Ali to me? They don't know each other. Perhaps this is my delirium. I rub my face on Ali's shirt. He seems real. His solid frame is exactly how I remember it and he's warm. His heartbeats soothe me, despite all the physical and emotional turmoil whirling round every part of me right now.

Ali kisses the side of my head. "Yes, there are people who care about you, Liam." I hear the smile in his voice. A sense of security and protection gradually seeps into my consciousness and takes hold of me. "Chris knew something was up when he realised you'd been gone a few days. He found my number on your phone and he called Sasha. We searched in Elephant and Castle and up here. Sasha said he'd find you, that you'd always run away and hide in squats, and he was right. They are waiting outside."

My eyes widen. In my drug-addled mind, I thought no one would even notice I'd gone. *Oh, shit.* I couldn't make rent. That was the problem. I'd flee and get high as a kite.

He hugs me again, tighter, and kisses my forehead. "What were you even thinking? Leaving your room like that and not taking your phone? What if we couldn't find you?"

"I'm homeless again." My voice is muffled as Ali continues to wrap me up in his strong body. "I couldn't make rent. I spent everything on the flight to Ireland and on coke."

I push Ali away. "Why have you come for me? I need to work. I'm sorry, Ali. I can't be yours because this…" I point to my heart. "Anyone can buy this. My dad knew it. He knew what I'd been doing in London. I saw it in his eyes. That's what'd disgusted him. And Patrick. My older brother. They didn't want me there."

Ali sighs again. "I'm sorry about your dad. But he was wrong and your brother's wrong. You're not disgusting. And you don't sell your heart, not just to anybody. You're a good man. I wouldn't have wanted you otherwise."

Ali still wants me. A dream can't feel so real.

I stare at him, but I can't seem to understand anything. All I sense is the teardrops falling on my lap. I silently sob. After I came to London, I'd never cried so much until Ali came along and made me feel again. He'd forced me not to act all confident and brave when I was in fact broken and sad.

"Oh. Make it stop. Make it stop." I grab hold of Ali's shirt front, which is already soaked through with my tears and snot. "Why? This is what I deserve." I gesture to the squat and circle my finger to indicate what a dump it is. It's what I know. Despite the fucking mess, it's something I'm comfortable with. My tears keep coming.

"Why?" Ali answers steadily. "You don't need a reason to be upset. I think you've had a breakdown, Liam."

Breakdown, relapse, binge, craving. A big fucking mess. Fucking walking disaster. But Ali lets me cry myself dry while ruining his shirt.

When I finally stop, he asks, "Will you go to a detox? Sasha can ask his counsellor for an emergency placement. Perhaps we can persuade them you're a danger to yourself?"

Hearing those words, I chuckle through my tears. "I know I'm a danger to myself."

Ali smiles. "Yeah. And to me."

"What do you mean?" I have to clean some of my snot with the bottom of my T-shirt. It doesn't matter anyway since the clothes I'm wearing are dirty and probably need to be fumigated.

His grin broadens. "Well, I'm dangerously close to caring too much about you."

I shake my head. Ali's a big softie but I can't think about romance right now. "Will you wait for me if I go?" I ask.

"Of course, Liam. We'll talk after the rehab. Okay?" When he pulls away, he whispers, "You ready?"

I'm not but I nod.

He stands first and offers his hand to pull me up. My legs are wobbly from the withdrawal, and from sitting down for too long on the bare concrete floor. I manage in the end. Ali hugs me for a second and he kisses me gently.

When we pull apart, I right myself as much as I can. I'm still wearing Ali's jacket. I try to return it but he shakes his head. "You came out wearing only a T-shirt as well. You're definitely a danger to yourself. If the drugs don't kill you, you'll get hypothermia."

I'm too exhausted to disagree.

Ali offers me his big palm. "Let's go, then."

We hold hands and lace our fingers together as we walk out of the filthy unit.

Outside, the morning chill envelops me. Luckily, I still have Ali's jacket. Chris and Sasha are standing around and smoking in front of Ali's car. Chris smiles when he sees me. "There you are."

He hugs me and then moves away to assess the damage. "Try not to pull a stunt like that again, please, Liam. I'm getting too old for this shit."

Ali rolls his eyes. "What? At the grand old age of twenty-five?"

"Twenty-six," Chris counters.

Ali chuckles and I'm glad they're trying to lighten the mood. I can only assume that I look like shit and they've all been scared to death by my disappearance.

Sasha gazes at me and nods. He's a man of few words. But then he sees my and Ali's entwined hands and grins too, as though he approves.

I smile at them then, but I most likely end up with a lopsided grimace.

PART FOUR
HIS AND HIS

CHAPTER 11

SASHA CALLED HIS drug counsellor Sean. Apparently, I wasn't quite bad enough to warrant a long wholesale rehab. It's crack. There's relatively little anyone can do to help you get off it, unlike heroin. I'd binged, then crashed, and my confused mind told me to go cold turkey. I told Ali and Chris about my last few days, about Lambeth Bridge and the dark and thick Thames water. Sasha only frowned at me, like he always used to do. I know he'd forgiven me but I was quite a scumbag to him. Realising how I'd hurt someone like Sasha added to my self-loathing.

Sean said I suffered a mental health crisis. I'd call it a meltdown. He was concerned that I was also a suicide risk. I was eventually admitted to the rehab programme for two weeks.

For over a week, I've not said a word during the group sessions but now Sean, who leads the group, is focusing on me and looking expectant.

I blurt out, "I killed Skip." Eight pairs of eyes widen. "I mean… she was my pet rabbit."

I expect laughter or horror but there's none. And then words flow out as if a door has opened.

My dad always wanted me to help him with the farm. I did but he'd told me off for something I'd done wrong. I answered back.

"I want to go out. I'm supposed to meet Cillian."

"What is this? That boy is a sissy. If you want to be my son, man up."

He took his belt out. I stared at him. I'd stand up to him. He hit me on my back and my legs so the marks wouldn't show. I bit my lip and refused to make any noise. Crying is a sign of weakness. I wanted to hate him so much. Not being able to only made me feel worse, as though I was out of control of my emotions.

I glared at his red face and saw uncontrollable fury. He stopped then, and I ran away. My legs took me to the wood where I hid well until it was pitch-dark. When I returned to the house, everyone had gone to sleep, so I climbed back in, feeling the ache of my thighs with every step.

"I'd forgotten about Skip till the next morning and she was dead in her cage." Her body felt so cold and lifeless. Small and vulnerable, just like I was.

One of the other participants, a young woman, gasps. Sean merely nods.

"But you probably didn't kill it," the young woman pleads with her eyes, willing us to agree.

I realised that. Sometime later, I thought perhaps Skip was already ill. It didn't matter, though, because part of me had died with her.

"Still," I concede. Just then, Sean announces time's up for the session. I find myself exhaling, as though I've been holding my breaths through our session. It may have helped talking about the death of my rabbit. I feel as if I've taken my cocky, confident mask off, and there's no crack to lift my spirit. My emotions laid bare.

Sean tries to reach out to my core when we're in the one-to-one session. He is a big ex-junkie covered in tattoos and piercings.

"Have you talked to your dad about your sexuality?" Sean asks.

I shake my head. "No. He…he died recently. When I was by his deathbed, I came out to my mum even though they already knew I was gay."

"How did you feel after you did that?" Sean taps his pen on his small notepad but he never writes anything down when I'm in session with him.

I cock my head and think about the question. "I still knew they didn't accept it." I've had time to think about it all and how being home made my relapse worse. "You know in films and novels, these characters are always so perfect, and even when bad things happen to them, all the problems will eventually be all wrapped up and sorted. They will reconcile with their families and so on. I'm this character who never gets to resolve everything and he has to accept that he's not perfect. So, speaking to my mum was as good a conclusion as it could be for my story."

"Hmm. Actually, none of us are like Hollywood movies with happy endings," he tells me calmly. "Why did you come off crack? It was quite a difficult thing to do by yourself."

"Sasha and my mum both said something about me being happy and finding someone who loves me. I was thinking about this guy. This great, loving man who cares about me, despite my imperfections." I gaze at his open face. "I wanted to get clean, so maybe I had a chance with him."

Sean continues to watch me without judgement.

"When I was thinking about jumping in the Thames, I realised he'd help me to value myself."

Sean's lips turn up and then he smiles. "I'm glad you came to that conclusion."

"I know I need to stay clean for myself, though, whether he wants me or not," I admit quietly.

Sean nods.

When it's time for me to leave the detox, Sean hands me a leaflet for a local self-help group. A Narcotics Anonymous meeting.

I read the text. "I don't know. I've only got one dead rabbit story."

Sean shakes his head. "You don't have to tell stories. The group helps the participants to support each other in their journey of recovery." He regards me for long moments. "Liam, you have a lot of experiences. Probably too many for a twenty-two-year-old. If you don't want to go through the steps and talk in front of people, you can always write them down."

"Oh." I've never thought about doing that.

"You can even let other people read them. Like your man, for example," he gently suggests.

My man? Not yet. I nod. "Yeah, I'll think about it."

"Or, just go to the meeting to see whether it's helpful. And come to me anytime you're at risk of a relapse. You know I'm here."

I nod again. It's not easy being out, but it has been two weeks of emotional hell. I look forward to seeing Ali again.

Ali stands by his little black car, waiting for me in the car park of the treatment centre. In the squat, I was coming down, and too self-absorbed and emotional. I didn't notice that he'd got some white hair about his temples since my last appointment with him when we went for that Chinese meal. He looks sexy as hell. I stare at him with uncertainty.

"Let me take you home," he says steadily as he gives me a hug and a light kiss on my lips.

"I've got nowhere I can go." It has been on my mind while I've been in detox. I suppose it distracted me from the withdrawal. I think it's been over six weeks since I paid rent, so I've lost the bedsit. I was thinking of kipping on the sofa or in Chris's bed until I find my feet again. I'm sure he'll be all right with it.

Ali frowns. "I've paid your rent for two months." He holds his hand up. "I won't hear your protests now. We can talk about it later." Not waiting to see my reaction, he heads towards the driver's side and opens the doors for us.

Reluctantly, I follow and get in the car. As soon as I've sat down and Ali pulls away from the kerb, I turn to him. "That's a lot of money, Ali. I'll pay you back." I'm already worrying about how I will have to start from scratch again. I don't want to be indebted to anyone, too, least of all to Ali.

He drives on and shakes his head. "You don't have to but I know you're a stubborn git."

I direct him to my address. As we get out of his car, I take his hand and lead him to my building and the flat. Nothing seems to have changed in the apartment and my flatmates have left my room as it was. It's only been three weeks or so but so much has changed in me—physically, mentally and emotionally. It feels good to be free of drugs once again. I was an emotional wreck at the detox but now I'm as stable as I can be to face Ali and whatever he wants to talk to me about.

We manage to avoid all my flatmates as I steer him to my spartan room and I sit him down on my bed. "Don't move."

I need to wash the rehab off me. I grab a towel and go to have the quickest shower I can manage. When I come back, Ali hasn't moved. I put on a fresh T-shirt and a pair of ripped jeans and sit in the scratchy falling-apart armchair and watch him. I feel self-conscious as I have never brought anyone back here, let alone a john or an ex-client if I have to describe Ali now.

"So, how are you feeling?" His face is open.

I hide my hands in between my legs. "Good. It's great to be clean again." Ali must know I don't mean shower-clean. "I feel bad to have relapsed but the last few weeks have taught me a lot about myself, too. It's given me time to think."

"I was worried about you." Ali touches his five o'clock shadow. "What...what can I do to support you?"

"With my addiction? You've done plenty." I can't repay him enough as it is. "I'm sorry to worry you."

"Don't apologise. I wanted to. I missed you so much, Liam. The thought of losing you was unbearable. It's lucky that Chris phoned me and we found you."

I swallow. I feel bad for bothering my friends and Ali but it's also good to know I've got people around me who genuinely care. It's probably the first time I've felt accepted like this.

Ali reaches out and takes my left hand and wraps his around it. "What happened in Ireland? You called me but rang off when I answered and tried to talk to you."

I sense the tears surging, again. I'd wanted no one but Ali to be in Ireland with me but it'd have been futile. I had to face my family alone even if it destroyed me. "Dad died the day after I left. He still couldn't accept me at the end."

"I'm so sorry." He wipes away the tears around my eyes.

"I need to get over it. I had some good chats with my mum, older sister, and my younger sister and brother. I think we'll keep in touch." Finn and Niamh both said they want to visit me in London. Well, maybe not when I'm in such a mess but sometime in the future. When I've sorted myself out.

"That's nice." Ali nods.

My breakdown was brought on by my trip home but I had already been in a downward spiral before.

"What about you? I thought you'd something to talk to me about." I'm apprehensive about what it is Ali may say but I'd much rather hear it than let it hang in the air.

Ali swallows.

"You told me to try dating. Well, I did. I signed up to the apps. I really tried. It was impossible for me not to only think of you when these guys talked about hooking up. The hot dude fifty metres away? Which positions? I only knew I liked the stuff we did!"

I laugh. That is so Ali. I agree with him totally because I also compared him to all my other sex partners. But I really doubt I'm the only guy who's ever been good in bed. "So, did you actually hook up with anyone?"

"I went on a couple of dates with the men Sue and Michael suggested." He winces.

"Yeah? What were they like?" I ask, even though I'm jealous. I know it's selfish but I secretly hope they were bad dating experiences. At the same time, I still think Ali is better off with someone much less complicated than me. Preferably, someone who is not penniless and has a history of drug addiction. And young and foolish.

He smiles again, amused by the telling of his own story. "So, Sue's cousin was interesting. He's as shy as me and the two of us were just awkward. He's a librarian who's only interested in books and theatre. I mean, I like reading, too, but I couldn't seem to talk to him about anything else."

I nod. It's unfortunate. Two shy men together are probably not a good pairing.

Ali continues, "Michael's friend. Uh. This guy works in an office by day and moonlights as a drag artist."

I have to grin at the thought of Ali's date with a drag queen. "He sounds hilarious."

"He was!" Ali chuckles. Damn. How I miss his easy laughter. "I saw him perform. RuPaul has some serious competition there. He was fine until we started touching and kissing." He stops to see my reaction.

I can only bob my head to encourage him to continue. He's quite free to see other men, even if I don't like the idea too much. "Quite honestly, I couldn't have sex with a joker. I like your humour but you're much more than that."

"You mean..." I try to imagine the scenario. "He's funny in bed? How?"

This time, he properly winces, wrinkling his nose. "He kept cracking jokes while we kissed, and he had these names for the body parts that were going to turn me off undressing myself in front of him. I just couldn't possibly fuck someone like that! He must have thought he was still on stage."

"It's probably nerves." Perhaps the guy was over-compensating.

"Still." He scratches his day-old stubble. I don't know why he's a little unshaven these days, but I kinda like the new Ali too. I honestly couldn't care less even if he turned into an ape and didn't wash for days. "Is there someone for you? I thought you might be seeing Chris or still have a thing for Sasha. I don't want to assume."

I can't believe Ali is so considerate and patient. I want to be as honest with him as possible. "No. Sasha was the one I shared the squat with but he's just a friend now. And he's seeing someone. They're pretty serious. Chris and I are fuck buddies but I don't have feelings for him."

Ali nods. "Do you have feelings for me?" He seems so hopeful when he asks the question, his eyes shining under the glare of the bare light bulb.

How can he think I am not interested in him? After all the good times we've shared and seeing how much he cares about me, I have to admit to my feelings for him too. I nod.

Before I can say any more, he launches into it like he has rehearsed the speech but I know it has come from his heart.

"I really want to get to know you better. I still need to find out more about Ireland, about why you left. How people back home looked down on you. Who broke your heart? I need to hear you play the flute. What makes you tick? I think I know how you like it in bed but I want you outside of the bedroom as well. I know you're half my age and more, but I can relate to you. If you really don't want to see me like that, you only have to tell me to fuck off."

Ali's gaze consumes me, as if he wants to get through to my soul. As an afterthought, he adds, "And don't even think about the money issue."

I gape while he tries to catch his breath. Ali is not usually the most expressive but he sure brings tears to my eyes. Again. I hurriedly look away to regroup.

I can't help but notice our differences. I am hyper-aware of how poor I am compared to him. I can see my bedsit through his eyes; the furniture is cheap, old and functional; the magnolia wall stained with smoking and spills. My few possessions show that I am an itinerant at best. The other lads are noisy as fuck. Chris seems to be having some kind of argument with his latest girlfriend. Dmitri, the part-time drug dealer, seems to have started a DJ set, playing dubstep in his room but it's loud enough to be vibrating throughout the flat. Mahmood the private cab driver plays video games in the sitting room. Alberto isn't loud but his fried bacon makes the place smell like a greasy spoon. Why do they all have to be in when I need to think straight? If that's even possible for me.

"Now that you know I'm available, you want me to be your boyfriend?" I ask tentatively.

Ali swallows and utters quietly, "Yes."

The man is crazy to want me but he has been forewarned about my inadequacies.

"You said I'd find a good man. I think I have already," he adds. "Why do I need to keep looking when you're right here?"

I survey my room again and think about it, about how very different we are but also all the good times I've shared with him, being paid for the privilege or not. He was ready to jump on the plane to come to Ireland when I needed him, if I wanted him to. I still don't think I deserve Ali, but I also want to know more about him, to find out about things I've missed. I have the twenty years when he led a very different life to catch up on.

I still can't understand what he sees in me and how I can make it work. I've had no experience of an ordinary life, an adult relationship and responsibilities. And Ali should have all those things. *But fuck.* I want the man and he wants me. He makes me feel valued and cared for. How can I pass up a man like Ali?

I grin despite my reservations. "My name's Liam Patrick Finton Murphy. I grew up on a small farm near Bantry in West Cork."

He comes over and squeezes himself into the same armchair. He hugs me and kisses me. I had really missed those strong arms.

"I'm Alastair McClelland of Scottish and Irish stock."

I laugh and shake my head. Even if we're heading towards a disaster, it sure feels good to be with him on an equal footing.

"So, I really need to know more about Ireland. And when you're ready, perhaps you can tell me more about your family and growing up in rural Cork."

"The farm belongs to my brother Patrick now since I'm the irresponsible one. I've never wanted to tend to the family estate like Paddy does anyway."

Ali nods.

I remember the television show. "I saw your mum."

"What?" His eyes widen.

"On a TV chat show." Even though there are only four million of us in Ireland, I *don't* bump into Irish celebrities.

"Oh." Ali blinks, between being curious and not wanting to know. "What has she got to say for herself?"

I kiss him on the cheek. "She regrets not having time for her family." Even if I haven't seen him as a child, I can well imagine the cuteness. How can anyone leave a boy like Ali is beyond me. I feel for Ali, for the loss he must experience knowing that his mother wants the love from everyone else but her own son.

"Uh." Ali narrows his eyes. "I heard she's a good actress."

I agree. From what I saw, she sure was. I hug Ali tighter and kiss his cheek as he leans into my embrace.

"Do you know why I have my other tattoo?" Ali rubs his palm over the armful of forest.

I love his ink but I haven't thought about its meaning until now. "Scotland?"

He smiles. "Yeah, the Scottish Highlands to be precise. I remember my dad taking me for a walk in the Drumrunie Forest. Our ancestors were from around the area. I was only seven or eight but somehow I shared my dad's pain. Seeing the hills and the open space in Scotland helped. The landscape took some of his sadness away." His eyes glaze over with the memory.

"Maybe you can take me there, too?"

He nods, his eyes misted over once more. "I'd love to."

Then I recall what he said earlier. "You want to hear me play the flute?"

"Yes, please." I extricate myself from his arms and want the tenderness back straightaway.

Ali returns to the edge of my bed so I can get up for my flute. Chris had brought it back to the flat when I left for the rehab.

I did get some sheet music from the shop with his birthday gift card. But I can always remember my best pieces by my favourite composer by heart. I take the flute out of the case, check the tuning and play Erik Satie's three *Gymnopédies*. The pieces with a languorous sadness have been written for the piano but I play them with my alto flute.

As I play, I think about the rejection I felt as a child, about Cillian and Sasha; betrayal, regrets and unrequited love. I can never express these emotions in words but the music can. At one point, I notice all the noises in the flat have died down. Other than that I am utterly lost in my performance, letting my thoughts infuse every note.

When I finish and put the flute down, Ali's eyes glisten with suppressed tears. "I played them at Emily's funeral," he tells me.

I would have loved to play the songs at my father's funeral, to mourn him—a father who'd rejected me and who'd not got to know me at all because of all his prejudices. And now, all I can remember was the alcohol-fused rage and his fists. The disgust in his eyes. Even if he'd appreciated how I excelled in music, he never expressed his feelings. And that makes me sad and angry. If he could only show me that he was proud of me in some way. Ali has brought out the pride in me that has long been buried, and he makes me believe I am worth something.

I put the flute down and cuddle him, remembering how welcoming and solid his body feels and realising how much I had wished to be his boyfriend, rather than someone who was paid to be there.

We are interrupted by a tentative knock on my bedroom door. I want to ignore it but then decide to open the door just a few inches. Alberto and Chris's heads squeeze between the door and the frame. Chris begins, "Ah, that was…it was beautiful, man."

"Exquisite." Alberto adds, "Bravo."

The guys don't know how good I am because I have always chosen to practise the flute when they are not around. I have entertained them with the tin whistle before but not so much with the flute. They love the Irish music I play, especially when they are wasted. Chris and Alberto crack me up when they dance to it as if they're in a club.

I open the door wider and turn to Ali. "Alberto. My flatmate. Ali. And you know Chris. Ali and I are seeing each other." Ali beams at the introduction. The two guys nod and Alberto mumbles hello.

Chris raises his hand. "Good to see you again, man." He grins mischievously and winks at me, as if he was Puck who'd used the magic juice on us and now he is amused by the fruition of his matchmaking.

"Now that we've established I'm quite a musical genius, fuck off, so I can snog Ali."

They smirk and retreat. Chris leaves with a parting shot. "Do more than that if you want. These walls are so well constructed, they're practically soundproof." *The sarcastic sort.*

I shut the door and turn to see Ali chuckle in silence, his shoulders shaking. He drags me onto the bed and we kiss, and enjoy each other's bodies and presence for the first time without the shackles of a transaction. I feel the excitement of first love despite all my doubts.

"I want you to fuck me, Ali," I whisper. "Forget soundproofing." I've suffered enough when Chris fucked through half of London.

Ali smiles, pushes me down on the narrow bed and admires me with obvious glee.

Today, I want to be Ali's boyfriend, not someone he's hired. Today, I'm going to let him take the lead and please me.

He slowly kisses me, as though we had all the time in the world. His hands search for my body and take my top off, breaking the long tender kiss. His mouth moves down my chest to my abs. I've lost weight in the last few months while I was on crack. The teasing of his tongue has made my dick so hard, it's uncomfortable. He palms his right hand on my bulge and massages it.

"Would you fuck me, instead? You're so hard. I want you inside of me." His green eyes shimmer, betraying so much passion.

Yeah, it's been a month. I'm ready for some action, especially with Ali. "Yes, I'm going to fuck you real good."

He drags my jeans down and gets rid of my briefs, revealing my erection, standing tall and ready. Ali licks his lips and regards me in a shy way. I love how he is still unsure of sex.

"Have you got lube, condom?" he whispers.

Unfortunately, I have a lot of them. I open my bedside table drawer to reveal a collection of supplies and a variety of sex toys. They remind him of my profession but his eyes only narrow for a split second. I grab a vial of lube and a condom.

Ali removes his shirt, trousers and boxers. I can't describe in words what his naked body is doing to my groin. I have wanted him so much it hurts. What Ali does next only reminds me of how sensual sex with him is. He opens the bottle of lube and generously dribbles it on his palm and fingers, and he opens his legs wide to fondle his arse, smearing the lube everywhere.

The concentration on his face is delicious. So much for taking it easy. I stroke myself as he plays with his own hole with two fingers to stretch it.

I want to fuck him so much, I think I must have growled with impatience. I lift myself up from the bed and push him down. He opens himself wide but I want even more. I grab his ankles and push them back, so he's almost folded in half.

"Are you ready for this?" I demand.

"Yes! It's been too long." *Damn right it has.*

I enter him then. I am still surprised by the tightness and warmth that envelop my cock. I know where he's most sensitive, so I shift and hit the spot.

"Fuck!"

I smile. "Yeah, that's what we're doing." I start to pull out and glide back in.

"If you carry on, I'll come in about a minute."

"You can but if you manage to hold out, I'll give you a blow job that ends all blow jobs."

Ali simply adores my mouth on him. He gasps. "I'll try."

I don't know how I'd survived without him. The heat of his hole engulfs me as I continue to move in and out. I pick up speed, shoving him against the headboard every time I plunge forward. I soon tense and come. I fall on top of Ali who kisses my forehead tenderly.

Ali's erection awaits, so when I calm myself down, I go down on him, pulling out all my tricks to make him feel good. My hands cup his arse and pull him deeper into my throat. We move in unison faster and faster. Ali was right about him being close. It doesn't take long for him to shoot hot cum down my throat.

Afterwards, we cuddle close on the lumpy single bed.

"Did I shout out when I came?" I ask.

Ali laughs. "I think you might have done."

I join him and chuckle. "You know, these walls are paper-thin."

Ali shakes his head. "It's not like they don't expect us to have sex."

"Yeah. But I've never asked anyone back here before." I kiss him. My hands are still on his hips and I'm getting hard again.

"Why not?" Ali frowns and moves a strand of stray hair away from my face.

I sit up to light a cigarette. "I don't know. I guess this is my sanctuary. It feels private. Anyway, I didn't have anyone special."

Ali admires me with his bright eyes. "Then thank you for sharing your space with me."

"You're welcome, boyfriend." I smile. The term feels alien on my tongue but I'll need to get used to having a proper grown-up relationship soon.

CHAPTER 12

A few weeks later.

WE SHOPPED FOR food in the supermarket near Ali's house. He's making a vegetable curry for dinner. He's a great chef, often displaying the same patience he uses for his creative work in the kitchen.

I love watching him cook. He hums along to the tunes he's playing in the background, making his cooking seem like dance and movement. I will listen to an eclectic mix of music. Ali likes bands that are really mellow, like slow-core and sometimes music involving string instruments. That kind of music suits him.

Soon, the kitchen smells of a heady combination of spices and basmati rice.

He half-turns to me and asks, "Help me set the table?"

I know where everything is in his kitchen now. It makes me feel proud, as though I belong in his house. We eat heartily in companionable silence. I am a very lucky boy because Ali enjoys cooking. "I never had a curry until I came to London, and vegetables were only side dishes at home."

Ali smiles easily while forking up some rice and curry. "Your childhood sounds like a blast."

I smirk. "Isn't it just?" It was what it was. I was a wild child and from the age of eleven or so, a pariah because I made no secret of being gay. That's a negative for a farmer's son in a little village in the country. "What about you?"

"I learned to cook!" He laughs. Ali has already sampled my limited culinary repertoire and he is not impressed. "I've been independent ever since my mum left us. I learned to look after myself and sometimes my father as well when I was older."

The more I know about Ali, the more incredible he seems to me. Every day, it's as if we're turning another page of our story and revealing ourselves to each other. I am yet to meet his dad, though, who has been living in Scotland since he retired from writing scripts for the BBC.

"What's your dad like?" I ask, in order to prepare myself to meet the father of the most important person in my life. I feel nervous about the prospect. Parents and I don't mix.

"He's a liberal intellectual." *What the fuck does that mean?* "So, I don't think it will be a problem when I come out to him. I'll definitely want to introduce this wonderful sweet guy I'm dating to him."

Sweet? "Who's that? I didn't know you got another boyfriend on the go!" I grin, amused by my own joke.

Ali laughs and hits me in gest. "You just can't take a compliment, can you?"

I doubt I'll make a good impression as his son's first boyfriend but I will worry about that when the day comes. I stretch and hold his hand over the table. If there is one thing I can do as his boyfriend, I want to make Ali feel less lonely. I bring his hand to my lips and kiss it gently, and he responds with his signature grin. With my disastrous love life so far, I know this is a chance for me and I want to do right by him. We gaze at each other, our eyes lock and it feels so natural and good.

~~~

I love waking up with Ali. The next morning, I sneak out to the bathroom for a leak and brush my teeth. I know it's cheating but I don't ever want to be complacent like people who have been together for years. It's my way to show him respect. I want Ali to taste the mint and not a dead rat when he wakes up. When I get back under the sheet, he hugs me, his head automatically seeking out my shoulder and rubbing against my blade. He whispers, "Don't go, Liam." I love his neediness.

Ali's right hand reaches down to stroke my arse cheeks and meanders up to my balls and massages them. I can feel his woody near my crack, already smearing pre-cum on my arse. I want him, so I arch back to give him more friction. He plants kisses all over the back of my neck and his hand closes around my dick, his finger pads teasing my slit. I twist round to kiss him some more; our tongues search for each other. I lick my fingers and reach back to stroke his erection. Ali's lips meet mine again and he moans into my mouth as my teasing arouses him.

I stretch and reach out to his bedside table to retrieve a condom. I know with his pre-cum and the lube on the rubber, there is no need for more. Ali drags me back underneath him as if impatient. While he puts the condom on, I jerk myself off. The breaching of my ring sends pain and pleasure through me. Ali doesn't fuck me too gently anymore. He knows how I adore his hard body and the urgent intrusion of his dick. I arch back, meeting his cock until he is buried deeply in me. He starts to speed up, one hand closing around mine to jerk me off, the other holding me tight.

Now I can hear what Ali is mumbling: my name. He whispers for me again and again as he loses himself in me. I hold onto his headboard with my left hand and spread myself even further, still baffled by my desire to make him come, to feel his quickened thrusts and the tingling and building of my own need to release.

I put my right hand over his and both of us stroke hard and fast until I cry out and come, my jizz squirting all over our joined hands.

It feels as if Ali has been holding back and now he bites my shoulder and presses me onto the mattress while he pounds me hard, pulling out and thrusting back in until his orgasm shakes the bed and me into white heat. We collapse in a sweaty mess. It's the kind of sex that makes you think we're desperate. Perhaps we are, desperate for each other's bodies, wants and needs.

"Liam," Ali whispers my name once more as he calms down.

He pulls out eventually but continues to hold on to me, and all I can hear is our heavy breathing and our heart beats that have synchronised.

I don't know how long we stay like that before I feel the shaking of Ali's shoulders and the wetness on the back of my neck. I turn around to see Ali's eyes full of tears. I tighten my embrace and cup his head against my neck to let him sob into my skin.

"Hey, it's okay. It's all good."

Some people have a meltdown from intense sex, so I guess Ali is emotional. But he pulls off a little and raises his glittery eyes to look at me. "I should have told Emily...I was gay and I didn't love her the way she deserved. I lied to her. I don't know how I'll ever forgive myself for it." More fat drops of tears fall down his flushed face. Ali tries desperately to rub them with the back of his hands as if wiping away his guilt.

He chokes on his tears, his words broken up by grief. "I couldn't tell a dying woman she'd married the wrong man."

"Shh, shh." I let him cry himself dry while holding onto me as though I am his lifeline.

"I don't think what you did was lying. When you married her, you didn't know you were gay. And later, you protected her. You loved her the best you could and she died knowing you did. There's nothing wrong about that."

Ali's tears keep falling as he struggles to control his emotions. "I know. She would have understood it too. I made it worse because I didn't have the courage to be open with her. And now she's gone and I never had the chance to be honest with her."

When he eventually stops crying, he shifts and we lie facing each other. I ruffle his hair. "We wouldn't have met if you'd realised you were gay earlier, right? You'd probably be married to a hot man instead."

He smiles even though his tears are still fresh on his face. "I have a hottie in my bed. I'm good, thanks."

I shake my head. I am still in denial that I'm in a proper relationship.

Ali leans closer and kisses me. "If there was one thing I learned from losing Emily, it was that there's no time to waste. When we find happiness, we grab hold of it and never let go."

We gaze at each other. The happiness he believes in fights with self-doubt and fear to fill my heart. I'm not as brave and determined as Ali. Not yet. But everyday I'm meeting the feelings of self-loathing and depression head-on. Instead of thinking about drugs, I sometimes write down my thoughts and stories, as Sean suggested.

Much later, I reluctantly sit up because it's time for Ali to get to work. We have a quick shower together and Ali goes through his morning routine while I have a coffee before leaving. I stay with him three or four nights a week and I often spend a whole day with him during the weekends.

As I stand in the hallway ready to go, Ali tries to stuff cash in my pocket. "Fuck, Ali. You can't pay me anymore. You gave that up when you wanted me to be your boyfriend." Pulling the notes back out and mentally counting them, I frown.

He shifts uncomfortably. "But it's for your taxi fare and the beers you bought."

"That's bullshit. They don't cost two hundred." I call him out.

Ali isn't rich but he is definitely comfortable since he receives decent wages and doesn't have to pay rent or mortgage. He is also incredibly generous and he doesn't care about the money. I can't let him treat me like he is my keeper, though. I don't want that. Neither does he, now that we're no longer client and escort to each other. If anything, I need to pay him back the rent he paid. I'm not yet fully back on my feet for that.

Ali in the morning is a lovely sight and now he plays with his slightly damp hair, uncomfortable with discussing money with me.

"If you don't take it, you'll have sex with two more men. I'd prefer you didn't."

We are in a bit of a bind. We have not come to an agreement about it whatsoever. Ali is the best boyfriend I can hope for, but knowing what I do with other men when I am not with him can't be easy to bear. I have minimised the number of the jobs I accept. And it is beginning to feel wrong. I don't like the thought that I may be hurting him. I need my independence, however, and I will do what is necessary to keep it. Call me a proud prick.

I look away and take my first cigarette of the day out of the packet. "Ali McClelland. Too bad. I just can't let you become my sugar daddy." I put the notes back on the hall table.

He shakes his head. "I'll never be your sugar anything! You stubborn git." He grabs me and kisses me with force, enough to make me see stars.

When he lets me go, I give him a wide grin because I am giddy from his kisses. "Not everyone lives in a nice house in Islington. I only have my pride."

"And I love your pride." Ali smiles. "But I'm not rich despite having this house. Emily's parents gave it to her as a wedding present. And when she died, it was passed on to me. I'm grateful for it but it doesn't define me."

I sigh. "I never said it did."

"And you'll make me a very happy man if you come and share it with me. The house has three bedrooms. You can even have your own space." He waves his hand as if to emphasise the point that there is plenty of room.

I keep putting off the discussion of 'our future' as I know what it means. If I move in with him, I won't need to be an escort anymore to pay rent and I can maybe get a low-paid or part-time job. I can even go back to study music at college. It is a big step. I am scared, properly frightened. What if it doesn't work out? On the other hand, I've got nothing to lose except the newfound control of my life at the expense of selling my arse. I promise myself I'll give it more thought.

I frown. "I know that. I may only have one room but if I come live with you, I'll feel as though I'm dependent on you. We've been through this before."

Ali shakes his head. "I wish you didn't think that. I want to have you share this space. It doesn't mean I'm superior or anything."

"I'm just pointing out how different we are," I argue.

"Opposites attract."

"We're not magnets." I chuckle.

"No. But you're like one to me, though." Ali has to have the last word.

~~~

Larry's one of my regulars. I guess he must be in his fifties because he's greying. Nothing remarkable about Larry. I don't think he's married or out but then I haven't enquired about his personal circumstance. The probate lawyer is a gentleman who likes vanilla sex. That's why it's a good deal for me. The same foreplay, the same position. Good tip.

Anyway, he always ends with a sigh. "Oh, Liam. You're gorgeous."

I've already moved off the bed after he withdrew. I beam at him. "Thanks."

He hands me another twenty as a tip and I thank him again. Same routine.

As I'm putting my clothes back on, he wraps himself in a silk dressing gown, one of those kimono types. "Liam, you're a little distracted. Anything I should know?"

I stare at Larry. Do I appear different to the johns after gaining a boyfriend? I've always assumed that I'm good at hiding my feelings when I'm on the job. Perhaps not. "I'm fine. Why? Did you not like my service?" I wink.

He exhales again and sits in his plush armchair. "I'm not naïve. I know I'm only a client to you, like the clients I work for are only interested in what I can do for them." He cocks his head. "Just that…you're quieter than usual after coming back from Ireland. Did something happen at home?" I've told my regulars that I'd visited my family when I did a disappearing act on Ali and my friends and I was in rehab.

I didn't know he cared but I can't exactly offload my problems with my johns. "I am fine. Perhaps I'm a little tired. Sorry, if I seem more subdued than usual."

He smiles. "It's okay. Well, like I said. I know I'm not exactly your sexual partner by choice. You've always made me feel really special during our sessions, though. Thank you, Liam."

"Thank you." I grin. "You're special too, Larry. Glad to be of service. Same time next week?"

He smiles finally and nods.

~~~

Another day, another new john.

I've stopped servicing new clients but this guy seems friendly enough with his request and texts. So, I find myself in front of a nice house in South London. The man has booked me for a fuck. It should be straightforward.

Once inside, I ask for cash upfront as I always do. He sneers and holds out the money but then withdraws it when I try to get it.

"How about kinks? Blindfold? Handcuff?" he asks casually, as he strokes the bulge through his trousers. I consider the man. He's big, muscular and a few inches taller than me.

It's not that I never provide those services but his smirk gives me bad vibes. His size doesn't help if we ever get into a fight. I have to go with my instinct. I don't beg anymore and I strive hard not to show I am scared. "No, mate. I don't do that. I suggest you call someone else. Sorry. Deal's off." *Cut the losses, Liam.*

I move to leave but he grabs my right arm. Fuck. He's a strong fellow with an iron grip. I still think I can handle him, though.

"Get off me! I'm leaving."

He drags me back and hurts my arm.

"Okay. Fine." He huffs and holds out the cash again. "How about we just play rough?"

I stare at the money and back at the man. It's not going to be pretty but I've come this far. *You should have walked away.* "Another sixty."

He digs out the extra notes and stuffs them in my jacket pocket as well. "Seriously, we'll have some fun, baby."

No, it's never fun. Not like this.

He seizes my hair and shoves my face against the door. I push him away but he's heavy-handed and powerful. As I elbow him to try to get away from his grasp, he pulls me back. The creep laughs louder when I struggle. The fucking gym rat and his steroid-enhanced bulk.

"Yeah, I like a feisty one. Try fight me, bitch."

I can feel a bruise developing on my cheek but I know the man is all bravado. He wouldn't have paid me at all if he'd intended to assault me. I let him manhandle me back into the front room and onto the couch, resisting enough only to give him his money's worth. The more I fight, the more brutal he will be, so I let him play rough and pray I can stop him when I reach my limit.

Towering over me, he commands in a gruff voice, "Take your clothes off."

I do while he also undresses himself. Waving his hard-on in front of my face, he tells me to suck his cock. As I do so, he moans and grabs my hair, hurting me and forcing me to look up to him.

"You have stunning eyes. Very slutty." *Yeah, right.*

He face-fucks me fast while I try to relax my throat so as not to gag. I can taste his pre-cum on my tongue and throat, and it's bitter and acrid.

When he is getting close, he pulls out and then with his strong hands lifts me up to turn me over. He leans down and his face is so close, I can feel his hot breath on my cheek and his erection against my arse.

"Got a condom, slut?" I grab my trousers and dig one out. I hear him tear it open and soon feel his cock inside of me.

He grabs my neck. My head is pressed against a cushion on the sofa. I feel as though I can't breathe. I manage to lift my head up to clear my airway. His grip on me tightens. I try to tune out so I don't feel the pain, don't hear his groans.

The john wanted it rough and he got it. It's hardly worth the extra money. Sasha used to say it was an occupational hazard. I should count myself lucky he wasn't a complete psycho, but someone who wanted to act out a fantasy on the unsuspecting prostitute.

I stagger out of the house, forgetting where I am. The time that follows is hazy. I remember the busy Tube and all the commuters pushing and shoving through when I stop in the middle of a busy carriage, feeling disembodied from reality. I must have boarded an overground train later.

The end of the platform drops off to the track. It's raining and the wind gushes past, just like the fast train that flew by some minutes ago. I've thought about this for more times than I dare to admit. *A body on the track.* They always say that in the tannoy. I often wonder how it feels to be that body. One foot. Two feet. Wait for the next fast train.

One foot. Two feet. Into the void below.

The ringing brings me back momentarily. The train glides past so fast that the platform shakes. The wind blows my hair away from my face. I take my mobile out of my jacket pocket and press speak.

"Liam, where are you?" Ali sounds hesitant. "Have you forgotten you're supposed to come here tonight?"

I open my mouth, then shut it, suddenly afraid to make a sound.

"Liam. You there?"

No, not really.

"You're scaring me. Are you all right?" He's worried. "Where are you? Are you at home?"

I look around, wanting to see if there are ghosts hiding in dark corners. "I'm here."

"Where?"

I glance at the shadowy bushes across the track, trying to remember where I am and why I've come here. A train stops further down the platform with squeaking wheels.

Ali's shouting now. "Liam, are you at a train station? I can hear the announcement. What are you doing there? Which station are you at?"

I squint back towards the main platform where a few stragglers are moving towards the exit.

"What the fuck are you doing there? Liam! Talk to me, damn it!" I don't think I've ever heard Ali raise his voice like this.

"Drayton Park. I'm at Drayton Park." My voice sounds distant.

"I'm coming to get you. Don't you fucking move! Don't you dare!"

Finally, he clicks off. I stare at the phone in my hand until the light goes off. I sink down on the floor, draw my knees up and bury my head in my lap.

I don't know how long I sit like this before I hear footsteps running towards me. Strong arms pull me back, away from the platform edge.

"Fuck's sake. Have you taken something?"

Ali's come to save me. Save me from myself. I stare at his face but my vision is blurred with the tears.

"No," I whisper.

He wraps me in his arms, so my face is pressed against his broad chest. "What happened? You scared me."

"Nothing," I answer automatically. Then the memory floods my brain. "I'd a rough trick. I'm okay."

Ali's quiet for a moment. "Let me take you home." He pulls me up. With his arm around my shoulder, he walks me toward the stairway and the exit. His little car sits at an odd angle right outside the station. He must have driven up and jumped out without a thought to how he'd parked it.

We're quiet during the short drive. I stare out of the window at the passing streets and people in twos, in groups, chatting and looking happy.

When Ali said home, he'd meant his house. He gently guides me to the bedroom where I sit on the edge of the bed, still dazed and confused from my episode. Ali kneels down in front of me.

"What did he do to you?" His eyes are red, as though they're in pain, in sympathy with my heart.

I shrug, wanting to play it down. "He was rough. It got a bit out of hand."

Ali sighs. "You have a bruise on your face and finger marks on the back of your neck. Did you agree to it?"

"I'm sorry. I should have left." Tears fall down my face. "I didn't want you to see me like this."

Ali sits down next to me and wraps his arms around me again. Then he kisses the side of my head. "Don't put yourself in that situation again. You're worth much more than that."

"I'm not."

"How can you say that? After everything?" Ali turns me round to face him. "You can't throw it all away. Think of me."

He stands up and with his back to me, he breathes heavily. I can see the tension in his spine. "How can you even contemplate leaving me?" His voice trembles. Then his shoulders shake when he starts crying.

I stand up then, wrap my arms around his chest and rest my head on his back. "I'm sorry. I wasn't thinking."

I wish he'd listened to me when I told him how fucked up I was. "I said you shouldn't want to be with me." My voice is muffled against Ali's warm back.

"Too late. I'd fallen for you." Ali replies between his sobs.

We stay like that for what seems like an eternity.

I take a bath. Ali gives me a sleeping pill and I sleep curled up in a ball. He wraps me in his larger body.

The last thing I hear before I fall into a slumber is his soft voice. "Please consider my offer. Stay with me."

During breakfast, Ali tells me he has to go to work but he's going to drive me back to the flat. "Give me your phone. I want to call Chris."

My mouth is stuffed with a piece of toast. "He's probably sleeping. I don't need babysitting."

Ali glares at me over his cup of coffee, so I hand him my mobile. He finds Chris's number and presses the button. It takes my flatmate a while to answer the phone. Ali walks over to the kitchen counter and has a quiet conversation with Chris.

Back in my room, I take another sleeping pill that Ali has left me and rest until the afternoon.

~~~

I find myself sitting in our lounge, mind wandering off to fuck knows where, while sucking on a joint.

Chris jolts me out of my brooding when he plonks himself down on the sofa. The whole thing sags. He must be able to see the bruises on my cheek and neck, too. He shakes his head. "You know you can talk to me, yeah?"

Ali has asked him to keep an eye on me. I wish I could be a good friend to him; instead I seem to lean on Ali and Chris. I still know next to nothing about Chris and he seems to want to keep it that way. He has been an escort for as long as I've known him. I do wonder about his past but I have never asked because he has always been guarded. The only thing he mentioned was that his mum had a drug problem. Maybe it's why he recognises all my issues.

"Cheers, mate." I've considered feelings a luxury for so long, and fear talking about them might leave me vulnerable. The desperation never seemed to leave me completely no matter what I did or how much drug I took.

Chris broaches the subject. "How're you doing with that nice man of yours?"

"We're…" I contemplate the right answer here. "It's lovely. I got stressed out."

"You're stressed because things are too good?" I nod. Chris smiles. I'm glad he's amused.

"I told you not to pull that shit on me."

I regard the man and appreciate how lucky I am to have a friend. "I'm sorry."

I suck in a chest full of hash and exhale slowly. Changing the subject, I ask, "Why are you an escort? I mean, you're attractive and bright."

Chris picks up his joint. "Thanks. Do you know I haven't even finished school properly?"

"But you could go back to study if you wanted?"

He squints at the sorry excuse of our pendant light. "I don't know what I want. I was a child actor. Then I did some modelling and acting. I've always used my looks and my body, Liam. That's why."

I consider his predicament. "What about now?"

"Having done this for eight years doesn't qualify me for shit." He shakes his head once more. "Sure. I'll do something else one day. When I'm too fucking old to have sex for pay." He chuckles drily.

Is there a retirement age for our profession? I wonder. I have seen some mature escorts advertising themselves on the agency's website. Guys in their forties, maybe even fifties. I shudder. I can't do this for thirty years. That's for sure.

Chris focuses on me again. Though his gaze doesn't shift, his handsome face is dreamy as though he's imagining a future. "What would you do tomorrow if you could stop hooking?"

"Simple answer. I'd play the flute and do music." And hang out with Ali. That is the truth even if I am keeping that thought to myself for now.

Chris moves his sexy arse closer, so I can smell his cologne, scented like jasmine. "Do you love him?"

I squirm under that word; I feel so raw inside still. "Dunno. Do you think Ali loves me?"

Chris sighs in an exaggerated way and gives me an eye roll. "If you have to ask that question, you're a bigger idiot than I thought."

"What?" I stare at him, wondering whether I should be insulted.

"Ali loves you. Plain as day." He makes another joint and takes a slow and deliberate toke, as if he's about to tell a long story. "When I called Ali to tell him you'd gone MIA, he was here in a flash. He was out of his mind with worry. Without him insisting that 'we do something right fucking now' I probably wouldn't have phoned Sasha. I'd have left you to rot in that squat." He winks to show me perhaps he's only joking.

Ali saved me again yesterday, pulling me from jumping on the track. I appreciate how much he really cares even though I'm a bit opaque when it comes down to matters of the heart.

"The man loves you and you'd be a right twat to throw that back in his face." Chris is clearly enjoying his yarn. "So, don't you love him? The truth."

I stare at Chris. "Truth. Love?" I say them as if I've never heard of the darn words in my life. These concepts are so alien, too permanent and too perfect, and I'm damaged and broken. They don't suit me.

He groans. "Yes, you know. Something that most people believe in, other than us muggins. I guess you're as much a moron as I thought you were."

"What? I'm not a moron…" My head begins to hurt with the direction of this conversation. "I do love—" *him in my own way.*

Chris won't let me finish. "Then what's stopping you, my princess?" He comes closer still and kisses the side of my face. It is a peck, nothing sexual in it.

Okay, so. Chris has tricked me into saying I love Ali. *What do I do now?*

As I ponder about all this, Chris is still close and we are both lost in our thoughts. But then, the moment comes when clarity sails into my consciousness. Love may break my heart but I need to heal it first, and Ali has been helping me to do just that. And I hope I am treating him right in return and giving him all I have to offer. I can't run away from it any longer.

If I believed in God, I'd say it was a sign when the sofa creaked, then cracked, and collapsed in the middle. Chris and I end up on top of one another with the remnant of the monstrosity around us. We are buried under the mass of seat cushions, and broken slats dig into my hip and back. The piece of crap also throws up debris from hundreds of prior occupants and the pungent smell of tobacco and hash. Nice.

Chris bursts out laughing first as he scrambles to get up from underneath my legs. I manage to extricate myself from the wreckage and soon join him in stitches. The fucking blood-sucking landlord and his damn cheap furniture.

Chris finally stops himself after five minutes and he stares at me with the fierceness I often see in him. "Get out of here, Liam. I command you."

I don't think he means only to leave the sitting room, but my hand-to-mouth existence altogether. Be unafraid to love someone again.

I bark out one last laugh. "Thanks a million, Chris."

CHAPTER 13

DON'T NEED TO be told twice. I get dressed and walk to Ali's house. Seven o'clock. He hasn't come home yet. It is not unusual. Some days he works late if there is a big project on, or he may be swimming. I sit on his doorstep and wait, while smoking a cigarette. I know he hides a spare key under the post box. It is not very safe for him and I don't want to use it. Not yet.

I like this time of the day when the retreating sunrays shine at an oblique angle and the smog of the city becomes hazy. His road is quiet, almost serene like an oasis in the middle of the Big Smoke.

As he walks back, the orange glow of the setting sun is behind him and he appears like a miracle. He is gorgeous and he wants me. I still cannot believe it.

When he sees me, his eyes light up and I just fucking love his little crow's feet. I squint in the late sunset as he extends his big hand and pulls me up. "You didn't answer my calls. Chris told me you were resting most of the day. How long have you been sitting here?" *Too damn long.*

I gaze at Ali and realise how, since the first time I met him, this has felt like home. Ali values me. He doesn't judge and he never gives up on me. Since coming to London, I've felt so adrift, so lonely at times, and he's welcomed me with open arms.

I mumble, "I am happy to wait." I'd been waiting for someone like Ali but I hadn't realised it.

He stalls for half a second as he thinks about what I'm implying. Then he turns to unlock the door as he replies, "You don't have to wait any longer." Does he mean it as a double entendre?

I stamp out my cigarette butt under foot and try to appear nonchalant about it. "I'll have to give up or cut down on the tobacco when I go back to playing the flute seriously."

His hand on the lock falters briefly but then he opens the door and lets us into the warm cosy air of his house. I'd love to live there. I am kidding myself about independence. Liam Murphy has turned from a stray dog to a scaredy-cat when he realises he has fallen in love.

In the hallway, he moves a few strands of stray hair from my face and asks, "What do you mean playing the flute seriously? Are you saying what I think you're saying?"

"I am thinking of applying to college to study music." I kiss him and look into the jade of his eyes. "I would like to move in with you. To take up your offer if it's okay."

Ali smiles. "Yes, yes, yes." He hugs me, squeezes me tight and returns the kiss. "When can you move in?"

I can't help but chuckle at his eagerness. "I didn't pay a deposit, so I could pretty much leave any time. This weekend?" That was the problem when I got out of rehab the first time. I didn't have a thing to my name. That's the reason why I pay high rent for a shoebox. The landlords in London are all sharks as far as I'm concerned. It still makes me yearn for my squatting days, though the sub-human existence is not for everyone. I barely survived it. At some level, I enjoyed the freedom, without feeling as if I was at the mercy of a greedy landlord. Now, I've found someone who is offering me a sanctuary.

Ali nibbles my left earlobe, still holding on to me. "You won't change your mind?"

"No." Another little bite on my other ear. Hmm. Heaven.

His tongue traces to my neck, down to my Adam's apple and up against my lips before he gives me another sensual kiss and finally breaks away. As he is teasing me like that, my dick shoots up.

"That's good, because my dad's coming to visit the weekend after next."

Holy shit. He's tricked me. "Fuck. I can always pretend to be your lodger."

Ali pushes me against the nearest wall and kisses me with such force that my lips swell and I nearly run out of oxygen. He always has that effect on me. When he finishes with me, he cups my face in his hands and stares into my eyes. "You will do no such thing. I'll come out to my dad and introduce him to my live-in boyfriend who happens to be a musical genius. And…"

I am stunned by his words. I find myself staring at him, trying to comprehend what he's saying.

He moves his hands and they are now under my shirt and caressing my skin. "My father obviously had a thing about Irish people, marrying my mum. So, you'll talk to him all about Ireland and he'll be won over."

What the fuck. "Ali. You think all Irish people have the gift of the gab or some shit, right? I've never kissed the Blarney Stone and I am hopeless when it comes to speaking to parents. Why do you think I was practically chased out of my village?"

"Was that what happened when you left home and became homeless in London?"

"Yeah, that's about the sum of it, and I told you what went down when my dad died." And it still fucking hurts.

He nods. "I'm sorry."

I consider the beautiful man in front of me. "My shitty life brought me to London and to you." I know I have an addictive personality, and once a druggie…I'll always be vulnerable to it. The heroin and crack seem to be an invisible permanent thread that ties to me. But with my decision to move in with Ali, I feel a great weight lifted from my shoulders. I'm ready for a new life with him. "I think I need to speak to Sean, perhaps receive some counselling. And go to the NA meetings."

I bring out the small notebook that I've been keeping and give it to Ali. "I've been writing down some stuff. Thoughts, memories. Bad things, mostly, but I'd like you to read it."

He smiles and puts the notebook in his back pocket. "Good or bad. I will cherish it."

We close the distance between us again and kiss, a deep and greedy one. Ali pulls away after the long hard snog. "Liam, will you show me Ireland sometime?"

"Yes." It'll be strange but I've finally realised that coming from the country doesn't define me. It's left its mark but I am my own person. Home is where I choose to make it. In Ali's arms, I've come home.

There is something else I need to do too, apart from moving in. "Ali, I've been tested regularly, but I will go again as soon as possible. Tomorrow. I wanna be clean for you. For us."

His grin widens. "I'd like that. For you more than anything else." He weaves his fingers in my hair and his gaze is warm. "I never asked you. How did you really feel being an escort?"

I take a deep breath. If I'm honest, I try not to think too much about it. Shut my eyes, ignore any physical discomfort and get on with the job. I had no problem with sex and I sometimes did enjoy it. But the emotional attachment wasn't there; not until I met Ali did I realise how arousing it was to want someone so desperately. It was a job that I had mixed feelings about.

"I persuaded myself that it was only sex but it wasn't. I was dying inside, losing my sense of self. It's okay as a job but there are other things I can do. I'll find them." Ali's strong arms hold me tight and his presence grounds me. "All I know is I want you. Anyone else will only remind me that I'm not with you."

I kiss him again and again.

~~~

The next day, after I've gone for the STI tests at the drop-in in Central London, I text some of my regulars and tell them the news that I'm quitting. I haven't told them why, though. Larry sends back a message to wish me well.

Then, on the Friday, I put my worldly possessions in a holdall and pick up my flute. I look around the small room that I've called my home for nearly two years but I'm just glad to be leaving.

Chris is in the sitting room when I emerge from my bedroom. He smiles when he sees my bag and the flute case. "Well, I guess this is it, mate?"

I nod. "Yeah. Thanks for everything." I put my possessions down and give him a bear hug.

"Don't mention it." I look up. His smile masks the melancholy in his eyes. "Keep in touch, all right?"

"I will. You take care of yourself, too." I quit gazing at his handsome face. He's a good mate and once a fuck buddy but I've never seen him truly happy. I know that much.

He pats my back and urges me to leave. Yeah, before I lose my nerve.

I take a taxi to Ali's and he meets me with a wide beam. His house is so familiar to me now, and yet, I am anxious as hell. This is the beginning to the unknown. After he greets me with a kiss, I put my holdall down but remain standing in the hallway. "Are you sure about this?" I wring my hands. "I was a homeless druggie, a beggar and an escort. I'm prone to breakdowns and poor decisions. Have you picked up strays before and let them into your house?"

He laughs, not taking me seriously at all. "I don't give a flying fuck as long as you're here." He rubs my abs to soothe me. "Liam. You make me happy. Life's too short not to grab hold of happiness when it comes knocking at my door."

Fuck. He has done it again. Tears surge in my eyes. "And you just seem to make me cry like a fucking twat!"

He smiles, comes closer and kisses me. Before I know it, he wraps his arms around my waist and thighs and tries to lift me up and carry me. I am pretty lithe but I'm still too tall and heavy for him.

He manages to half-lug, half-drag me up the stairs and into the bedroom while laughing his head off.

"What are you doing?" I protest.

"I'm carrying you over the threshold."

After Ali dumps me on the bed, I start to take off my clothes in anticipation of some hot steamy sex with him, chuckling uncontrollably at the same time. I regard the man standing by the bed and shake my head at the whole ridiculously slushy scene. "I am a whore in the bedroom but I'm pretty useless around the house and I can't cook. Sorry, I'm not husband material at all." I wink to show him I'm not serious about all this.

Ali's eyes sparkle. "I love you anyway, Liam Murphy. It's not about sex or how good you are at making toast." He laughs. "I love your sense of humour. I love your vulnerability. You always listen to me when I need to talk. I like how you make me feel better. Shall I go on?"

I freeze. Boyfriend is one thing. I'm still scared by the declaration of love. I'm all these things to him? I had no idea! I want to run out of his house once again. My heart is thumping, from fright or excitement I can't tell.

But Ali's not letting my rambling thoughts fester. He makes short shrift of his clothes ready for his brand of love making. Why has it taken me months to realise he is the one I want? The only one. Watching his elegant face, I laugh like a fucking eejit.

"Come here." Now that we are equals, I'm not shy about being demanding in bed, and Ali happily complies.

He comes forward, standing in between my legs. He leans down and cups my face in his big hands and kisses me.

"You want to fuck me?" His erection jumps in front of my face even before I can answer.

I smile. "I always want to fuck you." We are versatile with each other despite my preferred position.

Ali throws his head back. "Then do it." He's in a reckless mood. He pushes me back onto the bed, and jumps on top and hovers over me while continuing to gaze at my body.

I have my arms above my head. I look intently back at him, into those green pools that draw me in. "Ali."

He covers me with his larger body, all strong and safe. Then, he slides down and wraps his fine mouth around my dick.

I moan with pleasure. "I'm not going to last long. Stop if you want me to fuck you."

He releases me and stretches over to get a condom and a tub of lube. His flushed face is full of lust, as always. Seeing him like that makes me forget myself and become completely absorbed in his presence, in his scent, in his powerful embrace.

He puts the condom on me and applies the clear gel. He then plays with his own arse with lubed fingers. *Oh my fucking hell.* After several minutes, I can't wait any longer, so I drag him towards me, my dick seeking him out.

Ali's not as used to bottoming but he doesn't hesitate to impale himself on me. The tightness sends me into a pivot. *Fuck.* I push up until I'm completely buried in his arse.

Ali's face tells me after the first few seconds of discomfort, he loves my erection filling him up. We soon start moving together. He's a power bottom, controlling my arousal like he's a pro. He grabs my hip while moving up and down my dick, hitting his own p-spot.

"Touch yourself. Please."

He closes his palm around his dick and strokes it.

Seeing his flushed face and hearing the sexy groans undoes me completely. I drive myself upwards, meeting his arse again and again until I see whiteness. "Fuck!" When I come, it feels as though a volcano has erupted inside me as I empty myself into the condom.

Ali's whole body is covered by sweat. I see the pre-cum flowing from his slit. His strokes quicken. "I'm gonna come." He seems to go into a frenzy, staring down at me. His cum squirts out onto my front and belly.

It takes me a long time to come back to planet earth. Ali has taken care of the used condom, and he flops down next to me, as zoned out as I am. Then he turns to me and I can see myself in his beautiful green eyes.

"I love you."

Oh, fuck. I'm not going to cry, again. I really am not. But the tears fall and they keep falling. I try to dry them with my hands. Ali takes over.

"I hope they're tears of joy."

Choked by my own ridiculousness, I mumble, "No one's ever loved me."

"I do."

I stare through the tears at Ali's open face.

"And you deserve to be loved. Those other people are obviously idiots."

My sobs become more desperate. *How old am I? Fucking twelve?* "Damn you. Stop making me cry."

He chuckles.

I manage to stop myself eventually. My fingertips touch his cool skin, and playing with the powerful muscles always helps to soothe me.

"I got the all-clear today at the clinic but I need to be re-tested in a month."

Ali grins and ruffles my hair. "That's good to hear."

My dick likes it too. It's already half-mast again, as an image of barebacking with Ali comes into my head. "I want to feel your dick inside me without a condom."

He cocks his head. "Likewise."

"Is this what a proper relationship's like?"

Ali laughs, his fine crow's feet dancing. "This is a proper relationship. And you can do whatever you feel like within it, Liam."

"All right!" I pounce on him, pushing him back onto the bed. "Let's do it again, then."

He laughs some more and lets me kiss him.

~~~

I've been living with Ali for about ten days. It's bliss. Proper lush. I guess it must be what a honeymoon feels like. We can't keep our hands off each other and I'd find myself grinning for no particular reason. Ali's the same. He reaches over to me in the middle of the night or the crack of dawn and when he finds me, he sighs with contentment.

Ali's given me the small room where I've deposited my worldly possessions. Of course, we sleep together in the master bedroom. I have been looking into college admission, and made some enquiries to retrieve my school certificate and the music exam results from the Royal Irish Academy. After finding out how much red tape there is to get re-issues of the certificates, I called Finn for help and he promised to track them down for me at home. Despite everything, I don't think Mum would have thrown them away.

Ali's place is beginning to feel like home after such a short time.

But it doesn't stop me feeling apprehensive. I stand near the door, wringing my hands that are clammy and cold. Ali puts his arm around my shoulder and squeezes.

"Don't be nervous." Then he moves to open the door.

Ali looks like his mum but as soon as his dad walks in, I can see their resemblance, too. It's the older man's gait and stature. He is a little shorter than Ali but he has the same ruggedness. His hair is brown and peppered with white, his eyes steely blue.

I feel like a young boy being inspected by his schoolmaster. I try to hang back, but there's no chance of escaping the older man's scrutiny. Ali senior regards me with keen eyes.

Ali grabs his dad's small rucksack and ushers him into the sitting room. "Dad, come in."

When we're all in the lounge, Ali clears his throat. *Oh, boy.* "Dad, this is Liam. My dad, Liam."

I offer my hand. "Nice to meet you, Mr. McClelland."

He takes my hand, his shake firm and heartfelt. "Good to meet you too. Call me Fraser."

I nod but I'm not sure how to behave in front of Ali's dad. Instead, I deflect. "Ah, would you like a cup of tea or coffee?"

When Ali's dad says yes to tea, I escape to the kitchen, leaving them to talk. But, I have no luck. Ali and his dad are sitting at the dining table in silence when I come back with the pot of tea, mugs and biscuits. Ali has already explained to me that Fraser McClelland was an acclaimed scriptwriter before retirement but he's socially awkward. He has basically been a recluse, living alone in the Scottish Highlands now that he has stopped working. I can see where Ali's shyness comes from.

So, I find the two of them staring into their respective space as I return and serve tea, all the time debating whether I should hide in the bedroom and leave them to it. But I also want to make the nice with Ali's dad.

Ali smiles. "Stop hovering and sit down, Liam." He wants me there when he talks to his dad.

I comply and pick up my hot cup of tea, burning my fingers in the process.

Ali clears his throat. His dad glances between us.

"Dad, Liam's my boyfriend. I am gay." Just like that.

Something stirs in my heart. I'm proud of Ali but I feel sad because I've never come out properly. At home, no one in my family specifically asked me but I simply made it clear that I liked boys. My sexuality was assumed, and expected to be a problem from the beginning. But it was also erased as a possible subject to be talked about. I never once uttered those three words at home until I saw Mum before my dad died.

I watch Fraser's face. There's no sign whatsoever of disgust, outrage, shock—any of the reactions that I used to get all the time. He takes a sip of his tea and calmly asks, "Had you known when Emily was around?"

Ali wipes his face with his hand. "Yes, for a few years, but I didn't tell her."

Fraser nods. Their eyes meet. That's all. No condemnation. No accusation of moral impropriety. It's the only response needed. This is what acceptance looks like and feels like. Even though I'm not the one who's coming out, I feel elated and relieved.

Ali beams. Now I understand why he's always so calm and unflappable. "Well, Liam's from Ireland if you haven't worked that out yet."

His dad turns to me. "Good. Whereabouts?"

"West Cork." I still feel like a little boy in front of an authoritative figure, though Ali's dad doesn't seem scary anymore. "Near Bantry, to be precise."

"Hmm. I have been there." Ali's mum's from Kerry, so it's not surprising that Fraser has been to where I grew up. But he doesn't ask me about myself. Instead, he suggests, "Why don't you help Ali make dinner? I'll just take a rest." With that, he stands and retreats to the second bedroom, which Ali and I have cleaned and tidied up in preparation for his visit.

I like the man already. I'm not exactly quiet, but I definitely prefer the serene acceptance that Ali and Fraser show each other. It's peaceful. And now, Fraser is sparing me from questions and embarrassment.

Ali and I enter the kitchen and we kiss, his hand ruffling my hair. "All right?"

More than all right. My fear of Ali's dad's reaction proved totally unfounded. "Yeah." I kiss him again. "Well done for coming out like that. Your dad's super cool."

Ali beams. "Isn't he just? I told you it'd be fine. Of course, he's a very reserved and guarded person. It may seem really hard to get to know him to start with. Don't worry about that, okay?"

Well, our first meeting wasn't bad at all, so I'm not that tense now. Ali rummages through his cupboards and fridge.

"So, what's for dinner?" I watch him pick out spices.

"A veggie curry, if it's okay," Ali offers. "My dad's quite a traditional eater. Y'know, the meat-and-two-veg type. But I know he's okay with my curry."

I've grown used to Ali's cooking and I'm not fussy anyway. We work together in silence for a while. I chop up the vegetables and Ali concocts a bunch of spices together to make the curry base.

Later, as Ali stirs the deliciously smelling curry and the rice is nearly ready, I ask, "How long is your dad staying?"

"Till Monday morning. Is it okay?"

"Of course." I only moved in last week, so I don't think it's my place to say who can stay here and for how long. At the same time, I've enjoyed being close to Ali and going to bed and waking up together. It will take a while for me to get used to the idea of having a proper 'home'.

"We're going to the theatre tomorrow night. The director is one of Dad's friends. It's partly the reason why Dad's come down." Ali adds, "Sorry. I only asked for two tickets. I'd arranged it long before I knew you were moving in. Now, it's totally sold out."

Why would I object? He doesn't need to apologise. "It's cool. I'll practise my flute and watch a vid or something. You guys have some quality time together."

"I'm hoping he can get to know you too but we still have some time, I guess."

The three of us dine in almost complete silence but it's not uncomfortable. Far from it, in fact. It feels like we're just a quiet family of three. Ali briefly tells his dad recent news. I love how his face lights up when he talks about me moving in and how I'm looking to go to college next term. He talks about his work as well. Fraser listens and nods, his face calm.

Ali's dad retires to bed early. Everything seems familiar, as if we have known each other for a long time. We're a family completely different from my Irish one.

CHAPTER 14

O N Friday, Fraser has gone out in the afternoon to visit some bookstores in London and Ali is working. I manage to do some food shopping in the neighbourhood and practise, in anticipation of auditions if my college applications are being considered seriously. Fraser returns in the afternoon.

I want to continue practising, so I ask, "Is it all right if I carry on playing for a little while?"

Ali's dad nods. "Of course. It's your home. Ali said you're really talented. I'd love to hear you play." *My home.* In so few words, he has made me feel really good to be Ali's partner.

We spend a couple of hours together in the lounge. He sits in the armchair and reads the *Guardian* newspaper and drinks tea while listening to my practice with a faint smile on his face.

~~~

Ali calls me about half past six.

"What's up?" I know he and his dad are supposed to go to the theatre tonight. Fraser had already changed and gone out to meet Ali about half an hour ago.

He sounds a little distant. "We've got this huge project on at the moment. I have to stay here to sort out an issue for the extra filming tomorrow. This problem's come up unexpectedly. The green screen's been booked for tomorrow, so…if it's not sorted, we won't be ready." It sounds all gibberish to me only because I have no clue about the filmmaking process. I promise myself I'll learn more about it so I can speak to Ali about his work.

In the meantime, I offer, "You want me to tell your dad you'll be late? He's already gone to the theatre, though."

Ali hesitates for a second. "No. I don't think I can make it at all. Why don't you go instead? He has the tickets."

I've not gone to the theatre before, and I'm apprehensive about spending a whole evening out with Ali senior. This afternoon with him was peaceful and easy. I just don't know him well enough yet.

While I am thinking, Ali must have thought I was reluctant to go. "It's okay if you have other plans. I'll call him. He'd be fine alone. He's a hermit anyway."

But I want to know Ali's dad better. "I'll go." I can hear him breathe a sigh of relief.

"If you are sure." He gives me the theatre's address. "We're meeting in the foyer. I'll call him and let him know."

"Okay."

"I've got to run. Have fun!" He rings off, obviously in a rush to get back to work.

Not wanting to be late for the start, I get ready in record time and take a taxi to the West End. I arrive with only five minutes to spare. Fraser's eyes widen when he sees me instead of Ali.

"Hi, Fraser. Ali's got a big job on." I am breathless even though I only ran from a hundred yards down the road where the taxi dropped me off. "Did he speak to you?"

He takes his phone out of his pocket. "Oh, I think I've turned it off." Right, it's the kind of thing an old recluse would do.

"Well, if you don't mind. I'm joining you." Now that I've thought about it, perhaps he'd rather be on his own. "It's okay if you prefer to watch it by yourself. Ali was supposed to call you and let you know I was coming instead."

He shakes his head. "It's all good. I'd be glad if you joined me."

We are almost late, so we enter the auditorium straightaway. Since Fraser's director friend has invited him, we have a couple of seats right in the middle of the front section. I don't even know what the play's about since Ali was in such a hurry when he gave me the instructions to get here. It turns out to be a piece called *Period of Adjustment* by Tennessee Williams. I've never been into literature and theatre at school but I find myself being drawn to the story about these two married couples, and how they try to work out their difficulties. Though the subject is quite serious, it is also underlined by humour. Ali and I are still in our honeymoon period, just like the newlyweds in the play. It makes me wonder how we'll be five years down the line. *Shit. Liam in a long-term relationship?* I'm elated and scared at the prospect.

It almost surprises me when the show is over and the actors come out for the curtain call, because I've been thoroughly absorbed by the performance and don't want it to end. All the audience stand up and clap, cheering the cast.

Afterwards, Fraser takes me along to meet the director and the actors backstage. He and his thespian friend must have been close, as they hug and briefly exchange their news. Ali's dad was a respected scriptwriter, so lots of people seem to recognise him and want to speak to him, but I can tell he is not comfortable with so many people around and wanting a piece of him. He stands back with his hands in his pockets, trying to stay away from the centre of the action.

"Hey, Fraser. Are you coming with us for supper?" his friend asks, turning away from the excited crowd who also crave his attention.

Fraser smiles and replies, "No. Thanks for asking. I'm getting too old for late-night eating and drinking. I need my sleep."

They hug and promise to meet again soon. Ali's dad and I emerge from the theatre into the chilly air of the night. The West End is still buzzing around us. I start walking towards the Tube, but he puts a hand on my arm. "Are you hungry?"

I've completely forgotten about dinner in my rush to the theatre. I rub my chin. "Yeah, I haven't eaten yet."

He looks around for a moment. "Is Italian okay? I know a place."

"Of course," I answer. "I thought you were ready for bed, though?"

Fraser laughs softly. "I told them that. These after-performance hangouts are tiresome. I don't care for them."

He cocks his head to show me where we're heading. We begin strolling north and soon cross Oxford Street. *Shit!* I always avoid the area now. It brings back too many memories, mostly bad ones. I try not to be obvious. Ali's dad doesn't need to know I'm an ex-junkie beggar. Still, I feel light-headed and my stomach churns when I cross the main shopping street. I try to steady myself and carry on with our journey.

Fraser glances sideways to me but otherwise he does not seem to notice my discomfort. He guides me to a little nook off Charlotte Street and we come to a stop in front of a small Italian eatery. Most people would have missed it if they didn't know it was there.

Once inside, we sit down. It's no more than a greasy spoon but with the primary colours of the Italian flag. The Formica tables are all scratched and faded. We're handed these plastic menus with edges that have peeled off; a chalkboard also lists a few dishes—their daily specials. The proprietor is a large Italian patron who greets Fraser as if he knows him. Perhaps he does.

Ali's dad reads the menu quickly and orders in what sounds to me perfect Italian. "Any preference for wine?" he asks.

Ah. I'm not a wine drinker and wonder for a second if he's a connoisseur. "No. I mean, I don't really drink wine, so anything's fine by me."

He nods, scrutinises the drinks menu and orders a white wine. "Why don't you get an Italian beer, too, for yourself?" He must have known that I'm more a beer drinker because that's what I have at home.

"And what will you have to eat? Everything's good here, I can assure you." He speaks with authority and I believe him.

I don't really eat out except when I'm with Ali. I'm a readymade spag bol kind of guy but I also recognise the lasagne. Ali has also cooked it at home. I decide to try that.

After ordering and the proprietor bringing the drinks, we lapse into silence again. It turns out that Fraser has ordered a salad of mozzarella, tomato and basil as starter for both of us, and it's delicious.

"So, how did you meet Ali?" he asks while spearing a mozzarella ball with his fork. I'm surprised by his question. It's usual for a parent to be interested in his son's relationship, but he hasn't shown any curiosity towards me during the last couple of days. I know it's not out of lack of concern. It's just the way he is.

Common sense tells me to give him the clean version, but, here in the little restaurant, my belly full of good food and fresh beer, I gaze at my boyfriend's father. He's everything that my family didn't give me. He's approachable and open-minded. All of a sudden, I see clearly. I understand Ali more through meeting and spending time with his dad. I know in my bones what it's like to be free to be whoever I am, to be loved by people around you without conditions, to be understood without judgement. Even though not everyone in the world is like that, I'm lucky to be with Ali and Fraser who make me feel comfortable in my own skin.

I take a sip of my beer first, as I need to fortify myself. "I was an escort and Ali hired me when he tried to figure out his sexuality." To be sure I'm not hinting that he'd done that while his wife was still alive, I add, "We've known each other for about ten months now."

Fraser considers me. "Hmm. I see." It's exactly the kind of response I was expecting from the older man. A reaction, or lack thereof, that I'd have loved to have received from my own parents. Now I know I have my new family.

Fraser simply continues to finish his salad and the glass of wine. The main courses come and we eat in companionable silence.

We finish the simple but delicious meal. It's past eleven by the time we step out onto the street again. The night air smells damp. I look up to consider the new moon, my heart filled with contentment.

Ali's dad turns to me. "You fancy a drink?"

I honestly expect him to want to head back and go to sleep. He must be a night hawk. "Sure. I'd like that. Isn't it a little late? Most bars are closing for the night."

He smiles. His eyes sparkle, appearing almost mischievous. Then, he tilts his chin to indicate I should follow. I do and he leads me towards Bloomsbury. I'm less familiar with these areas of London. I used to find squats south of the river instead.

Fraser and I negotiate alleys and narrow streets, and he soon finds a basement bar that is sunken below the pavement level and shrouded in darkness. I would have missed it if I'd walked past by myself. It must be what a speakeasy bar would have been like.

The Stag looks closed and dusky in a good way. We descend the metal stairs to the door. Instead of ringing a bell, Ali's dad taps on the window, on its stained-glass picture. I see a man peering through the coloured glass and a few moments later he comes to open the door for us.

"Frase! Long time no see. Come in, lads." *Lads?* The man's also Scottish but with a much stronger accent than Ali's dad's.

Fraser introduces us. "Hamish, Liam. Liam. Hamish."

I take Hamish's extended hand, which is big and firm.

"What are you having?"

Fraser and I both ask for ale but Hamish gives Fraser an extra Scottish whisky. We take our drinks and sit at a small table round the back, so the bar will still appear closed to the outside world. It's a typical ye olde small alehouse. I rather like it since it reminds me of Irish pubs back home. Proper Irish pubs—not the cliché, tourist variety with their shamrock and canned jigs that one finds in London and, I am told, all around the world.

Hamish joins us with a large whisky in his hand. "So, what brings you back, Frase?" Hamish is a little younger than Ali's dad. He's handsome and tall with a full mop of grey hair and sharp, brown eyes.

"To visit Ali and his boyfriend." Fraser introduces me again. "It turns out he's been falling for the wrong gender all that time."

Hamish laughs heartily. "Ah." He grins at me with warmth. "Ali is quite a slow learner when it comes to matters of the heart, like his dad." His eyes are on Fraser and I swear I can see something that resembles a mixture of love and regret. Whatever it is, I'm not privy to it; it's a private bond between the two men.

Fraser smiles and breaks Hamish's gaze. "Oh, come on. He loved Emily in his own way."

"Aye." Hamish nods and is quiet for long moments, perhaps considering what Ali might have been through. Then he turns to me. "I used to be an actor. Fraser and I have been friends for a long time. Don't mind us if we turn loud and vulgar."

I hasten to reply, "I'm good here. You talk about old times… or something."

"Or something." Hamish laughs some more and winks. It makes sense he was an actor. He seems to have the flamboyance to go with the profession. "Hey, Frase. How's Scotland?"

"It's a small country with lots of empty properties bought by wealthy foreigners."

Hamish chuckles. "Aye. My nan's croft in the highland was sold for an obscene sum of money when she passed away."

Fraser nods in agreement.

"How about Ireland?" Hamish asks me. "I can't help but notice the accent. Hope I'm not assuming."

"I'm Irish," I reply. "It's a small country with lots of empty properties owned by wealthy foreigners. A lot of Irish Americans, in fact."

"Ah!" both of them exclaim in unison.

The banter flows easily. I let the two friends talk and catch up, while I sip my beer. Once I've finished a pint, Hamish automatically pulls me another. I really enjoy the company, even if I don't join in the conversation much. After numerous pints of ale and Scottish whiskies, I think Ali's dad is pretty drunk by the time we stumble out onto the street to the taxi Hamish ordered for us. The two men hug and Hamish kisses the side of Fraser's head, lingering for a second too long.

It's nearly two by the time we arrive home. I sneak into our bedroom, have a quick wash in the bathroom and climb into bed. *Bliss!* It's the most divine thing to snuggle up to Ali in a warm bed after a long day. I lay my head on his shoulder and wind my arms around his chest.

"Hey, guess you guys had fun. Did you go clubbing or something? It's really late." He sounds sleepy but amused.

I whisper, "Funny. After the play, your dad took me to an Italian café for supper and then for drinks in the Stag."

"Oh, the Stag. You met Uncle Hamish, then."

"Uncle Hamish." I think about it. Yeah, if Hamish and Fraser have been long-term friends, it's natural that Ali knows him.

"The two of them are like chalk and cheese but they've been mates for as long as I remember." Ali turns around now to face me. It's too dark to see him properly but I can still make out his green eyes once I get used to the shadows. "Hamish has a big heart and a bigger mouth."

Yeah, the Scot is larger than life, all right. "Did they? I mean, did your dad and Hamish have a thing?"

Ali frowns. "A thing?"

"It's just…" I can't put my finger on it but I am sure they are more than really good friends.

"Oh!" I would have loved for it to be brighter, so I'd see the effect of the revelation on his face.

"I don't know for sure. It's just a hunch." I don't want to rock the boat.

"Now I get it. I mean, I've always known how close they are, but if they'd loved each other that way, my dad never acted on it. I'm certain of that."

Like Ali hadn't told his wife he was gay.

"Your dad asked me about us as well and I told him I was an escort. He seemed totally cool about it."

"Aye." Ali has picked up a little bit of Scottishness after his dad's been around for a couple of days. "Wait, you told my dad I was buying your services?"

"Yeah, sorry!" Come to think about it, it was quite a gamble. "Your dad's a gem, you know that?"

He nods. "Yeah, he's a fine gentleman. Shit! Hamish and my dad!"

I chuckle. "It's probably why he so readily accepts you and me."

Ali replies by way of a kiss.

"Wow. You think my dad went through a similar experience to mine?" He sits up and turns the reading lamp on. I have to shade my eyes under the light. The pints have clouded my judgement a little.

"Similar experience?" I squint.

He rubs his chin. "Maybe he realised he liked Hamish but couldn't act on it or didn't want to cuz it was frowned upon to be gay then?"

I sit up too. "You don't think…" I trail off, not wanting to pick open an old wound.

His eyes widen. I can see his brain working. "What?"

"He might be in the closet. Would he have driven your mum away?"

Ali thinks about that. "Nah! My aunt told me why she left. I trust her. Apparently, Dad was devastated. He really loved my mum back then. If my dad's gay or bi, it'll have more to do with why he hasn't remarried and how he's so closed off."

I kiss Ali. "Well, he certainly doesn't have a problem with you being gay and with my history. I'd call that open-minded. Why don't you ask him about Uncle Hamish?"

Ali grimaces. "I doubt he'll talk about it but I may try sometime. Liam."

"Hmm?"

He pulls me close and whispers into my ear. "You're amazing, you know that? I've known my dad all my life and you came along. Five minutes later, you've fathomed this out about him."

"Ah, I told you about my Irish charm." I laugh. Then I attack his mouth with a passionate kiss. When we finally pull away, I plead, "Now, can I sleep? All that culture, good food and beer is making me tired." My eyelids are definitely getting heavy.

"Okay." Ali turns the light off again and we burrow under the warm cover. "Good night, Liam." His voice lures me to a restful sleep.

~~~

By the time Fraser leaves on Monday, I've grown to admire the man and I can truly see how Ali is the way he is. If I had found acceptance like that in my family, I'd have turned out quite differently. But, no point thinking about my past that way when I share a present with Ali and look forward to a future.

I've been practising all afternoon for a college interview if I get one. I love the early summer sunshine that illuminates Ali's front room and how it highlights my sheet music stand.

The ringing startles me since I've been totally focused and lost in my performance. No one uses the landline anymore. I've almost forgotten that Ali has a house phone. I consider ignoring it. After all, Ali hasn't given me instructions in the event that there is a phone call. But then, it is my house too. Should I answer or not? It may be urgent.

I run over to the corner of the sitting room and pick up the receiver.

The voice sounds surprised. "Ali, is that you?" A woman. A posh-sounding one.

"Ah, no. He's not here right now. Can I take a message?" I'm not sure if I remember how to speak properly on the phone.

"Who are you?" She's abrupt and not at all friendly.

"I'm sorry?" I should be the one asking that question. "Who should I tell Ali has called?"

There's a short pause before she speaks up again. This time, she's not so much rude but annoyed. "Tell Ali it's Claire. He knows who I am!" She clicks off.

I stare at the phone for long moments and put the receiver down, feeling ridiculous. The woman has just made me feel as if I don't belong in Ali's house. I'm not a fucking secretary. I should be the one feeling annoyed for having been interrupted during my practice.

The phone call really rattled me. I pack my flute away and glance at the clock. Nearly seven already and Ali's not back yet. I want to make something simple for dinner, so it'll be ready when Ali comes home. *Home.* I can't help but smile to myself as I get the ingredients for a pasta dish, using a readymade sauce. Surely even I can't fail at heating up a packet of sauce and boiling some noodles.

As I cook the pasta, I hear the door open and Ali's soft steps towards the kitchen. He hugs me from behind. "Wow, you're turning into a good househusband, domestic god. Or whatever. Making dinner while you wait for me to bring home the bacon." He rests his chin on my shoulder. I can feel him chuckling.

"Fuck off! You don't even eat bacon." Ali eats much more healthily than I do.

I try to picture us. I am holding up the spatula in one hand and a sieve in the other, indeed looking rather domesticated. *Wow, it is the new Liam!* I half turn. "Well, I'm going to see about the bar job soon. You know, Sasha's bouncer mate set me up. I'm not going to stay at home and wait on you forever."

Ali smiles and kisses my cheek. "The job's in Soho, right?" He pulls away and turns around to lean against the kitchen worktop so he can face me.

"Yeah. It's only going to be a couple of nights over the weekend to begin with." I stir the pasta, which is nearly ready. "It'll suit me just fine when I start college."

Ali stretches over to pick up an apple to eat. He must be hungry, working so late. "That's good. You don't want to work too much anyway. You won't have time for coursework and practice."

"I know. I just want to contribute."

He shakes his head. "I've told you. It's not necessary. Your being here is hardly going to break the bank. You still skip meals! Even the food bill has hardly gone up because of that."

"I'm still going to pay my way."

"Stubborn git." He always calls me that. It was why when I begged, I'd hated myself so much. At least I'd played the tin whistle. I'd pretended I wasn't a total charity case.

"That's why you love me." I don't know where that comes from but when I look across to Ali, he nods.

"That I do."

Fuck! I cough. Can I bring myself to declare that I love Ali yet? I stare at him.

Ali grins. "You don't have to panic. I don't expect you to say it back just because I do. We're good. Okay?"

Now, if he puts it that way. I swallow. "Okay."

I dish up and we tuck into our dinner in silence for a while.

"Hmm, this is good." Ali speaks with a full mouth. It's only tagliatelli with some tomato sauce. I've added a bit of fresh basil and cherry tomatoes from his backyard garden. I'd seen him make it before. That's why I thought I'd give it a go today.

"It's only sauce out of a packet," I reply with modesty. I managed not to overcook the pasta too. Yeah, that's a success.

Ali beams. "It's progress from beans on toast, anyway. How's your practice going?"

We talk about my college application and the pieces I'm preparing for an audition. Part of me dreads having to perform in front of people—proper music professors—but I'm also excited. The idea of going back to study is driving me to work hard every day. I've not even felt any cravings for a long time.

After eating, Ali makes a cup of tea and he moves his chair closer to me at the table. He sits down and takes my hands in his. "Liam, I read some of your notes today."

"Oh." I've been nervous because my writing depicts my life on the streets and drug-taking. It tells Ali what it was like in rehab and how I loathed myself. In fact, I still have low self-esteem and little confidence. I've written about my childhood and my time with Cillian, and how hurt and rejected I'd felt. My happy-go-lucky self is a total fabrication.

I gaze at him sidelong.

"I nearly couldn't get back to work after lunch because I wanted to read more. I bawled my eyes out sitting on a park bench in Soho Square during lunch hour." He kisses my cheek tenderly. Tears stream in his eyes. "A guy asked me if I was okay."

He tries to chuckle through his threatening tears. "I knew it'd have been hard to be homeless, but I couldn't have guessed some of the things you'd experienced. Like…like when people beat the shit out of you for no reason."

I remember writing that down. I was sleeping on the street. I had some cardboard on the freezing ground and a sleeping bag. Drugged up and not so alert. Twice. Some drunks just thought it was fun to kick the homeless beggar after they'd downed a dozen pints. The second time I'd gone to the hospital with bruises and a concussion. It was why I started to find squats to sleep in. I'd accepted that kind of things happened to homeless people, as if I deserved the same treatment people gave to stray dogs or garbage. I wasn't prepared for how affected Ali was.

"I talked about it with Sean. He also thought that I might have panicked when I had that rough trick. He suggested it had something to do with my experiences on the streets, too. I hadn't even realised the link." I card my fingers through my hair. Talking to Sean had helped. I go to NA now but I haven't opened up there because it's full of strangers.

Ali sighs. "I'm sorry I didn't realise. You're strong, Liam. You've come through these horrendous experiences. But you're too harsh on yourself when you can't cope."

I stare at him, trying to make sense of it all. "Sean asked me to be aware of triggers. Yeah, I did bury my head in the sand whenever anything bad happened. I would take too much drug or let my emotions build up until it was tipping point. I'm an idiot."

"You're not." He moves to hug me.

I hold onto Ali tightly. "And you've helped me. More than anyone or any drugs had before. These days, I can almost forget about my craving."

He kisses my forehead. "Good. I'm glad. I love you, Liam."

Ali has thrown me with his declaration of love and this conversation about my past, so I've completely forgotten about the woman's phone call. Until the next morning.

PART FIVE
THEIR PASTS AND FUTURE

CHAPTER 15

I REMEMBER WHEN I smoke my first cigarette of the day on the patio. I've been trying to cut down but I'm not doing great in that department. Still, five to ten a day is better than twenty and the possibility of a relapse. As I come back in from the morning chill, I find Ali eating his toast and staring at his mobile.

"I almost forgot. A woman called last night asking for you and she sounded quite pissed off."

Ali raises his eyebrow. "Did she leave a name? A message?"

Crap! My memory. "Jane? Helen...Sarah? It's not a very unusual name."

Ali chuckles. "So, it's a common name?"

I nod. "Don't laugh at me for my poor memory. That's what drugs do to ye. I'll probably have poor health and a premature death. Don't tell me I didn't warn you!"

He laughs. "It's okay if you age prematurely. I won't feel so old then."

"Fuck you!" I push him in gest. Then, it comes to me. "Claire! That's it. Told you it's not very memorable."

Ali turns serious all of a sudden and frowns. "Claire? Why is she calling?"

"We didn't exactly have a conversation. She was quite rude and demanded to speak to you. I couldn't ask what she wanted before she put the phone down. Sorry." I gaze at Ali's furrowed brow. I tease. "Who is she, anyway? An angry ex-girlfriend?'

Ali scrolls his contacts on the phone while he explains, "Ha-ha. Emily's sister. She can be a bit abrupt but..." He makes the call and waits for her to answer.

The ring tone drones on. "No, she must be busy. Property lawyer." As if that explains her behaviour. Ali ends the call. "I'll try her again later."

He leaves for work and I tidy up some weeds in the garden. It makes me feel even more domesticated. I'm quite handy in the outdoors since I grew up on a farm. I like Ali's herb and edible borders. I spend half a day trying to make myself useful and pick out things we can eat before the slugs get to them. I also pick a few wild strawberries. I devote the rest of the day to practising my flute.

Ali comes home early. "Hey, Chinese delivery from your favourite courier!" His voice is full of amusement.

I put my flute down to laugh at him. I've forgotten to eat lunch, again, so the smell of rice makes my stomach growl with delight.

He chuckles as he puts the few food boxes on the table. "Come help, then, since you're hungry."

"Yeah, I skipped lunch." Blame it on my time on the streets. Sasha and I used to go without food for days, sadly. My stomach has probably shrunk.

He tuts. "How many times have I told you to remember to eat? How can I let my boyfriend waste away under my watch?"

I follow him into the kitchen, and I bring out the plates and necessary cutlery while he opens the fridge to pull out a couple of beers. "I know, I know. Sorry!" I'm sorry to worry him but his concern melts my heart. I am still not used to having someone caring so much about my well-being.

We are halfway through dinner when the doorbell rings. "Are you expecting anyone?" Ali gazes at me.

I shake my head, thinking it's probably a salesperson and that it's annoying to be disturbed at this time of the evening.

Ali puts his chopsticks down and gets up to have a look through the spyhole. When he can see who it is, he turns around to whisper to me. "Shit! It's your favourite woman, Claire. I was really busy all day. I only tried her phone once more today but I couldn't get through."

Oh! Perfect. She sounded like a real bitch on the phone. Can't wait to meet her.

Ali opens the door and lets her in.

This Claire is dressed in a sharp suit. I recognise the resemblance from Emily's picture, except her sister seems older and harder. Her blonde hair is immaculately styled and her blue eyes are cold and piercing. Emily was always smiling in the photos I've seen, an image crystallised in my mind. I'm sure she's in Ali's heart in the same way. They must have made a really sweet couple, despite everything. I sometimes wonder about all my inadequacies compared to her.

"Come in, Claire." Ali ushers her but she only walks past the lounge door and stays there as though she's wary of being too close to us. "I've tried to reach you a couple of times today."

"I've been busy." She's as blunt as when she was on the phone yesterday.

Ali smiles. "Is everything okay? Are Mum and Dad around?" Mum and Dad. I guess he's referring to Emily's—his in-laws.

Claire's eyes dart between me and Ali. I automatically move forward to stand alongside Ali. "No, it's not okay! You cheated on her, didn't you? You fucking bastard."

"What—" Ali is clearly surprised. The loud smack on his face stuns him further. He steps back.

I want to grab the woman and ask why she slapped Ali, but he holds me back. "What the fuck? You can't just hit people!" I shout.

"Yeah?" Claire stares at us, then points at me. "Who's this? Your toy boy, huh? You never told us you were gay, Alastair."

Toy boy? That's insulting.

"It's not what you think—"

Ali starts to defend himself but Claire cuts in again. "Then what is it? You were in the closet. I only heard from one of Emily's friends. You're just going to hide it from us, aren't you? My sister died not knowing the truth. You're here, in her house, having dinner with your boyfriend!" She is shaking with anger.

She continues to stare, her eyes full of unshed tears, shimmering and refusing to fall. I feel for her. I really do. She thinks she's standing up for her dead sister. But Ali had his reasons too. I take hold of his left hand, which is trembling.

"I regret not telling Emily. Every single day. Believe me, I never cheated on her. I swear." He wipes his face with his right hand.

Her voice quakes. "This was our family home. My dad's gift to Emily. You shouldn't have it if you weren't her real husband. And you're fucking a young kid now?" She points to me again. "You're disgusting, Ali!"

I am not a young kid. I'm a fully grown adult with a mind of my own. If anything, I'm probably too mature for my own good. I want to scream at her but I must let Ali deal with her first; except, Ali is so shocked that he has no words for her.

They eyeball one another. Finally, Ali replies softly. "I didn't want to hurt Emily, and I couldn't come out to you and Mum and Dad when you were already grieving for her. I didn't tell anyone I was gay until about a year ago. Would you let me speak to you, and to Mum and Dad properly?"

She shakes her head. "Don't you dare call our mum and dad. Not after what you'd done to my sister."

Ali sighs. "What can I do?"

"Nothing! You've done enough to our family." She's already making her way to the door when she gives us her parting shot. "My parents will hate you living here with your boyfriend. I'm going to challenge Emily's will. Testamentary capacity or fraud. You will hear from me again."

With that, she leaves as abruptly as the way she arrived, and bangs the door shut behind her.

Ali stares at the door, stunned silent. After several moments, he runs his hand over his face. "Oh, shit. She really hates me now."

I hug him. He's still shaking. "It'll be all right. When she calms down, perhaps you can call and speak to her." I don't know her at all but I want to offer him something.

He shakes his head. "Claire is not one to back down. If it makes her feel better, I'll just give up the house. I don't care. I do want to talk to her and their parents, though."

But Ali shouldn't have to give up his home because of a misunderstanding. He'd shared it with his wife for many years. Claire had made it sound as though Ali deliberately married Emily to get the house.

"Then you will. Talk to her and your wife's parents. You don't even know if Claire's told them yet."

He pulls away. "I will. I need to come out to them anyway and explain. I don't care about the house. Except..." He kisses me lightly. "Sorry, you've just moved in."

"Hey. I was homeless, for fuck's sake. What do I care?" We'll find somewhere else to live. In the short time I've been here, I've come to think of home as us, not a particular house or a place. "I don't think she liked me, though. I'm sorry I've made it worse."

Ali shakes his head. "No, you haven't. She shouldn't have called you a 'toy boy' or anything like that. Actually, it's all my fault."

I roll my eyes. "Okay. Let us both stop trying to take the blame. I'm sure you can clear things up with them. What she said was not fair, regardless of what she's going to do with this place."

"I know." Ali goes into the lounge and sits down. I follow and join him on the couch. Ali puts his head in his hands and leans forward, his elbows on his knees.

When he looks up again, his eyes are red. "I should have gone to her parents and Claire first before I came out to other friends. I should have guessed that word would get back to them."

"Hey, don't beat yourself up over it. We all make mistakes and have regrets." I've had more than my fair share of them. And I'd never managed to reconcile with my own dad.

He nods. "Emily's mum and dad live most of the time in Spain now. I didn't think it was a good idea to call and come out to them over the phone, you know?"

I understand. It'd be weird to do that.

"What a fucking mess," Ali whispers. I have never seen him so dejected. I want to do something about it but I don't know how.

~~~

I take my pint upstairs of the pub to find Sue and Ali sitting by the stained-glass window. I've come to meet them, fresh from having attended an 'interview' at the gay club down the road. I'll be starting work this weekend. That makes me feel pretty good; maybe I'm finally respectable enough to enter the world of proper work. For the interview, I put on my escort uniform—a dark shirt and skinny jeans—but they seem to have worked on the manager of the club today.

Seeing Ali still lights up my insides. I wonder when it will stop. Perhaps I have struck gold and it's happily ever after for me this time. What I don't like is the worry lines on his face that have appeared ever since Claire's phone call and visit several days ago.

Sue stands and gives me a firm hug. After we sit back down, she gives me the updates. "So I asked Jeff—my husband. And he'll look into it. He said straightaway that they'd probably missed the time limit for a legal challenge."

Ali adds for my benefit, "Jeff's a lawyer as well."

I'm not sure if I've understood the legal gobbledygook but I've got the gist that Sue is getting advice for Ali over Claire's threat to challenge Emily's will.

Ali sighs. "Like I said, I don't care about the house or the will. I only want to speak to their parents, but Claire won't listen. She's not answering my calls or texts. I phoned their house, and the maid kept saying no one's in. Claire's obviously been censoring my calls."

Sue gulps down some beer. I notice she's got a full pint in front of her. It seems quite a lot of alcohol for a petite person. I've met her a few times now and come to think of her as a friend, too. I'd describe her as a little woman with a huge heart.

She tells Ali, "But they can't just take away your home. It's yours and you didn't steal it."

Ali shifts uncomfortably. "It amounts to the same thing for Claire. I don't want to argue over Emily's will. I only want to speak to them and explain myself and apologise. If we have to lose the house, so be it." He puts his hand over mine.

It seems Ali's friends are angrier about this than he is. He looks miserable instead. I can't bear it. As they talk, an idea comes to me. I don't know whether it's a stupid one or not. I'll sleep on it.

Sue can't understand Ali's determination to do right by Emily's family either. "What's up with this sister? Why is she being such a bitch?"

Ali sighs. "No. I can empathise with Claire. She's a little abrupt but this is entirely my fault. Claire's unmarried and still lives with her parents when they're in London, so she's particularly protective of them, of the family." He rakes his fingers through his hair again. "I should have come out to them before I told anyone else, but they were already grieving. They didn't need to hear about my shit as well."

"You haven't seen the parents at all?" Sue asks.

"No. I was hoping to see them at Christmas but they decided to stay in Spain. So, I only sent a card and small gift. If they've been back to London since, they haven't contacted me." Ali frowns.

Sue shakes her head but decides to drop the topic for now. Instead, she turns to me. "What's up, Liam. Have you got better news, my cutie pie?" She gets hold of my cheeks and shakes them, as if I'm three years old.

"Hands off me," I protest.

"Seriously, I'm just glad Ali's found someone so gorgeous and nice. I adore your Irish accent."

I'm not sure if I qualify for her description. The accent is not something I can shift easily, and I'm quite fond of it myself.

Ali blushes. Beautiful. "Sue, stop being such a fag hag," he tells his friend off.

She laughs. "I love seeing you happy, Ali. If it makes you uncomfortable, I won't harass your boyfriend again. I promise." She holds two fingers up as if to pledge.

I cough to change the subject. "Okay, okay. Stop bickering, children. So, I've received a notice to attend an audition and interview for a music degree. And..." I pause for suspense. "I've just landed myself a part-time bar job down the road."

Ali grins wide. "Fantastic!"

Sue clips my shoulder. "Congratulations!"

Ali gives me a hug and kisses me. I've been so worried about being a freeloader. He knows how much being able to contribute means to me.

~~~

My first day in my new job is exciting, but as I'm made to feel so welcome, it's less dramatic than I've anticipated. The Estrella is a popular gay bar in London's Soho. I've been given the Friday and Saturday night shifts first, since those are the busiest times. During the day, it's more a chill-out café bar, but the weekend nights are for the hardcore clubbers. My colleagues all seem nice enough. The barmen are mostly young college guys doing part-time jobs to supplement their student loans. I'll fit right in if I have my place at the university after the summer.

Before the place gets more frenzied—usually after eleven at night when the trendy, cocky guys and girls turn up—I take a break. I walk out onto the noisy street and light a cigarette. Finding a quieter side road, I take out my phone and search the contacts, press the green button before I rethink my options.

Larry answers quickly. "Hey, Liam. Long time no hear."

I smile, thinking about the gentle client and his vanilla sex. He's one of the better ones, though I don't miss the work. Not really.

"Hey, yourself. You well?"

"Okay, I guess." He drawls, "Are you, uh, available again?" He was one of the few johns that I bothered to text to tell them I'd quit.

"Larry, I'm sorry. You know. I've got a boyfriend now, and..."

He doesn't sound disappointed at all. "That's cool. Congratulations are in order. You deserve some happiness, dear." Really, was I *that* unhappy?

"Thanks. Talking of which… I've got a question but I can call another time if you're busy."

"It's fine. I'm just relaxing at home. What's up?" Yes, he was definitely one of my best clients.

I tell him about Ali's situation.

It's something that the probate lawyer should know well. Larry immediately offers his opinion. "As far as I can tell, there are only two grounds they could have done this. That your boyfriend's wife was not of full capacity when she made the will, which doesn't sound like the case. Besides, they had only six months to contest it under this scenario. They're out of time. Second, they can prove it was fraud. If the sister really wants to go down that route, she'll have to claim that your boyfriend deliberately deceived his wife, marrying her purely to benefit from the will, et cetera. It's not a valid claim, correct?"

Wow. I'm not sure I've followed the argument so far. "Of course not." I hesitate. "But…what are you saying?"

Larry draws a breath. I can hear him take a sip of something, probably one of the liquors that he's rather fond of. "I'm saying that unless the sister wants to go through the headache of a court case, they don't have a leg to stand on. You understand, Liam?"

I'm definitely glad that I plan to study music and not law. "So, they can't sue Ali over the house?" Let me confirm this once and for all.

"No. Unless they want to prove that your boyfriend deliberately married his wife for her wealth, dear," Larry concludes. "It will sound so much like a ghastly wicked stepmother fairy tale. Who's going to believe that?"

"No, he definitely did not marry her for her money. He didn't even know he was gay and he thought he loved her!"

"Defensive already? You really love this guy, don't you, Liam?" Larry is teasing me.

Do I? "Hmm. If you say so." I'm not going to admit it to Larry. If I'm going to tell anyone I love Ali, Ali should be the first person to hear it, except Chris, who'd already coaxed it out of me.

He laughs. "Well, I'm not going to embarrass you anymore. Has it been useful? Now, a thousand for the consultation."

"What?" He can't be serious. I can always fuck him ten ways since I definitely don't have a thousand quid for legal fees. *Will Ali forgive me for my sacrifice?*

"No." He carries on chuckling. "Free for you, dear. I'm glad you found yourself a man. Good luck with everything, okay? Now, I'm going to get back to my boring TV drama because my favourite escort has hung up his boots, as it were."

I laugh too and thank him. I wanted to find out where Ali stands legally and Larry has certainly delivered. There's only one more thing I need to do for Ali to sort out this mess.

CHAPTER 16

O NE DAY DURING the following week, when Ali's out at work, I search through his papers. I shouldn't do that but I think my plan might work and I wouldn't let a little detail like his privacy stand in the way. His document drawer is pretty neat. I suffer through reams of bills and statements, many going back years but I'm not interested in them. On some of the older papers, I can see Emily's full name. Dickens, just like the writer's.

After half an hour or so, I've given up on the content of the drawer but I notice a green concertina folder hidden under our bed. I pull it out and find more documents organised under different subject tabs. They seem like just more bills but a few greeting cards are stored in the front. There, I come across the order of service for Emily's funeral, with her beautiful face in the photo on the front.

"Hi, Emily. You don't know me. My name's Liam and I'm Ali's boyfriend. If you've been watching us from wherever, you know that already, though." I swallow. "I'm sorry about what happened. Ali really loved you. I have no doubt about that. But..."

I read through the hymns and the music, including Satie's *Gnossienne*. At the funeral, Ali read a poem called 'Remember Me' by Margaret Mead.

To the living, I am gone.
To the sorrowful, I will never return.
To the angry, I was cheated.
But to the happy, I am at peace.
And to the faithful, I have never left.

It's as though Emily is speaking to me, telling me that she can be happy for us. Her sister's anger is not going to bring her back. I hope it's true. I find myself tearing up, even though I didn't know her. I can imagine how moving Ali's recitation was.

"Ali and I are happy and I think you would be supportive of him. Your sister's angry because she's hurt but Ali has no intention of causing her pain. Or your parents. Please, wish me luck. Give us your blessing."

I note down the names of her parents and their address. Holland Park. I put the card carefully back in its place, alongside everything else I've disturbed.

On the Friday night, I inform Ali, "I'm going to see Chris and his new bloke Alex tomorrow. Is it okay?" I hate lying to him but it has to be done.

Ali looks up from his electronic book reader. As if he's not geeky enough at work, he enjoys reading sci-fi novels at home. "Oh, what are you guys up to?"

"Flat-hunting." They have mentioned they're thinking about a one-bed for the two of them. It's a bit silly to rent two rooms in a grotty flat when for the first time Chris may actually settle down with someone. It's a miracle. "They want to move in together."

I even phoned Chris to make sure I had a watertight alibi. He called me a 'big crazy' and I could hear Alex laughing and saying that he'd thought the name was reserved for him. And Chris told him to 'shut the fuck up'. I'd never understand how the feisty man ever found someone who could tolerate him. I guess Alex being a six-and-a-half feet tall ex-boxer with muscles and tattoos to die for may explain Chris's change of heart.

Ali smiles. "Wow, nice." Then he frowns. "You may as well get some practice. We're probably going to need to find another place soon enough. Claire sent me a letter from her firm, requesting that I gave up the deeds. I'll probably go to their office next week when I find the time. Maybe then she'll let me speak to her." There's no time to waste, then. It sounds as though Ali's already accepted that he's going to lose the house and he's going to voluntarily sign it over. I know he doesn't care about the property but I want to see what I can do.

I have no idea what I'll achieve by going to Emily's parents' house, but there's only one way to find out.

~~~

The house is about fifteen minutes' walk from the closest Tube station and in a surprisingly secluded part of Holland Park. This is a well-heeled area of West London. The last few times I'd visited were for appointments. I remember those rich men and their expensive houses.

When I see the Dickens's house, I can't help but whistle. I had a sense that Emily's family was wealthy but I couldn't imagine anything as grand as this. I can barely make out the large property hidden behind the hedges and a manicured garden. Two stone lions flank the forbidding tall black metal gate. Jeez. That's enormous by London standards where people like me live in shoeboxes. It makes me aware of how far I've come with Ali's help, that I'm standing here in front of a huge residence. Some days I still think about life on the streets, about barely making a living. I tear up sometimes when Ali comes home, to our shared space, and we embrace and kiss. It feels strange to have stability and security in the form of Ali. A year ago, I couldn't have imagined ever being able to live like this.

Facing the expensive house, I'm apprehensive. Before I can have second thoughts I raise my hand to ring the bell, fully expecting no one home or being told to fuck off straightaway. I can't hear the actual bell since the house is so far away. Minutes later, a small Asian woman appears.

She speaks to me behind the bars of the gate, as if she's trying to protect herself from a dangerous intruder. "Yes? May I help you?"

"I'm looking for Claire. Miss Dickens?" I reckon that's the correct address. I don't want to assume, but the Asian lady in front of me seems to be their maid who's been sent to answer the door. Who can afford a maid? These people really are a class above.

Her frown is obvious. "Do you have an appointment?"

Yeah, right. Of course not. "No, but could you please ask? Tell her I'm a friend of Alastair's." I hope she'll be curious enough to want to see me.

"Hmm. Wait a moment, sir." *Sir?* What the fuck am I doing here? I'm definitely a fish out of water.

The woman doesn't look happy but she returns to the house. I must have waited ten minutes before the furious Claire approaches the gate.

"What are you doing here?" She crosses her arms in front of her chest and stares at me. "Did he send you? He's a fraud and a coward now?"

"Just listen to me, okay? Ali doesn't know I'm here." I haven't planned my action in detail but now that I'm here, I am not backing down. "My name's Liam, and I want to speak to you and your parents, if they're around."

"Why should we do that? Are you scared of our legal action?" Her scowl deepens.

"No. Ali's quite prepared to give up his house. And I'll be wherever he goes. He doesn't fucking care about your legal action." I know I'm swearing, but frankly I don't give a shit about Claire's feelings right this minute. "*I* want to speak to you because *you* won't listen to him."

"I don't care who you are. I have nothing to say to you. Neither have my parents." Her face is closed. She's already turning around to retreat back to the house.

"Who's that, Claire?" An imposing older man steps up from behind her. I can see the resemblance immediately even though Mr. Dickens' hair is totally white. He's probably close to eighty years old.

I jump in. "Mr. Dickens, I'm Alastair's boyfriend. I know you probably don't want anything to do with me but I want to help Ali. I need him. I only want a few minutes of your time."

Emily's dad turns to Claire but I can't see his facial expression. I turn out my pockets. "Look. I'm not armed or anything." It's probably a stupid thing to say but I can only imagine rich folks like them being scared of riff-raff like me.

The older man gazes at me, his sharp eyes travelling the length of my body. I feel as though I'm that homeless kid again and a wealthy pedestrian's ogling to discern whether I'm going to taint him with my poverty. I expect the worst.

But Mr. Dickens presses the gate open, ignoring the protests from Claire. "You'd better come through."

Ahead of us, Claire runs back to the house in a huff.

I follow her dad. As the older man and I walk towards the imposing building, he turns and offers his hand. "Leonard Dickens."

"Liam Murphy. Just call me Liam." My heart's thumping with nerves but I need to do this for Ali. I'm not going to feel intimidated. Their servant is waiting by the front door to welcome her 'master'. The house isn't only huge, it's a mansion. A large covered garage stands to the side that can probably house a fleet of three sedans. The entrance hall is all dark wood and velvet curtains. A chandelier hangs low.

Leonard leads me to their front sitting room. They probably call it a parlour. I have no idea about posh people's houses but I can only imagine the places featured in period dramas. A well-dressed lady stands to greet us. She's younger than her husband, probably in her late sixties. She wears an elegant pale-blue trouser suit.

Leonard meets his wife's frown with an explanation. "This is Liam Murphy. Ali's boyfriend."

She covers her mouth but doesn't immediately respond.

It's probably a huge shock for her. "I'm sorry to turn up unannounced, Mrs. Dickens. Ali has been trying to reach you but…" I look over to Claire, who's now standing by the tall bay window, still with her arms across her chest and watching me with suspicion.

Mrs. Dickens sighs and points to one of the plush armchairs. "Take a seat, Mr. Murphy."

I sit down. "Please, call me Liam."

"Would you like a drink, Liam?" Leonard offers.

"No, thank you."

Mrs. Dickens sits back down in a sofa and gazes at me with wariness. Claire is still outright hostile. Leonard re-joins his wife and introduces her formally, "This is my wife, Teresa."

I stand, approach her and shake her hand. She's tentative and reluctant but good manners are ingrained in this class of people. She fixes her eyes on me.

Considering them all, I wish I had planned this better and rehearsed a fucking speech. But it's too late now. "I know you're angry with Ali. I probably would be too if I were in your position. But Ali didn't set out to hurt anyone, least of all Emily and her family. I've seen him torment himself every day. Believe me."

Teresa tries hard to hold back her tears as she trembles. I really do feel for them, but I am more determined to save Ali from his misery. He doesn't deserve to be treated like a villain.

Claire glowers. "Why didn't he tell my sister he was gay, then?"

"You can ask him yourself if you'd answer his calls. Whatever he'd decided back then, it was because he loved your sister and didn't want to hurt her. When she became ill, he didn't want to leave her. He'd wanted to care for her. He'd have been an even bigger bastard if he came out and divorced her, right?"

Teresa has started crying, her shoulders shaking with grief but she does so silently. She takes out her handkerchief and dabs her eyes.

Leonard considers me. "Tell me about yourself." I remember Ali said Leonard has a property empire. I normally dislike landlords, given my history and the dumps all around London I've stayed in. But I've got to handle this carefully. The man in front of me doesn't strike me as too unscrupulous. At least he's willing to hear me out. I swallow to brace myself.

"I'm nearly twenty-two. I know you may think my relationship with Ali is weird, what with the age gap." I bite my lip, realising what I'm going to admit for the second time. "I love him. I love him to bits. We met last year and I was the first man he'd gone out with. So, please don't think Ali had affairs when your daughter was alive." I turn to Claire briefly, as she's the one who assumes the worst of Ali.

Teresa's still sobbing. I continue, hoping they'll understand. "I'd been homeless. I was in a bad place when I met Ali. I was fucked up. I didn't think I deserved anyone, so I rejected him at first. But Ali...his calm and openness. Ali saved me and grounded me. He's given me a home, but it has little to do with bricks and mortar. I've come to believe that a home should give us our basic needs. We all need to find someone who cares about us. In return, we care a great deal about them. We can overcome the rest."

Leonard looks at me intently. "What's this got to do with us?"

I shake my head. "Nothing. It has everything to do with your daughter, with how Ali tried his best to treat her right. Perhaps he should have been honest with her. You probably think you have the right to judge him. At least hear him out. Ali's a decent man and you all know it. You've just forgotten about that because he's come out."

"I'm not homophobic," Claire interjects.

I swallow. "I'm not saying you are. Ali didn't know he was gay for a long time. It doesn't change the fact that he loved Emily and he did his best."

It's gone all quiet in the house, a grandfather clock ticking in the background. The occasional sniffling from Teresa makes the air heavy.

Eventually, Leonard breaks the silence and asks Claire, "Are you still angry?"

Claire shifts her feet. "I was imagining all kinds of things that Ali might have done behind her back. It just doesn't sit right with me."

"I totally appreciate your concern, but Ali doesn't do sneaking around. You know him well enough to understand that."

She bites her lip but doesn't respond.

Leonard sighs. "You mentioned something about the house, Claire."

She nods with a degree of defiance. "I was looking into challenging the will. It's deception."

Her father gazes at me for long moments. "It sounds to me like Ali was telling Emily white lies and we all tell them, don't we? They were together for twelve years. Emily was happy. She would've been heartbroken if Ali had left her. What do you think, Terry?" Leonard turns to face his wife.

Teresa dabs her eyes again with her kerchief. She glances round the room, settling on my face. I feel naked all of a sudden. Will she think I'm just some punk who wants to stay in a nice property? But after a while, she utters, "We don't need the house."

"Neither do we. We'll survive. Ali's not going to fight. That's not the point. He wants you to listen to him and to ask you for forgiveness." At least that's what I think he needs. "A lawyer friend tells me it'd be a strain on everyone to go through the court. And you won't win." I direct this at Claire.

She ventures, "But—"

Her father stops her with a raised hand. "It's fine, Claire. We're all still grieving, but going through a futile court case will be hard on your mother, on all of us." He turns to me. "Have Ali call us and we can meet. My wife and I are going to be in London for another couple of months before returning to Spain."

I breathe a sigh of relief. I was so nervous even though I'd made myself face these people for Ali. I address Teresa. "I didn't know your daughter but I'm very sorry for your loss."

She nods.

Leonard stands, so I follow. He shakes my hand again. "Thank you for coming, Liam. I can see you care a great deal about Ali. I wish you both well."

I smile, my heart full of pride for what I've done, for forcing a meeting with the family. "Well, thank you for listening to me."

~~~

When I get home, Ali's working on his laptop at the dining table. He glances up. "Hey, how did the flat-hunting go?"

I sit down at the table, facing him. "I went to Holland Park."

He frowns. "Oh, Chris is moving to Holland Park?" He must be wondering how Chris and Alex can afford the area.

"No, Ali. I'm sorry I lied to you. I met with Claire and her mum and dad."

Surprised, Ali shuts the lid of his computer. "Claire? As in Emily's sister?"

I nod.

"What? How did you even know where they lived? And they agreed to see you?"

I bob my head again. "I found their address in your papers. Sorry. I turned up unannounced. It was a gamble but I reckoned I might as well try. It didn't look like Claire would give you a chance otherwise."

With knitted brows, Ali gazes at me. "So, what did they say?"

I smile. "Leonard said you should call him and they'll arrange to see you."

"Leonard?" Ali's shoulders relax, then he gives me a half-grin. "What the fuck did you even say to him? Sounds like he's your new best friend."

I shrug. "Not quite but you know...I'm not as useless as I appear to be."

"You're not useless at all. You truly astonish me sometimes, Liam." Ali moves next to me, grabs me and gives me a big wet kiss. "You must have talked some good shit."

I wink at him. "No. Just the truth, and nothing but the truth."

~~~

Ali has driven us out to West London. I understand straightaway what we're there for when he stops at the gates to the cemetery. The sun's shining but we're the only people here. We walk through grass long enough to be cut as birds chirp from the overhanging trees. The small grave is covered by a black stone, still shiny and untarnished by age. Emily smiles at us from a photo that shows how radiant she was. I can see how Ali would have fallen in love with her. The flowers in the glass vase have wilted, though. Ali puts some fresh water in and replaces them with a bunch of blue and white flowers that he's brought.

He kneels down on the cool marble, his hands on his knees. I sit next to him on the soft ground.

Ali's voice shakes slightly as he starts. "Emily, it's been a couple of months since I came. I've got a lot to tell you. I saw your mum and dad. They're back from Spain. I guess they have already come to see you since someone has left flowers."

He drinks some water from a bottle, as if he needs to fortify himself. "They may have told you about me. Or, if you really are looking down on us from above, you'll have seen. I loved you. I did. But, it wasn't the kind of love that you could expect from a husband. For that, I'm sorry. I hope you've forgiven me because I never intended to hurt you. I should have told you that I made a mistake. Do you remember that time when I met Matt at work? I saw him quite a lot outside of work and he abruptly left the company.

"I realised then who I was. It was totally my fault that I hurt both you and Matt. I didn't know what to do, to try to make it work, to do the right thing. I couldn't, so I continued to lie to you. I never regretted being with you, Em. You'd given me so much over the years. I only regret depriving you of the kind of love that you deserved."

Ali reaches out to me and takes my hands into his. "Your mum and dad told me they were shocked when Claire told them. After you died…" Ali starts to cry, teardrops falling as he hunches his shoulders. He wipes his eyes with the back of his hands.

"After you died, I thought my problems were too trivial. How could I burden them with my sexuality when they were already coping with losing a daughter? I guess there's never a good time to come out to your in-laws who'd assumed that you're straight."

Ali tries to force a smile. "We talked for a long time. I don't think they can truly forgive me, but they've accepted that I lied to you because I wanted to protect you from the truth." He has to stop and rub off his tears again.

He squeezes my hand. "I think you'd have accepted it eventually and you might have even been supportive of me.

"I hope you can see me now, trying to hold on to happiness again. I think you'd have approved. I've found someone I truly love." His voice no longer shakes, and his hands are steady and strong on mine though tears keep falling down his face. "Your parents wished us luck. I felt like they were doing it on your behalf, you know."

I look at him, then at the image of Emily again. I think she'd have been glad to see Ali happy. I silently thank her, for her blessing that I was able to speak to her parents. I don't think anyone's past is ever perfect but being able to reconcile our regrets will help us heal and face our future. I sit there with Ali in the silence of the cemetery, feeling sad and hopeful at the same time.

~~~

As I sit in the long corridor waiting for my college interview and audition, my stomach threatens to churn and eat me from the inside out. The other students are dressed as though they're already in the orchestra, and they look like cookie cutters from encouraging families, with wealthy mommies and daddies driving them to music lessons and rehearsals. Of course, I have Ali now, and we've become a small family. I still feel totally out of place, an imposter in a proper university, waiting with these bright young things. I may have been only twenty-two but I feel like another generation when I consider the fellow applicants around me.

Fortunately, Ali insisted that I buy a new white shirt and a pair of trousers. I opted for dark blue jeans to complement my freshly ironed white shirt. *Will they take one look at me and show me the door?* I am convinced that I am twitching despite myself because that's how I feel inside.

The chair of the interview panel calls for me. I follow her into the room, which is more utilitarian than I'd imagined. An upright piano stands to one side, and a group of three sit behind a long table. They introduce themselves: double-barrelled-surname professors whose names I am too nervous to try to remember. Two men and a woman, the latter chairing. She has properly coiffured hair and a pair of rimless glasses that makes her seem serious and intelligent. Her keen eyes are on me and my unconventional choice of attire.

The lady coughs, as if to refocus herself on my performance rather than appearance. She begins, "I hope you found our department all right?"

I mumble something about living locally. Seriously, I'm here already, right?

Seemingly satisfied, she smiles and looks to the other two academic staff. "Okay, why don't you play your chosen pieces when you're ready?"

I nod, and take my flute out of the case and stand in the middle of the room, feeling more naked than when I used to walk into a stranger's bedroom and peel my clothes off.

I'm more confident with the performance than chitchatting, anyway. I've selected some difficult pieces to showcase my techniques. Vivaldi, Debussy and a modern piece, *Suite Modale* by Ernest Bloch. The latter reminds me of Asian music and it's an unusual choice.

I play them almost perfectly. The panel then tests me on the scales and sight-reading. I make a couple of minor mistakes during these tests. I can only hope that they are not detrimental.

Then comes the interview with the posh trio. I'm even more anxious than when I played. My hands feel cold and clammy. They ask a bunch of questions about my interests in music, my academic record and schooling in Ireland.

Towards the end, the woman peers over her glasses at me. "Mr. Murphy, can you tell us what you've been doing between school graduation and now? It's been nearly five years."

It's a reasonable question. I swallow. "When I first moved to London, I was homeless. Then I worked for a while. I survived." It's a gross understatement but I have no wish to rehash my troubled life in front of these college professors.

She considers me and nods in encouragement. Her two colleagues look at me and back at my application in front of them, expressing disinterest or indifference, I can't tell. One of them scribbles something on a form.

"And now?" She arches one of her eyebrows like a question mark.

"I have a home," I reply.

She glances at my details again. "I see you've applied to the college scholarship. It's rather competitive."

I nod. "Yes, I understand. I will get a student loan and work part-time as well, but I've applied for the scholarship to support myself, so I'm not dependent on my boyfriend."

She gazes at me for a second. Something softens in her face. "Of course." She folds up the papers in front of her—presumably my application—and stands up. She extends her hand to shake mine. "Thank you for coming, Mr. Murphy. We'll be in touch with the outcome very soon."

I address all three of them. "Thank you for the opportunity."

As I walk out of the university, I feel proud of my performance. Even though I don't think I truly fit in among the fresh-faced students, I desperately want to be there, to be back in education and pursue a subject I am passionate about. I can only hope that the interviewers could see that.

~~~

Ali switches on his laptop. He beckons me to sit down next to him. I gingerly do so.

"Come on. The sooner we look at the result, the sooner we can go celebrate." He kisses my cheek. The university has sent me an email to inform me that I've received a decision for my application, but I've been on tenterhooks all day, not wanting to read the result by myself. I've waited until Ali's home from work.

I raise an eyebrow. "Yeah, what if it's a rejection?"

Ali tuts. "Have some confidence in yourself. Here, tap in your username and password." He puts his laptop in front of me. Even the stupid college admissions system has to have these 'security details'.

I am sure my hands are shaking as I input the information but my application page comes up as if by magic. I avert my eyes, feeling the butterflies in my stomach.

"Liam Murphy…date of birth…BMus Honours…" Surely, Ali's taking the piss by drawing out the suspense. Now that we've started, my heart's thumping fast. I need to know even if it's bad news.

"Just skip to the part where it says rejection," I urge him impatiently. My hands clasp onto his arm as I lean close, but not too much, so I don't have to see the actual words.

Ali gives me an eye-roll before reading on. "September entry. Unconditional offer."

"What?!" I grab his computer and try to read it myself but he pulls it back.

"Wait. I haven't finished yet. There's something more here…" He reads on, "Performance scholarship, £4,000 per year. That's brilliant. Acceptance and scholarship. Congratulations, Liam."

He draws me into an embrace and kisses me.

My head's still whirling. I have to see for myself, to make sure Ali isn't joking.

"Let me see!" I wiggle out of his strong arms and read the screen. Yup. Everything is as he said. I sigh with relief.

He stands, pulls me up and swings me around. "Will you stop doubting yourself?"

When he releases me, I grin. "Yeah. I was just a bit worried they didn't know what's going to hit them."

He chuckles. "They'll love you. You're funny and brilliant. And you play like the Pied Piper of Hamelin."

"Ah, he played the pipe. It's in the name," I counter.

"Same difference." Ali's elation is catching. He pats himself down. "Right, we're going out for a drink and food."

"Can we go to Gino's?" That's the Italian place Fraser took me to. "I want the lasagne."

"Anything you want, Liam."

CHAPTER 17

I T'S KIND OF a surprise, though I had an inkling that Ali would bring me here. It's my birthday treat. I can't believe we've known each other for two and a half years and Ali still wants me. Last week, he carefully instructed me, "Pack your passport and enough clothes for a few days. Uh, I'd prepare for four-seasons-in-one-day kind of weather."

I'd rolled my eyes. It didn't take a genius to work out what he was up to. He wouldn't be wrong about the weather either. I still let him give me a 'surprise' when he dragged me along to London Heathrow Airport to catch the Ireland-bound flight. I've just finished my last exams before the summer break.

It feels strange being back in Cork because I've got Ali by my side. I remember how lonely and scared I was when I came back for Dad. I was hurting so much by the time I left. I still hurt, but it's manageable now. Ali senses my apprehension and reaches out to squeeze my hand.

Looking around the small provincial airport, I'm not sure if the 'welcome home – fáilte' sign is meant for someone like me, a prodigal son who doesn't want to be back. We have no check-in luggage, so we pretty much go straight through immigration and customs. I have my Irish ID with me, just in case.

I'm happy to show him my home country. I'd promised him that. We promise each other many things, whispered in the dead of night and all to be delivered in good time.

Ali smiles as we walk into the small and quiet arrival hall. "I've rented a car. I guess you'll have to be my navigator." He leads me to the car rental counters.

I grimace. "If you trust me." I'm pretty directionless, though Ali has managed to anchor me whereas no one has ever been able to before.

After collecting the key to the rental, we walk in silence towards the car park, Ali's fingers entwined with mine. It's early summer but the air is clear with a touch of chill.

Sitting in the small car, Ali hands me the satnav. "Here. Can you turn it on to see if it shows where we are? I've put Ireland on and updated the maps."

I hold it as though it's a burning hot potato, and fiddle with the buttons and screen.

Ali inserts the car key. Seeing me with the GPS, he laughs from the driver's seat. "Give me it, then. I'll get us there." He grabs the offending machine back and punches in an address. I lean over to see.

"Castlemaine?" I frown. It's a bit of a nowhere town in County Kerry. "What the fuck are we doing there?"

Ali's mischievous smile widens as he deftly manoeuvres the car out of the car park. "We'll see."

"How long are we here, anyway?" I ask casually. He'd said a few days.

Ali turns and smiles. "I managed to get the whole week off work. Five nights. I'm so excited!"

I can't help but grin, too, because his enthusiasm for our first proper holiday is catching. Strangely, I'm also looking forward to it even though I was hoping Ali would take me to Italy or somewhere more exotic.

Despite Ali's request for me to navigate, I don't need to do much, so I gaze out of the car window at the greenery that starts to appear only minutes away from the airport. Yeah, I come from a small country. Four million population and a quarter of them live in Dublin. Cork and Kerry in the West are mostly rural if you don't count the small cities.

As we drive through the edge of Cork, I think about my family. I wonder if Finn and Marie may want to meet with us, and what they'll think of my man. I could visit my mum, too. *My man.* I grin. Ali watches me sidelong and smiles as if he knows what I'm thinking.

I'll see what he has in mind. Perhaps he'll get to meet my family on the way back.

The scenery soon lulls me into a brief nap. I wake as Ali pulls into a farm and stops in a small car park. I look around. "Great. You're bringing me to a vacation on a farm. You do remember I grew up on one, right?" I laugh, opening the door and swinging my legs over to get out of the car.

Ali also jumps out and opens the boot for our luggage. He's still smiling. He passes my bag over. "Come on, then, farmer boy."

I hit his arm jokingly. He only laughs and leads on. We pass the farmhouse where I assume we're staying but we carry on. Ali seems to know where he's heading as we walk down a narrow, overgrown path by the house to a secluded field behind the farm buildings.

A restored gypsy caravan stands on the edge of the green, all bright and shiny in the hazy sun. I can't believe it. I quicken my steps, almost running towards it. It's painted red, yellow and black, with a few steps leading up to the front door and a small flower garden in front of it. The caravan is deceptively big with its long back. I turn around to see Ali watching me with a massive grin on his face. I hug him, my arms around his strong body and I kiss him greedily.

When we break away, he asks, "You like it, then?"

"No, I hate it." I smirk to show that I'm joking. Anyone else in my family would have hated it. Who would want to sleep in a restored caravan, anyway? These things really are only for gypsies who are unfortunately despised by the general populace here. My family probably wouldn't understand why some hipsters from London would appreciate an old caravan disguised as rustic charm. I just fucking love the fact that Ali has gone to such lengths to find something that he knows I'd love.

I am still breathless from the kiss. "Well, are you going to open it or do we have to break in?" I'm pretty good at breaking into houses, a skill learned from my squatting days.

He smiles again and goes up to the wooden door. The little key has been left there. It opens into a small sitting area. A double bed occupies the far end. The décor is a bit too floral for my tastes but I really don't care as long as I'm with Ali.

Before I can even react to the confined space, he closes the door with his heel and shoves me to the side of the caravan. His mouth and tongue ravish me. He peels my T-shirt over my head and flings it on the floor. He licks my earlobe and his lips trace my sensitive bits down my neck; the sensation of his soft tongue wrapping round my nipples makes me moan loudly. "Lube, Ali." Before I blow my load without either of us touching my erection.

We stopped using condoms with each other when we both tested and were sure we were clean. I thought I was an absolute top before I met Ali, but I adore his dick in me now, especially when he fucks me raw. *Shit.* My erection really is going to jump out of my tight jeans in the most painful way. Ali unzips and pulls my trousers and briefs down in one sure sweep. He leaves my cock standing tall to retrieve the lube.

Ali opens his case and quickly locates the small bottle. The sensation of the cold gel on my arsehole cools my heat down temporarily. It's quickly replaced by the swollen head of Ali's cock. "Oh, fuck!" I murmur.

Panting, Ali's voice is croaky and sexy. "Yeah, I'm on it."

He breaches my tight ring. Pain and pleasure fill me and warm my insides with desire. I can never have enough of Ali like this. I stretch my arms tall over my head, and steady myself against the top of the curved wall. Ali's hands hold on to my hips tightly, as he pushes in deeper and deeper until he's buried to the hilt. Before I can catch my breath, he pulls out and rams in again.

For a brief moment, I wonder if we're rocking the whole caravan and it may topple over. I don't give a shit, though, when Ali feels so good. "Don't hold back. Just fucking come!" I start jerking myself off when he quickens his thrusts. If we were not tearing the place down before, we definitely are now.

He bites my shoulder as he reaches his peak. Then he yells and I come, my jizz squirting all over my hand and dripping onto the side of the caravan. Ali's hot breath on the back of my neck tingles me. I've never felt more at ease, happy and safe in his arms.

"I love you, Ali."

He kisses my neck and shoulder. I turn around and our mouths and tongues meet.

"I love you too."

~~~

We eat dinner at the farm's restaurant. We are the only diners, perhaps because the school holidays have not yet started. There are few tourists at this time of the year. The proprietor is an Australian woman in her sixties called Laura. She married an Irishman many years ago and has been here ever since. Her husband isn't around but I don't think it's my place to ask. We introduce ourselves, making polite conversation. Ali tells her about his job, and I talk about my study and part-time work. She catches my accent, so I admit I'm from Cork.

"Well, here's the menus, gentlemen." Her accent remains strong. "But first, would you like to order some drinks?"

I don't need to look at the drinks menu. "Have you got Bushmills?"

She smiles. "Yes, I believe I do. Two glasses?"

I nod.

Ali puts his menu down for a second. "Is this something to celebrate with?"

"Uh-huh." I grin. "And it won't break the bank either, I promise." I know Ali likes an occasional glass of whiskey. I still feel guilty spending 'his' money even though he's made it clear that it's 'our' money. Semantics. Either way, you can't take the poor beggar out of me. Besides, I'm already going to be in debt for a lifetime with the college fees and student loan.

When Laura returns, she puts down the two glasses of Irish whiskey and asks if we're ready to order. Her menu is full of local produce. The majority of the dishes are vegetarian, right up Ali's street. We both order the veggie food.

Ali takes a sip of the whiskey. "Hmm. This is delicious."

I follow him and let the liquor burn my throat. "Yeah. Out of all the Irish whiskeys, Jameson is most famous, but this is good stuff and cheap. What do you think, compared to the Scottish malt?"

"I don't want to hurt the pride of an Irishman." He hits my chest in jest. I shake my head. I don't really care so much about national pride and he knows it.

Ali's smile makes his eyes twinkle, though. "Is this all right? You don't feel too weird being back?"

I can't help but gaze at his gorgeous face and beam. "Why would it be anything but all right when I'm with you?"

He grabs my hand across the small table. We look intently at each other as if we've only just discovered how amazing we are.

After dinner and coffee, Laura brings another two glasses of Bushmills. "On the house."

Ali looks up. "Would you like to join us for a moment?"

"Sure." She pours another small shot for herself and sits down. "How was the food?"

"Oh, it's delicious and the ingredients taste very fresh indeed. Thank you," Ali replies.

"Thank you for coming." Laura nods. "We don't get too many visitors this time of the year, but I prefer it that way. I like to use locally produced food anyway, so I don't buy in too much in case it gets spoiled."

"My family's farm is near Bantry. I don't suppose you source from them." She asks me the name and I tell her.

"I've heard of it but it's a bit far for me to drive all that way," she tells us. "And I don't buy in bulk to justify delivery."

We all sip the whiskey and savour the taste for a moment.

"But you're staying here instead of with your family?" Laura asks with a hint of curiosity. Her open face makes it less of an intrusive question.

I shrug. "Well, this gives us more privacy." I glance over at Ali and he's still smiling. I'm not prepared to go into it all to a stranger.

Laura cocks her head. "I don't want to assume but you're together, right? There's a honeymoon vibe here."

Ali chuckles. "We're boyfriends but it's only Liam's birthday, not our honeymoon."

She directs her gaze to me. With understanding, she asks, "Is that why it's not so easy at home?"

I take another gulp of the smooth whiskey. "You could say that."

"Well, hope you find the space you need." Laura considers me and immediately appreciates why we're here staying on her farm, rather than with my family. "I think, if I were your folks, I'd be very proud of you, making a life for yourself in London. Studying for a music degree, you said?"

I nod to thank her. "You know. Millions of Irish people have done it before, so I can't say I'm anyone special."

"But they're not you. You're special." Ali gazes at me with smiles and pride all over his face.

I reach out and grab his hand.

~~~

We already had sex in the caravan this afternoon. It was a long sensual one when we took time to enjoy our bodies, seeing them together, feeling our skin, kissing, caressing until we couldn't bear it, until we yearned for each other so much that it hurt not to be inside each other somehow.

Finally, we got up and showered. We had to run across the field to the shower block but it added to the fun of our temporary nomadic experience. Ali seems to have a plan for our first trip together and I'm happy for him to lead me. I think he's looking for a romantic version of my homeland that I don't necessarily share. Through his eyes, though, I experience this corner of Ireland in a totally different light. It is beautiful and tranquil. The green really goes on for miles and miles. Just like the depth of his eyes.

The place is no longer about the pains of growing up, of always feeling like a failure and disappointment, of longing to be somewhere else, of unrequited love. I feel...forgiven. Finally. Skip might have died because of me but it was always partly my dad's fault for beating me up. Yet, I tried to earn his love over all those years. I blamed myself for everything. I wasted four years of my life in a cycle of self-loathing, drug abuse and depression. I stop dressing. My hands stall. I find myself sitting on the edge of the bed in a flood of tears.

Ali sits next to me, turning me to face him. He hugs me tightly, and kisses my hair and cheeks. "It's okay. I'm here." He knows why I'm so emotional being back in Ireland.

I look up to him, my vision blurred through my tears. "It's okay cuz *we* are here."

"Yes, it is. Exactly." He kisses me again.

"I'm not a disappointment."

He rubs the back of my neck tenderly. "You're far from it, Liam." Ali whispers as though he's revealing his secrets. "When I was planning this trip, I thought I'd arrange to see my mum. I was about to call my dad for her contact."

I pull off a little to meet his sad eyes.

"Then I remembered. I was seven or eight. Forty years ago. I realised that she would never come back. She didn't want to be a parent, so she wouldn't be any good to me even if she did return. I promised myself that I wouldn't be upset by her. I'd find love elsewhere. And when I did, I'd know." He leans down to kiss me.

I close my eyes to savour the moment of his tenderness. Tears fall down my face. I've been crying for both of us.

When I calm down a little, I take his right hand and put it against my chest. "Take this instead as your connection to this country. My Irish heart."

~~~

We hide in the sand dunes, wrapping ourselves with the thick blankets that Ali has borrowed from Laura. She even gave us a small patio heater when we told her we were coming to the beach.

We've been kissing for a long time, our shirts discarded and trousers disappeared.

Ali asks, "Is this okay? I mean, do you have laws against nudity in public or something?"

That makes me laugh. "Probably, but I wouldn't worry about it. We Irish generally disrespect the law until we have use for it. And no sane person will ever come out onto the beach this late in the day." It's only about eight but the beach has long been deserted; even the hardcore surfers have gone home. Ali and I managed to find a remote dune where we wouldn't be disturbed.

"You've thought of everything, Alastair the Scout." I tease him.

"Not really. Don't forget I'm a city boy. But I wanted to bring you here. Do you remember what you told me about Ireland when we first met?" he asks.

I only vaguely recall talking about things I'd missed about Ireland. I was treating him like a professional then and wondering why I talked to him about things that I wouldn't divulge to other clients. "What did I say?" I play with his wild hair.

"You said you missed the stars and dark nights, and the smells and sounds of Inch Beach. That's why I wanted to come here with you."

This is perfect. Being on the beach under the dark sky, and listening to the light breeze and sound of waves with Ali.

I can see the glimmering green of his eyes, shining despite the dusk. He kisses me with such a lot of heart, making me tremble inside. I hold onto him, caressing his skin with my palms. I pull Ali close and turn him around. I squirt some lube in my hand and prepare him. We're still reeling from our earlier round of sex. Our bodies are probably going to scream tomorrow. But I want him, more than anything else in my life.

Turning his head around to kiss me again, Ali whispers, "Fuck me, Liam. You're overthinking."

Am I? Ali has not only turned me into a romantic fool and now I'm a fucking thinker. To remedy that, the only thing to do is to fuck hard and ignore everything else on my mind.

Naturally, I also reward Ali with a blow job.

As I lie down beside him exhausted, I start to chuckle. "We're covered in sand and semen, Ali."

He props himself up on the elbow and watches me with a big smile on his face. "Sand, semen, sea and sexy. When I am old and senile, forgetting everything, will you remind me of this moment?"

"Yeah. You really think you'll want me for that long?"

Ali nods. "Yes, as long as you want me."

He leans in and kisses me, then he stands and pulls me up.

When we get back to the caravan, we sit on the steps admiring the dark blue sky.

Ali's arm wraps around my shoulder. "You can see more stars in Ireland."

I gaze up and try to remember what I know about the summer constellations. I take his hand and we move together to trace the stars. "Yeah. You can follow the curve of the Plough's handle. The bright star at the end is Arcturus. You can't quite make out the Milky Way but there's a vague band up above, for sure."

Ali repeats, "Arcturus."

"Guardian of the Bear," I muse. "See what I've left behind. I've come a long Milky Way to find my guardian."

Ali chuckles. "Except I don't really guard you. I like to let you be free, my Liam. How does it feel now being back home?"

I consider him and think about his words. Ali is my guardian but he doesn't keep me in a locked box. His love protects me and lets me be whoever I am. Free. "This is where I grew up. You. Are my home. And wherever you are, Ali, I'll be there."

Ali pulls me close and we kiss. A light breeze grazes our skin. We're surrounded by the rustling sound of the long grass and the lingering scent of sea and sand.

– END –

ABOUT A. ZUKOWSKI

I am a London-based British writer who grew up in the gay village and red light district of Manchester, UK.

I was trained in screenwriting at the University of the Arts, London; National Film & Television School and Script Factory, UK, followed by a series of misadventures as a film journalist, writer and producer of short films. My stories are based on personal and emotional experiences, and feature strong LGBTQ-identified characters.

Connect with the Author

Twitter: http://twitter.com/saszazukowski

Blog: http://azukowskiblog.wordpress.com

Goodreads: http://www.goodreads.com/author/show/16509569.A_Zukowski

Tumblr: http://azukowski.tumblr.com

FB: http://www.facebook.com/aleksander.zukowski.353

OTHER BOOKS BY A. ZUKOWSKI

THE BOY WHO FELL TO EARTH

#1 London Stories

Jay Palmer is two months away from his sixteenth birthday. He doesn't realise how his life will be changed forever when a gang of thugs leaves a badly injured boy on his doorstep. The biracial boy and his white single mum Maggie nurse the stranger, sixteen-year-old Aleksander Zukowski, also known as Sasha. Sasha ran away from care two and half years ago. He sleeps rough, is addicted to drugs and sells himself on the streets of London to fund his habit. For the first time in his life, he has a reason to change.

Sasha confirms what Jay already knows about himself but it won't be easy for Jay to come out to his macho mates in a largely black neighbourhood. Sasha has an uphill struggle to stay clean when his past threatens to throw him back into the abyss. Are the two boys strong enough to stay together against all odds?

"This was a poignant coming of age story…a well-written and enthralling read that I couldn't put down." ~ Bayou Book Junkie

"It has a force that keeps you on the edge of the seat and a grittiness that opens your eyes and makes you think." ~ Sinfully Gay Book Reviews

~~~

We ended up sharing a joint again that afternoon. I carried on my one-sided conversation while he patiently listened to me, his newly cleaned hair shining in the sun. He had his back to the door frame, his eyes closed to catch the rays like he was on holidays enjoying himself, trying to get a tan. For the first time since we picked him off the front lawn, he was relaxed. I was absolutely mesmerised by the shape of his face, the lines of his nose, the vulnerability of that bruised body. I leaned forward and touched his lips with mine.

His eyes snapped open, but he didn't seem shocked or upset.

Still. I moved away, awkwardly. "I'm sorry. I didn't mean to," I muttered.

He gazed at me, his eyes quietly assessing me. His facial expression was calm and receptive. "It's okay."

My eyes went wide. "Okay? Hmm." I busied myself with a little loose thread on my top. I hadn't even kissed a boy before and now I had done this to a stranger, someone who didn't yet have a name. What the fuck was I doing?

He lit the joint and drew on it deeply. He breathed out, cocked his head, and looked at my face, as if he was trying to work me out. "Does your mum know you're gay?"

I stared at him. I hadn't considered coming out seriously. Hell, I hadn't even come out to myself, so why would I have spoken to Ma about it? "Uh, no," I answered.

He took another toke and passed the joint back to me. He didn't comment further.

All my doubts evaporated. He'd acted like it was nothing special and, like he said, it was okay. Kissing a boy you found attractive was fine. I couldn't believe I'd come out for the first time to a total stranger after kissing him.

BLUE JAY

Forthcoming queer romance

#3 London Stories

Boxing was all Alex had ever known. His entire being now shattered beyond repair. One night and five years in the nick changed everything.

Chris has been selling his body for too long. Weariness seeps into his bones, and eats away his soul, if he ever possessed one.

Chris is too fine looking, like an actor or model. There's not much else he's good at. The gaze people give him tells him that. The contempt on his new flatmate's face is nothing new. Some days she shaves and puts on a soft dress that she loves and she'd touch herself, thinking about Alex's strong muscular arms and the tattoos. Yet, Chris avoids the big man. The six-and-a-half feet giant with a boxer's broken nose and a scar across his right cheek.

Alex wishes he didn't have to flat-share with the pretty boy who rubs him up the wrong way. All the fucking time. The dark gaping hole in his heart is enough to deal with. In the world he's known so far—growing up poor in Essex and fighting in the ring to be the best—he'd never be interested in someone like Chris. The sooner he gets out of this housing arrangement the better because he can't afford to lose himself in these dangerous thoughts—the same ones he's been hiding for longer than he cares to admit.

Featuring Chris from *Liam for Hire*.

COURTING LIGHT

A novella, part of the Seasons of Love anthology

Our days were numbered but precious.

Courting Light is the story of Josie, an eighteen-year-old about to leave home to start university in London. She volunteers at a summer camp for disabled children. When Josie is paired with the autistic teenager Lucian, she faces intense experiences that are truly eye-opening. To her surprise, Lucian is not the only one who captures her attention. Over the weeks, Josie develops powerful desire evoked by the camp's enigmatic young leader with a shaved head and tattoo on her skull.

BEATEN TRACK PUBLISHING

For more titles from Beaten Track Publishing,
please visit our website:

http://www.beatentrackpublishing.com

Thanks for reading!